WITH

3 1192 00402 7957

821.912 Warne.S
Warner, Sylvia Townsend,
Collected poems /

MAR 24 1983

COLLECTED POEMS OF
SYLVIA TOWNSEND WARNER

Sylvia Townsend Warner

COLLECTED POEMS

edited with an introduction by
Claire Harman

EVANSTON PUBLIC LIBRARY
1703 ORRINGTON AVENUE
EVANSTON, ILLINOIS 60201

CARCANET NEW PRESS / MANCHESTER
THE VIKING PRESS / NEW YORK

Copyright © 1982 by Susanna Pinney and William Maxwell,
Executors of the Estate of Sylvia Townsend Warner
Introduction and Notes copyright © 1982 by Claire Harman Schmidt

All rights reserved

First published in Great Britain by Carcanet New Press Limited, 330
Corn Exchange Buildings, Manchester M4 3BG, and in the United
States of America by The Viking Press, 625 Madison Avenue, New
York, N.Y. 10022.

Published simultaneously in Canada by Penguin Books Canada Limited

Warner, Sylvia Townsend
    Collected poems.
    I. Title   II. Harman, Claire
    821'.912   PR6045 .A812

    ISBN 0-85635-339-6   U.K. edition
    ISBN 0-670-74993-1   U.S.A. edition
    Library of Congress Catalog Card Number: 82-50704

Carcanet New Press Limited acknowledges the financial assistance of
The Arts Council of Great Britain.

The Espalier (1925), *Time Importuned* (1928), *Opus* 7 (1931),
Boxwood (1960), and *Twelve Poems* (1980) first published in Great
Britain by Chatto and Windus Ltd.

Printed in England by Short Run Press Ltd., Exeter

CONTENTS

FOREWORD

DURING the last few years of her life, Sylvia Townsend Warner was preparing her *Collected Poems*. She was meticulous in the selection, revision and arrangement of her unpublished poems but never, in the time she had to devote to the task, fully satisfied with it. On 30 January 1978, temporarily defeated, she wrote to the publisher: 'My envelope of poems is not at all selected. I have just shoved them in, so you can have a Dies Irae with them.' At the time of her death, later that year, these unpublished poems were grouped in sections according to theme, and marked 'People and Places', 'Personal', 'Miscellaneous' etc., but were too disordered to present as they had been left, which was as the author herself had clearly felt.

I have reverted to a chronological presentation, where dates are known, integrating a selection of previously uncollected poems from periodicals and anthologies. Undated poems have been interspersed with the others where there is either a thematic link or a clue as to their chronology. Dates and place names which appear on the author's typescripts and the dates of publication of previously uncollected poems will be found in the notes.

The collection of unpublished poems in this book is not exhaustive, and I hope that more material will come to light in the future.

I am grateful to The Monotype Corporation Limited for their permission to reproduce on the cover of this book an engraving by Reynolds Stone from *Boxwood* (which appeared on p.17 of their edition of 1957, facing poem VI by Sylvia Townsend Warner). I would also like to thank J. Lawrence Mitchell and Dr M. A. Hill for their assistance and the executors of the estate of Sylvia Townsend Warner, especially Susanna Pinney, for help and support.

C.H.

INTRODUCTION

WHEN, in an interview in 1975, Sylvia Townsend Warner introduced herself as 'that odd thing—a musicologist', the description was only half ironic. She had some thirty publications to her name. Five were collections of poetry, seven were novels and ten were volumes of short stories. She was a long-standing contributor to two very different magazines, *The Countryman* and *The New Yorker*. She did not expect many people to remember that her first calling had been as one of the editors of a scholarly ten-volume survey, *Tudor Church Music*, the research for which lasted a decade. But by choosing to overlook her literary achievement and to side-step the expected confession to being a Lady Novelist (a title which she considered 'an accusation'), there is another point to be made: Sylvia Townsend Warner never set out 'to be a writer', nor, when she had clearly become one, did she adopt a professional posture. That she avoided what is called literary life might recommend her work; certainly it freed it from the distortions of fashion, though she paid for that and her individualism with 'years of—I will not say neglect—inattention'. That this woman of strong character, gifted beyond the ordinary and fastidious in all things, was reticent to bandy terms is a mark of her integrity. 'Lady Novelist' would be self-deprecating; 'neglect' self-pitying. A term she was especially particular about was 'poet'.

The Times of 2 May 1978 had less reason to be particular: 'Sylvia Townsend Warner—Poet and novelist of distinctive voice'. An obituary is, I suppose, as good a place as any in which to begin a public career, especially for a writer who had good-humouredly exclaimed, 'I propose to be a posthumous poet!' Sadly though, one would have had to take this poetry on trust in 1978, since apart from *Boxwood*— a book of secondary importance—her poems had been out of print in commercial editions for forty years. Since then *Twelve Poems* has been published (1980) and, remarkably enough for the slimmest of volumes, continues to strengthen and substantiate a reputation which was beginning to rely solely on long memories. But 'Poet' comes before 'novelist' in the obituary for more than chronology's or politeness's sake. In that forty years, she had not been idle.

Sylvia Townsend Warner was born on 6 December 1893, in Harrow, Middlesex. Her father, a distinguished scholar and teacher, was Head of the Modern Side at Harrow School, where she grew up a solitary and observant child in a benignly eccentric household (or so she describes it). She did not go away to school, but absorbed from her parents a wide range of knowledge and the habit of voracious reading. 'I wasn't educated—I was very lucky' she once said, and, unlike the heroine of her first novel, Laura ('Lolly') Willowes, she avoided being 'subdued into young-ladyhood'.

She was invited onto the editorial board of the Church Music project in 1917, when she was twenty-three. She moved to London, where she became absorbed in her research and 'the fascinating discipline of living alone'. She loved walking, especially at night, and her explorations of city and countryside fuelled a remarkably fertile period of writing which was about to begin. On a hot August day in 1922 she set off for a week-end in the Essex marshes. She stayed a month, preoccupied by the haunting Blackwater landscape and 'the discovery that it was possible to write poetry'. The landscape stayed with her—six years later she used it as the background to her novel, *The True Heart*— and the poetry stayed too.

During the next decade Sylvia Townsend Warner wrote three volumes of poetry, three novels, a novella, a book of short stories, other stories which were collected later, and many unpublished poems. The ten Church Music volumes also belong to this period. Her first book, *The Espalier*, includes poems written from 1922 to 1924. In 1923 she had been to Dorset to meet the novelist and eccentric, T. F. Powys, a formative influence in many of her early poems, and an even greater influence on her subsequent fiction. She met David Garnett around this time too. His enthusiasm recommended her poetry for publication to Chatto and Windus, who issued almost all her subsequent books. In *The Familiar Faces*, Garnett describes how Sylvia Townsend Warner took him to see the marsh-country which had so impressed her, and how, on the way there, she 'gave an extraordinary display of verbal fireworks. Ideas, epigrams and paradoxes poured from her mouth ...'. And yet, 'when she gave me her poems to read . . . it was not the sparkling epigrammatist of the morning who had written them, but the quiet, intimate companion who sat beside me in the cold train with her clothes and even her face spattered with mud from the Dengie Flats'.

The distinction which Garnett noted is not as fanciful as it may sound. Sylvia Townsend Warner's prose is always sharp and fast-moving; time and again she pulls the carpet from under the reader's feet. But in the poems, in general, she is content to leave the carpet be, to settle down on it before that potent Warner symbol, the hearth. With its many Georgian flourishes, and yet little of the vitiating sentiment and deliberated significance which characterise that school, Sylvia Townsend Warner's early poetry did not appeal to many of her contemporaries. Behind all that is derivative and superficial in the style of *The Espalier* and her second collection of poems, *Time Importuned*, one can begin to hear the tone which became distinctively her own as she sloughed off the poetical and moved towards the plain style of the late poems:

> With a hair plundered from the white beard of Merlin
> You shall be tied;
> With a grass ring plighted you shall come at nightfall
> To be my bride.
>
> The straight rain falling shall be the church walls,
> And you shall pace
> To where an old sheep waits like a hedge-priest
> In a hollow place.

('The Mortal Maid')

In a brief introduction to his selection in *Modern British Poetry* (1936), Louis Untermeyer, one of her few early champions, said of Sylvia Townsend Warner's poems: 'Each reader will discover a different quality on which to lay stress: the poet's marked accent, or her half-modern, half-archaic blend of naiveté and erudition; or the low-pitched but tart tone of voice . . .'. Although there are elements in the poetry which readers of Sylvia Townsend Warner's novels and prose would easily recognise, this tone—the before-the-hearth manner—is peculiar to the verse. Most of the poems in the two early collections end on a sombre note, a dying fall; even in the most straight-forward ones she effects a quiet key-change, often subtly disturbing. Her satires are sharp-edged, deliberately-aimed, their humour by turns wry, benevolent and black. The poems of reflection and observation suggest a wide range *xv* of ironic possibilities, some of which are taken up, while others are left teasingly unexploited. The exceptions are her didactic and political poems—few of them satisfactory—and her poems of passionate love, when the poised ambiguity, of necessity, disappears.

Louis Untermeyer added to his advocacy the phrase, 'like a feminine Thomas Hardy'. Sylvia Townsend Warner's poetry resembles Hardy's understating tone and themes sufficiently to suggest the comparison whenever it has attracted anything by way of commentary. Circumstance itself seems to encourage it; since the summer of 1981, Sylvia Townsend Warner has shared a place with Hardy and the Dorset Worthies in Dorset County Museum, and the implications are more than geographical. Many specific poems invite comparison—'A Woman Out of a Dream' can be set beside Hardy's 'The Voice', 'The House Grown Silent' beside 'The Going', 'The Alarum' beside 'Just the Same'. Their similarities are obvious, but not, unfortunately, very illuminating. She is a much more diverse poet than Hardy, and her tone, though 'tart' where his is sometimes sour, is not so 'low-pitched' as his. Her early books contain many embedded allusions to other writers: Shakespeare, Burton, Herbert, Browne, Marvell, Gray, Crabbe, Blake, Wordsworth, a very unhappy Lord Byron, Shelley and Keats among them. There is, too, an air of learned mischief about the poetry which is far from Hardyesque. Both writers were also novelists, both were accomplished ironists, though where Hardy's irony is pessimistic, Sylvia Townsend Warner's comes from her scepticism, and works to a different end. Still, as far as she was 'like' any other poet in her early years, she was likest Hardy.

Also commemorated in the County Museum is that Dorset Worthy whose influence over Sylvia Townsend Warner I mentioned before—T.F.Powys. Hardy, who is said to have jumped out of his chair with surprise at his discovery of Powys's fiction, might have been similarly unprepared for some of the poems in *The Espalier*, for example, 'Nelly Trim', 'A Song about a Lamb', 'The Soldier's Return' or 'The Little Death', which begins:

> What voice is this
> Sings so, rings so
> Within my head?
> Not mine, for I am dead,

And a deep peace
Wraps me, haps me
From head to feet
Like a smooth winding-sheet.

Before my eyes
Reeling, wheeling,
Leaf-green stars
Have changed to purple bars

And flickered out;
Spinning, thinning,
Up the wall,
That has grown very tall.

Sylvia Townsend Warner was in a sense writing Powys's poems for him—or at any rate, to please him. 'Peeping Tom' must have pleased him, and 'Mrs. Summerbee Grown Old', narrated by a character from an early novella which Powys dedicated to Sylvia. 'Farmer Maw' is also constructed out of purely Powysian material, and 'Ghosts in Chaldon Herring' (Powys's village) goes so far as to suggest Powys himself is speaking on one of their nocturnal walks. The vocative 'my dear' was one of his speech-mannerisms. 'Nelly Trim', too, draws on a local Chaldon legend.

In a more general way, Powys must be held responsible for the proliferation of graveyards and dark, empty houses in Sylvia Townsend Warner's early poems, and for the element of horror which mars some of them. His work strengthened her growing suspicion that 'the English Pastoral is a grim and melancholy thing' which she expressed in her own version of the Powysian perverse. In her writing, no convention is sacred, no presupposition assured. The world has been turned upside-down, and we must stand on our heads to view it clearly. The reversed viewpoint is central to the technique of some of her fiction: *Elinor Barley, The True Heart, The Cat's Cradle Book* and *Kingdoms of Elfin*, for example, and is a strong element in her poetry, from 'The Patriarchs' and 'Kill Joy' to the 'Seven Conjectural Readings', 'Journey By Night' and 'Gloriana Dying', where she is, figuratively and literally, 'examining my kingdom from below'. When John Ireland set 'Songs Sacred and Profane' he took his sacred texts from Yeats and Alice Meynell, but all the profanity from early poems of Sylvia Townsend Warner.

The Espalier attracted some polite notices, and one enthusiastic one in *The Nation* which celebrated 'that quality of freshness, of spontaneous feeling, that comes neither from invention nor imitation, and with it a certain irony and reticence . . .'. The reviewer recommends 'Wish in Spring' to the other poets under review (Humbert Wolfe, Siegfried Sassoon and Graham Greene) and ends with percipient praise for Sylvia Townsend Warner: '*The Espalier* is not startling, but it is poetry'. 'Wish in Spring' takes issue obliquely with Keats: if poetry came as naturally as leaves to a tree,

> . . . then I should have poems innumerable,
> One kissing the other;
> Authentic, perfect in shape and lovely variety,
> And all of the same tireless green colour . . .
>
> But as I am only a woman
> And not a tree,
> With piteous human care I have made this poem,
> And set it now on the shelf with the rest to be.

This is not an admission which many poets would care to make and yet it recurs in Sylvia Townsend Warner's poetry—most notably in the central section about spring and inspiration in *Opus* 7. Like Johnson with 'lexicographer', she might have defined a poet as 'a harmless drudge', for her manuscripts bear out how well she knew the value of even the smallest detail of punctuation and syntax when striving after a certain effect. 'I revise them endlessly, endlessly. I revise everything that I do', she said, but it is not only an acute ear at work—there is also much 'piteous human care'.

Her next book was one Sylvia Townsend Warner once said she would have liked to change more. Garnett's 'quiet, intimate companion' had been writing poetry, but the sparkling epigrammatist had amused herself in the evenings by writing a novel. When Chatto and Windus published *Lolly Willowes* early in 1926, it amused a great many other people too. The book took off as briskly as the lady on a broomstick who decorates the covers of some of the early editions, and it remains her best-known work—though not universally read; one bookseller, on hearing the author's name, rummaged in his memory: 'Ah yes . . . *Lonely Willows*'.

Lolly Willowes was nominated for the 1926 Prix Femina and became the first Book-of-the-Month Club 'choice' in the United States, where Sylvia Townsend Warner has long had a committed following. The next year she published a second novel, *Mr Fortune's Maggot* and in 1929 a third, *The True Heart*, all in the same whimsical vein. *Time Importuned*, like *The Espalier* an unusually large collection of poetry, was published in 1928. Like its predecessor, it was well-received in a few quarters—A. E. Housman was now an admirer—but the success of the novels overshadowed her fledgling reputation as a poet.

Her third book of verse was *Opus 7* (her seventh published work). A long narrative poem in couplets modelled on Crabbe's, *Opus 7* stands mid-way between the short-story, a form which she was beginning to exploit successfully, and full-blown satirical verse. It deals with an old crone called Rebecca Random who is forced, in the lean years following the Great War, to grow and sell flowers to pay for her gin. Her increasing inebriation, as the trade in flowers catches on as a local rarity, leads to weird visions and hallucinations. The poem ends in the churchyard at night with Rebecca teaching God and her dead customer Bet 'a lesson how to drink', and there she dies. The story is sustained by great comic vivacity, interspersed with solemn interludes on the themes of Time, Death, War and Gin and passages of high-rhetorical extravagance. It is a little masterpiece, hard to categorise and unaccountably neglected.

By the time *Opus 7* was published, Sylvia Townsend Warner had gone with Valentine Ackland to live permanently in the country. They remained together until Valentine Ackland's death in 1969. In 1933 they published a joint collection, *Whether a Dove or Seagull* (*not* a collaboration, as the foreword is at pains to point out). The title was taken from a piece by Valentine Ackland:

> Whether a dove or a seagull lighted there
> I cannot tell,
> But on the field that is so green and bare
> A whiteness fell—

The lyrical and romantic Miss Ackland we associate with the dove; the seagull is the plainer-speaking, rougher-edged Miss Warner. The poems of the two writers are printed together and unattributed in the text. There is a key only at the end as a slight concession to those whose 'frame of mind . . . judges a poem by looking to see who wrote it', and against whom this 'experiment in the presentation of poetry' is 'a protest'. The book was dedicated to Robert Frost, who was perhaps puzzled by it.

Sylvia Townsend Warner and Valentine Ackland joined the Communist Party later in the 1930s. Their gesture towards an ideal of impersonality in *Whether a Dove or Seagull* is largely political, as was the decision first by W. H. Auden, then Cecil Day Lewis, then Stephen Spender, not to title poems. Julian Symons commented in his survey, *The Thirties*: 'I think this refusal to use titles sprang partly from a wish to discourage the emphasis placed by anthologies on the individual poem; the book that contained the poems, the social attitude expressed in them, these were the important things. The poets and those readers sympathetic to them, were looking for unity; titles seemed to imply diversity.' The theory behind *Whether a Dove or Seagull* is clear, but it is a large and wandering book in which the reader soon loses sight of the grand design. Intended, ostensibly, as a public statement, it is in fact a particularly personal one in which love poem responds to love poem. Most of the book is conducted *sotto voce*, although there is the occasional *fortissimo* such as the elaborate pastiche about the Reverend Joseph Staines Cope or the long eulogy of 'Grannie' Moxom, which ends with an impassioned vision of the earth and woman transfigured. For all the merits of the book—it contains a number of fine poems by both authors—I have not included it in this volume. It exists on its own terms and not those of a *Collected Poems*.

After 1933 Sylvia Townsend Warner published in her lifetime by way of poetry only *Boxwood*, a book of Reynolds Stone engravings 'with illustrations in verse' by Sylvia. *King Duffus* and *Azrael* (the latter published posthumously as *Twelve Poems*) were privately produced and privately circulated. So *Time Importuned*, which appeared in 1928, was in effect her last conventional collection of poems. Judging by the quantity of unpublished poems which she left at her death, the decision not to submit material for another substantial book, or seek publication except, from time to time, in periodicals, must have been to some extent deliberate. But whatever her reasons, the poems she wrote out of earshot of an audience are extraordinary.

The unpublished poems read as a sort of journal—not the kind that is slavishly kept to, but a record of small events breaking on the surface of ordinary life. The recurrent themes are the everyday difficulties of good husbandry: maintaining a house and fighting a garden. (Her realist, 'seagull' side was primarily concerned with ousting weeds, not planting flowers. She wrote an article on the subject, remarking that 'the sparing mention of weeds by those who write about their gardens seems hypocritical'. Weeds can be seen disporting themselves with perverse vigour throughout her poetry; they plague 'Peeping Tom', preoccupy Rebecca Random, pre-figure a death in 'The Sick Man's Garden'.) Her sphere of action in these poems is limited; a house, a garden, a lane, a village churchyard perhaps, but in this everyday English world, poems of love and of loss acquire a settled truth. The large themes are in a sense most naturally at home in these settings.

Among the unpublished and uncollected work are several witty squibs, macaronics and pieces of sophisticated semi-doggerel as well as the masterly 'Conjectural Readings', 'Five British Watercolours' and long poems which deserve close attention, notably 'In a foreign country . . .' and 'Astro-Physics':

> To no believable blue I turn my eyes,
> Blinded with sapphire, watchet, gentian,
> Shadow on snow, Mediterranean,
> Midsummer or midwinter-moonlight skies.
> Unstained by sight, unravished by surmise,
> And uttering into the void her ban,
> Her boast, her being—*I know not a man!*
> Out of all thought the virgin colour flies.
>
> After her, soul! Have in unhaving, peace,
> Let thy lacklight lighten upon thee, read
> So well thy sentence that it spells release.
> Explore thy chain, importune suns to cede
> News of thy dark—joyed with thy doom's increase,
> And only by distinction of fetters freed.

We also find substantial satires and political poems dating from her trip to Spain during the Civil War in 1936. Most of these appeared in journals of the time and anthologies of war-poetry, but her most effective political poem, one that goes some way towards particularity, 'Walking through the fields . . .', is set not in Russia or Spain, but her Dorset home, and is spoken in her own voice, not shouted—as some of the others seem to be—through a megaphone.

In the calm, reflective atmosphere of the unpublished poems Sylvia Townsend Warner's plainer style emerges. It is usually associated with the 'late' poems of *King Duffus* and *Twelve Poems*, although these collections drew on material from a thirty-year span. (Almost half the poems in *King Duffus* were taken from sequences written in 1943 and 1948; from *Twelve Poems*, 'Dorset Endearments' appeared under a different title in *The Countryman* in 1948, and 'Graveyard in Norfolk', which is often presumed to be an elegy for Valentine Ackland, was first published as early as 1934.) Sylvia Townsend Warner's 'plain' voice is sometimes discernible in the early books too, especially in the poems which deal with the folk world, where she has no peers. However casual the effects of her plainer style, rarely were they arrived at casually. She wore her learning lightly, using it in the service of clarity, taking great care to find 'The common word exact without vulgarity / The formal word precise but not pedantic'.

A musicologist in her youth, she brought to her poetry the disciplines of her musical studies. The suggestive metrical and rhythmic patterning of 'Anne Donne' or 'M. de Grignan', for instance, or the slant-rhyming tercets of 'Faithful Cross', 'Journey by Night' or 'King Duffus', are elements of a complex auditory rhetoric:

My crown lay lightly on my brow as a clot of foam,
My wide mantle was yellow as the flower of the broom,
Hale and holy I was in mind and in limb.

I sat among poets and among philosophers,
Carving fat bacon for the mother of Christ;
Sometimes we sang, sometimes we conversed.

Why did you summon me back from the midst of that meal
To a vexed kingdom and a smoky hall?
Could I not stay at least until dewfall?

Even those poems where the diction is at its plainest can be complicated or counterpointed by the 'music'. This effects 'a paradoxical union of subtlety and simplicity,' as Untermeyer noted, 'with no sense of strain between these opposites'. In reflecting on her work for the Tudor Church Music project, it would be wrong to stress the 'musical' element at the expense of the 'Tudor'. Her lifelong friend Bea Howe once described her as 'pure Tudor'. Her love of conceit and word-play, her delight in language and her prosodic subtlety, have affinities with the work of Elizabethan and Jacobean lyric and devotional poets. There is also that abiding element, the distilled, epigrammatic wisdom, the 'sentence'. Her poetry has a range equal to that of her long and varied experience. In this she surpasses many, if not most, of her contemporaries.

Her best poetry remains fresh in part because of the spirit in which it was written. She never took for granted the visits of her muse. In a letter to Untermeyer in 1926, she said of her writing, 'I haven't yet got over my surprise that I should be doing it at all.' The same note of surprise surfaces in a letter written fifty-two years later, in reference to this volume: 'It is the most astonishing affair for me to be taken notice of in my extreme old age'. To those who were privileged to read her poetry in the years when it was not widely available, it does not seem so astonishing. They might say of Sylvia Townsend Warner what she said of John Taverner in *Tudor Church Music*: 'The honest admirer . . . must be ready to admit that such and such specimens . . . are not great works. The admission need cost him little, since he can say with conviction that the most insignificant of them betrays, somewhere and somehow, the master hand.'

CHRONOLOGY OF PRINCIPAL PUBLICATIONS

1925	*The Espalier* (poetry)
1926	*Lolly Willowes* (novel)
1927	*Mr Fortune's Maggot* (novel)
1928	*Time Importuned* (poetry)
1929	*The True Heart* (novel)
1930	*Elinor Barley* (novella)
1931	*Opus 7* (poetry)
1931	*A Moral Ending and Other Stories* (short stories)
1932	*The Salutation* (short stories)
1933	*Whether a Dove or Seagull* (poetry)
1935	*More Joy in Heaven* (short stories)
1936	*Summer Will Show* (novel)
1938	*After the Death of Don Juan* (novel)
1943	*A Garland of Straw* (short stories)
1947	*The Museum of Cheats* (short stories)
1948	*The Corner That Held Them* (novel)
1951	*Jane Austen* (a British Council 'Writers and Their Work' pamphlet)
1954	*The Flint Anchor (novel)*
1955	*Winter in the Air* (short stories)
1957	*Boxwood* (poetry) - first edition
1958	*By Way of Sainte-Beuve* (a translation of Proust's *Contre Sainte-Beuve*)
1960	*Boxwood* - new edition
1960	*The Cat's Cradle Book* (short stories)
1962	*A Spirit Rises* (short stories)
1966	*A Stranger with a Bag* (short stories)
1967	*T. H. White* (biography)
1971	*The Innocent and the Guilty* (short stories)
1977	*Kingdoms of Elfin* (short stories)
1980	*Twelve Poems* (poetry)
1981	*Scenes of Childhood and Other Stories* (short stories)

UNPUBLISHED AND UNCOLLECTED POEMS

A WOMAN OUT OF A DREAM

Why have you followed me so closely
Up hill and down dale,
And why in this onset of evening have you grown
So pale and so pale?

Why at the water's edge do you linger
With imploring look,
And what are those words which you write with a straying
    finger
In the weltering brook?

Many and many are the clear streams
At which there is no slaking
One's thirst, and many the passionate espousals of dreams
Broken in the waking.

QUEEN ELEANOR

'In this dusk land,
And with this dusk upon my sight,
What is that Shape I see,
Close at hand rising up?'
'Madam, a poplar-tree.'

'Erred then my eyes,
Dimmed with my body's darkening plight;
For it meseemed that lo!
I saw rising a tall rood.'
'Madam, the sleight of snow.'

'Does the snow fall?
Christ warm the wintry poor tonight,
When I, a Queen, require
Comfort withal! Where ride we now?'
'Madam, in Lincolnshire.'

'Why then, we'll fare
By God's great house, for man's delight
Carved over with God's praise.
Even so fair showed that tree,
New-wrought by my sick gaze.

'What it may bode
I am too weak to read a-right,
But in my fantasy,
By the roadside many such
Crosses companioned me;

'Yes, in all, ten—
Ten fair Crosses, snow-stone-white,
New-builded, have we passed;
Stone-slender, richly-wrought—
Vanishing snow-fast:

'Changed in a twitch
Of failing eyes to tree, or sleight
Of snow, ere I have seen
Her, who niched in the heart of each
Stands like a Queen.'

EAST LONDON CEMETERY

Death keeps—an indifferent host—
this house of call,
whose sign-board wears no boast
save Beds for All.

Narrow the bed, and bare,
And none too sweet.
No need, says Death, to air
the single sheet.

Comfort, says he, with shrug,
is but degree,
and London clay a rug
like luxury,

to him who wrapped his bones
in the threadbare hood
blood wove from weft of stones
under warp of foot.

'I THOUGHT THAT LOVE . . .'

I thought that love would leap from a cloud
To devour me,
Or with the loud
Unmaking challenge to be of a trumpet
Overpower me.
But love has befallen me like a sleep.

And calm as a weed I range in this flood
Where no will is.
My anxious blood
Forgets its scarlet and lies down in slumber
With the lilies,
And my thoughts for the change of clouds I exchange.

ORNAMENTS OF GOLD

Mother, why do you hang in each hurt ear
those bobbing rings of gold?
To tweak men's glances thither my face to behold.

And this other ring, so deep in your finger grown,
is that also for men to see?
Yes, and to warn their wishes from following me.

And why do you wear, not breeches, as men do,
but a long-skirted gown?
The better for cares to catch at, and pull me down.

And when I am woman grown, shall I dress like you?
Yes, child, you may depend,
Woman-kind shall go thus till our world's end.

'EARLY ONE MORNING . . .'

Early one morning
In a morning mist
I rose up sorrowful
And went out solitary,
And met with Christ.

5

I knew him instantly,
For his clothes were worn;
Carpenter's gear he carried,
And between us was growing
A winter thorn.

For leaf and blossom
It had drops of dew,
For birdsong, silence—
More lovely, more innocent
Tree never grew.

'Give me,' said I,
And my hands forlorn
Held out, 'be it only
One of these dewdrops
Hanging on the thorn.'

'Of all these dewdrops,
Hung betwixt you and me,
That must die at daybreak
I own not one of them
My own,' said he.

Hearing him speak thus,
Each dewdrop shone
Enfranchised diamond;
And with sunrising
All was gone.

'HOW THIS DESPAIR ENJOYS ME!'

How this despair enjoys me! How much more throughly
Than your love could, your faithlessness burns through me!
Now, only now, you have possessed me truly.

No more in joy's inadequate day I languish.
To this last dark my last light I extinguish,
And all my being to loss of you relinquish.

ECLOGUE

'Neighbour, let us to our church go
This Christmas Eve,
To see the shepherds and the kings kneel low
And Jesus in Mary's sleeve
And Joseph standing by well-pleased.'

'Babe nor mother should we find
This winter's night.
Our church now belongs to a king whose mind
Is grown too wise to delight
In toys and images like these.'

'Neighbour, let us to the tavern go
This Christmas Eve,
And kiss Nan under the mistletoe,
And give the mummers good leave
To quench their roaring thirst in our bowl.'

'Mirth nor mummers should we find
This winter's night;
For Oliver's men are strict to bind
In stocked or pilloried plight
Players of wanton games like these.'

'Neighbour, let us to our neighbours go
This Christmas Eve,
And raise those tunes of long-ago,
And a drink or a shilling receive
In thanks for the good news we have told.'

'Drink nor shilling should we find
This winter's night;
For schoolmistress teaches how unrefined
Must sound to all ears polite
Such old-time country staves as these.'

'Neighbour, let us to the pictures go
This Christmas Eve,
And see a lady her garters show,
And a cunning thief deceive,
And the townsfolk sitting there well-pleased.'

A BURNING

Blue as a forget-me-not beside the brook
flows the constant plume of the bonfire smoke,
tingeing the winter-wasted meadow where no folk
walk now, nor lovers couch under the oak,
that holds out arms bare and broke.

Blue as a forget-me-not . . . and though you are gone,
out of your field your smoke-proxy burns on,
and like a flower is living and lovely in the landscape wan,
and from dusk will gather the pallor of a swan,
and declare its red heart-beats anon.

But foul is its taint far-blown, and terrified
the cattle huddle all to the windward side.
Only I wander here, and snuff still unsatisfied
the stench of the bed they burn, the bed where you died,
the bed to me denied.

PLEASURE IS SO SMALL A PLACE

Too close, too weak is my embrace;
Though side lies warm by side
After rapture replied,
You are not yet my bride.

Out of my sight you sneak your face—
Ah, but unsatisfied
Are the looks, and denied,
Your cold heart would hide,

Nor can my flocking kisses erase
Footprints of longfelt care
That your lineaments wear—
Too plainly they declare,

'Pleasure is so small a place.
They who've been free to fare
Through a roomy despair
Dwell ill-contented there.'

Well, then—I quit you, arm unlace,
Take warmth away, grow less
Hourly, and stress
Me in your loneliness—

For leverage admits no grace—
Till vast of absence shall press
An unswerving caress,
And you at length confess

How mastering is my embrace.

'O STARING TRAVELLER...'

'O staring traveller, only the moon-shine
Piercing the branches paints upon that sign
A nebuly blazon. Here is no more an inn.'
'Yet you must let me in.'

'My fires are out. Only the night wind blown
Down chimney stirs the ash on the hearthstone,
My beds are all unaired and disarrayed.'
'I care not for the bed.'

'Spent is my wine. Cold are my chambers all;
And round about the house the trees grown tall
Creep closer in as though they meant to mourn.'
'I to a darker bourne,

'A colder bed, a poorer welcome fare—
And I had thought that I was almost there
When in the midmost of your grieving grove
I heard a noise of love.

'I saw the ghosts throng to your lighted door,
Indulged and confident as heretofore,
And you upon them like a hostess wait.
Am only I too late?

'I, who am living, must I stand outside
Of all your loves the only love denied—

9

Young, and alive, and bitterly alone?'
'O late my love, come in!'

ON THE EVE OF SAINT THOMAS

On the Eve of Saint Thomas
So innocent was the grass
Of footfall, of nightfall,
In its silver rind
That it came to my mind
How rightful to consider
Is the date of Christmas
Between the first doubter
And the first martyr.

Shove, Thomas!
Push darkness away from us.
And pull, Steven!
Haul down more light from heaven.

So solemnly the sky
Carried the moon's majesty
Through a mist of hoar-frost,
As through a transparency
Of earthly-veiled heavenly,
That I thought of Our Lady
Being so far gone
That the child in her belly
Shone like the full moon.

Endure, sweet Lady,
To the end of the journey!
And yet-awhile lie patient,
O Maker omnipotent!

TREES

How lovely your trees will be in winter! breathe they,
Who come this way
To warm our cold new house with belauding say;
And from this frowned-down window and that they peer,

As though in fear
Of the green ramparts standing round so solid and sheer.
Trees are always lovelier in winter, they say—
And look away,
Out-faced by that impenetrable array.

But now it is July, three months must go
Before the horns blow
And a night or two tumbles our Jericho.
Deep in the tree-tops the wood-pigeons coo,
Take two, take two!
And the trees have taken us for the whole year through.

Before the winter unarms them we must learn
The unconcern
That can walk under their towers of shade nor turn
Cold, that can tread their hundred summers beneath
Packed wreath on wreath,
And sink ankle-deep in leaf-mould nor think of death.

Best, since already they watch us and measure our pride,
Not to flinch aside,
Even at this hour when behind them their allied
Thunderstorm rears, purple cloud above green cloud,
But minute and proud
To stroll through the breathless garden with head
        unbowed.

BUILDING IN STONE

God is still glorified—
To him the wakeful arch holds up in prayer,
Nightly dumb glass keeps vigil to declare
His East, and Eastertide;

The constant pavement lays
Its flatness for his feet, each pier acquaints
Neighbour, him housed; time-thumbed, forgotten saints
Do not forget to praise;

All parcels of the whole,
Each hidden, each revealed, each thrust and stress,
Antiphonally interlocked, confess
Him, stay, and him, control.

Whether upon the fens
Anchored, with all her canvas and all her shrouds,
Ely signal him to willows and clouds
And cattle, or whether Wren's

Unperturbed dome, above
The city roaring with mechanic throat
And climbing in layer on layer of Babel, float
Like an escaping dove,

Or whether in countryside
Stationed all humble and holy churches keep
Faith with the faith of those who lie asleep,
God is still glorified;

Since by the steadfastness
Of his most mute creation man conjures
—Man, so soon hushed—the silence which endures
To bear in mind, and bless.

THE ABSENCE

How happy I can be with my love away!
No care comes all day;
Like a dapple of clouds the hours pass by,
Time stares from the sky
But does not see me where I lie in the hay,
So still do I lie.

Like points of dew the stars well in the skies;
Taller the trees rise.
Dis-shadowed, unselved, I wander slow,
My thoughts flow and flow
But whither they tend I know not, nor need to surmise,
So softly I go;

Till to my quiet bed I must undress—
Then I say, Alas!
That he whom, too anxious or too gay,
I torment all day
Can never know me in my harmlessness
While he is away.

'SLEEK AND CALM . . .'

Sleek and calm, securely drowned,
The house in the pond hangs upside-downed;
There wave the curtains, there the rose
Wafts up its petals like bubbles rising.
Nothing troubles that repose.

Within those water-painted walls
No chimneys smoke, no china falls,
No finger-biting care walks through
Those tranquil chambers, no flustered voices
Rock that lustred peace askew.

Wish in that house moves to its aim
As fishes through the water swim,
Unerring and unobstructed;
There meditation, a water-lily
Rounds undistraught and uncompelled.

That is the water's house—but mine
Was forfeit with a lease to sign.
Ownership's footfall like a stone
Rocked the fair image, the fondled fancy,
Reknit in the pond, but there alone.

'FAIR, DO YOU NOT SEE . . .'

'Fair, do you not see
How love has wasted me?'
'I am blind,' said she.

'Blind only that youth
Knows not to look with ruth.'

'Blind, sir, in good sooth.

'Once it was not so.
My glance went to and fro,
Till I grew learned in woe.

'Blind-song larks I saw,
A rabbit in a snare's claw
That the rats did gnaw.

'Men, too I beheld
By iron engines quelled,
And a sapling felled.

'Then to the witch I sped.
Take out my eyes, I said,
Plant bright gems instead.'

'AT THE FIRST MEAL'

At the first meal, at the first drinking of wine
Another than those two sat down to dine.
On game and fruit fared they; he for his part
More richly fed upon a heart.

His heavy relish and unstayed lagged out
The meal. Their frolic smitten to a rout
At dish or hand or cherry stone they stared,
For eye the other neither dared.

Yet they must keep talk going, as polite
Strangers bedfellowed by catastrophe might,
Lest he their words denied on silence leech
And make an after dinner speech.

'Lady and gentleman, it gives me true
Pleasure to see you settled in your new
And handsome house. Sure may your sojourn be,
And sharpened with felicity.

'So prime a guest, do not mislike my tact
(I see, indeed, you are but half-unpacked);

I to this breed you embrace so long allied
Must haste to greet you, Madam Bride.

'And with the licence of a family friend,
Madam, your husband's choice I much commend;
For you, though young, are as these gauds aver
Of all antiques a connoisseur.

'Blest will you be then, blest and blithe bestead,
Whom Sheffield candlesticks to laquered bed
Shall light, whose eyes shall seek out morning through
Brocades of seventeen thirty two.

'One who such skill has to authenticate
The pedigrees of porcelain and plate
Will not disdain among her household gear
A long hereditary care.

'That Care am I. From father to sad son
With strict entail forever darkening on;
A fancy-worm, a blackness in the blood,
A vapour from a hidden flood

'Raised with undoing agues for no reason,
The mind's self-murder and the spirit's treason,
Bidding the hand let go, the heart deny
Its hope . . . that Care am I.

'Inhabit here or there, warm as you will
New hearthstones, I beside your chimney still
Will shade your fire—as even now I daunt
This with my coming hither; plant

'Blossomed or gravestrew trees, my breath shall ply
Them into shapes of tedium on the sky,
Face to sun's rise or set, your avenues
My undelighted eyes peruse.

'Your walks and chambers shall reverberate
My footing, your spread table shall await
Me, your dull guest, your stables testify
How resolute a horseman I.

'I on your walls will hang with following looks,
Ground to your music, comment in your books,
Under your flowers a snake, and on your night
A deeper dark: no thing so slight

'But it shall be my heavy signet fraught
With cold intimidation to your thought,
Being some time so stared into the sense
That languished for my going hence.

'But most of all your happiest hours be mine;
Your dated joy the desperate sunshine
That wilds the waiting landscape under edge
Of gathered thundercloud, when hedge,

'Tree, house, man, beast, stand stiffened, small and bright,
Conjured in unreality of light
To vivid minikins, disproportioned toys
Under that doom in poise.

'To such a guest a careful hostess made,
Sir, though you see this lady's colour fade,
Her smile taught time-keeping, her wantonness
Remodelled like the wedding dress

'Into the graver suit, and tougher-hued
Of matron cunning and solicitude—
Which for all drench of tears and the heart's hurt
Oozing will scarcely show the dirt;

'And know yourself, even with the vows that won her
Compact with me to bring this change upon her,
Remember for your comfort that these thorns
Insure a hanging head from horns.

'I, your black dog, long watchful at your heel,
Will wait on her henceforth also; steal
After her walks, whine at her door, be fed
By her as though by proxy you bled.

'Thus chaperoned, thus guarded, thus surveyed,
She will step straitly who might else have strayed,
Sit stilled as now. Madam, I raise my glass
To see you brought to such a pass.'

So, on their silence thrust, the voice unheard
Spoke out and ceased. Untended, the fire stirred,
Shrugging itself to sleep, and warily,
Like one beside a sickbed, she

Turned her slow head and eyed the empty wall
As though the shadow of a shade should fall.
None but their own. No, no, look not on these!
Look rather where from packages

Rose, half-unwrapped, litter of homecoming,
The auguries of pleasant housekeeping,
Well-wishing gifts, and spoil from hearths long cold
Searched out to deck this hearth; but old,

All old, and full of whispering care, they flocked
Forth in a creaking saraband and mocked
With faint foul breath. 'See, neighbour, how aghast
Mopes she who thought to hire the past.

'Us she unearthed, us, pretty wolf, clawed out
To futile resurrection/and the flout
Quick proffers to the dead—but, as befell,
Hit on one ghost who walks too well.

'Install us as she please, 'tis all pretence.
Within a year we shall be bundled hence
To trim another dwelling, and another,
Until long use and wont shall smother

'Our guise, and her accustomed sight shall crawl
Past us to watch the shadows on the wall,
Painted as now—one fixed, one wavering,
Cypress a stone companioning.'

'OF THE YOUNG YEAR'S DISCLOSING DAYS'

Of the young year's disclosing days this one day—
The first of February and a Sunday—
I clasp in mind, and set down for safe keeping;
But why this one plain day more than another
Seems whimsy, unless it be that to me sleeping

You came embracing, said with your air of very
Truth: Sweet heart, this is the first of February.

Signalled thus, and thus with a kiss commended
The morning's visage looked from the blended
Duffle of winter's sober web with I know not
What of special grace, its date a portent
Pledged like the first aconite or first snowdrop,
Of its own choice and free good-will arriving
And flowered unreferred to the almanack maker's contriving

Everything I saw—the broad sky netted over
With small white clouds like a field of clover,
The fine lace of the treetops faintly stirring
Above the boughs unmoved as though not wind plied them
But only the pressed notes of the birds conferring,
The patient winter green of the lawn, the thrushes
Hopping ungainly large under the bare bushes,

All these, that January or March might show me
Unchanged on this eastern coast, where slowly,
Hooding her bright head, planting charily
Her shreds of colour in lew of balk or hedgerow,
Muffled in guise of winter, spring comes warily,
Took, at your word's wand, the light of the spirit
In its due day incarnate, all day to wear it.

Yes, and even the sea, coiling its endless
Tether along the strand, the friendless
Unharvested one, on whose cold green ungreeted
Fall the rich rains of February Filldyke,
Looked now at peace, as though this day had meted
There too a portion of promise, as though the ambered
Forests below that green their greening remembered.

'HERE, IN THE CORNER OF THE FIELD . . .'

Here, in the corner of the field,
Ten willows grow—
Five in a row, and five in a row,
18   And at the angle grows an elder-bush.

In summer when it is covered with flat-faced bloom
And the willows say, Hush,
It looks as though
Someone had cut and peeled
And planted willow-slips with an intent
Of making something like a room—
A cool green whispering room with grassy pillows
And one white-blossomed elder with fusty scent
For corner-knot and ornament;
Thinking that, when the slips were rooted and grown
And the elder in bloom,
He would meet a young girl wandering bird-alone
And love her, and bring her here, and bid her lie down,
And hear her sighs mixed with the breathing willows.
Or else, may be, he meant
To rest here with that lovelier bride
Of Thought-in-Loneliness—
Long, long to abide
Under the willows' lengthening caress
Till all his cares were healed
And he walked homeward, slow and satisfied,
To shelter of mute walls.
But if so indeed, then how long ago!
For year by year the elder-blossom is less,
And turns its fusty scent to bitterness,
And despairs of fruit;
Past-prime the willows have split, and drag from the root,
Scantier-leaved each summer the shadow falls,
And nothing lies now
On the grassy hummocks shapeless and overgrown
But a broken hurdle and a rusty plough.

WOMAN'S SONG

Kind kettle on my hearth
Whisper to avert God's wrath,
Scoured table, pray for me.
Jam and pickle and conserve,
Cloistered summers, named and numbered,
Me from going bad preserve;
Pray for me.

Wrung dishclout on the line
Sweeten to those nostrils fine,
Patched apron, pray for me.
Calm linen in the press,
Far-reaped meadows, ranged and fellowed,
Clothe the hour of my distress;
Pray for me.

True water from the tap
Overflow the mind's mishap,
Brown tea-pot, pray for me.
Glass and clome and porcelain,
Earth arisen to flower a kitchen,
Shine away my shades ingrain;
Pray for me.

All things wonted, fleeting, fixed,
Stand me and myself betwixt,
Sister my mortality.
By your transience still renewed,
But more meek than mine and speechless,
In eternity's solitude,
Pray for me.

'SQUAT AND SULLEN . . . '

Squat and sullen, the small house is left behind.
But as the wind
From the sea haunts round it, so haunts there my mind.

All the summer through that salt wind will not cease,
Combing the deep fleece
Of the grass, tilting the stiff rods of the irises.

Whether urgent or furtive, whether challenge or plea,
The wind from the sea
Will ply the narcissus leaves and assault the tree,

Will rattle the closed casements, and blowing under the door
Will stir across the floor
Wastepaper left there, as though there should be footsteps
20   once more.

Others going by will see the garden overgrown,
The house sulking alone,
Squat and rock-resolute amid the rising green wind-blown,

But never guess how my salt constancy of mind
Haunts in that constant wind,
Warding anxious and ownerly the freehold left behind.

COTTAGE MANTLESHELF

On the mantleshelf love and beauty are housed together.
There are the two black vases painted with pink roses,
And the two dogs carrying baskets of flowers in their jaws.
There are the two fans stencilled with characters from
      Japan,
The ruby glass urns each holding a sprig of heather,
And the two black velvet cats with bead eyes, pink noses,
      and white cotton claws.

All these things on the mantleshelf are beautiful and are
      married:
The two black vases throb with their sympathetic pink
      roses,
The puss thinks only of her tom and the dog of his bitch.
On the one fan a girl is coquetting and on the other a man,
Out of the same vein of fancy the urns were quarried,
Even the sprigs of heather have been dried so long you
      can't tell 'tother from which.

But amid this love and beauty are two uncomely whose
      sorrows
Isled in several celibacy can never, never be mated,
One of them being but for use and the other useful no
      more.
With a stern voice rocking its way through time the alarm
      clock
Confronts with a pallid face the billowing to-morrows
And turns its back on the enlarged photograph of young
      Osbert who died at the war.

Against the crumpled cloth where the photographer's
      fancy

Has twined with roses the grand balustrade he poses,
His hands hang limp from the khaki sleeves and his legs
    are bent.
His enormous ears are pricked and tense as a startled
    hare's,
He smiles—and his beseeching swagger is that of a nancy,
And plain to see on the picture is death's indifferent
    rubber stamp of assent.

As though through gathering mist he stares out through
    the photo's
Discolouring, where the lamp throws its pink-shaded echo
    of roses
On the table laid for supper with cheese and pickles and
    tea.
The rose-light falls on his kin who sit there with a whole
    skin,
It illumines through England the cottage homes where just
    such ex-voto
Are preserved on their mantleshelves by the living in token
    that they are not as he.

Uncomely and unespoused amid the espousals of beauty,
The cats with their plighted noses, the vases pledging their
    roses,
The scapegoat of the mantleshelf he stands and may not
    even cleave
To the other unpaired heart that beats beside him and
    apart;
For the pale-faced clock has heard, as he did, the voice of
    duty
And disowns him whom time has disowned, whom age
    cannot succour nor the years reprieve.

MANGOLDS

At field-gaps heaped, buttressing barn-wall and hedge,
Mounded along the main-road's grassy edge,
Dull harvest and unsung, the mangolds are gathered—
Lopped clods of earth looking, skull-pale in these dark-
    weathered
Closer-hooded days of autumn decreasing.

They wait, and the rains wash them, and the wind's teasing
Dries off from their stolid chaps and unstirred the last
Flecks of the mothering soil. Day-long lumber past
Lorries and farm tumbrils with the mangold load,
And the cars spurn the spillings along the road—
Limboed chance-falls, not worth the pitch and tossing
Of child's-play even. To-day at the level crossing
We watched our last of them: truck after truck full
Of the identical rough image of a skull,
Not for any sense socketed, not for any crown
Grown but to grow, to be uprooted, sliced down
For cattle-mash or in the winter fold scattered.
On through the emptied fields the train clattered,
The smoke thinned, the releasing signal jangled . . .
Where on earth, we said, is the need of so many mangolds?

In fields ploughing, mucking out barton or plashing hedge,
Bicycling home along the main-road's edge,
Dulled of aspect and speech 'go the labourers.
Legged clods of earth looking, numb-skulled with all
        weathers'
Buffeting, and broken on the year's wheel of toil unceasing.
Sun flays and the rain sods them, and the wind's teasing
Subdues on their sullen cheeks and inured the last
Rebellion of the blood, dyes them all to the fast
Sad Adam tint, wraps bone with likeness of clay
Even before the death-cart lumbers them away.
Heaped, mounded, buttressing, everywhere multiplied,
Where in earth, I say, can be safe hiding for these in their
        autumn-tide,
For these skulls to what end socketed, and with what
        crown glorified?

MAKING THE BED

Hearing you overhead
It was as though
In solemn dance and slow
You moved around the bed.

Step forward and retreat
And then a pause—

Hereditary laws
Of smooth adjusted sheet,

Plumped pillow truly placed,
Blanket tucked fast,
Ordered from first to last
The measure that you paced.

In tawny Egypt so
Or Hellas my mind
Still bent to look behind
Has watched the dancers go

Gravely before the God
With cadenced fall
And immemorial
Of feet in ritual shod;

Nor they, to custom yoked,
Guessed further than
You launched in your pavane
How (anxiously invoked

With plea of continuance)
Man's slow and few
Steps the unchanging sue
Through mazes of a dance.

Dance to your Daddy, then!
Happy my love,
With tweak and pat and shove
Make up the bed again.

Wont's votaress, dance on!
Prepare the dark.
Altar array and ark
Of life fetched and foregone.

'THE VINERY HAS BEEN BROKEN . . .'

The vinery has been broken for years and years.
Out through the shattered panes the grape-vine rears
A green head, thrusts sideways a trailing limb.

Inside all is discarded, musty and dim.
Sheafed penny notebooks hang mouldering on the wall,
Where ten years ago someone recorded the rainfall.
Ah!—in those days the rain drummed on a sound roof.
Milky-white were the walls, the casements weatherproof,
Everything was prosperous, neat, tight and trim:
Even the weather was more orderly then than now;
And pruned was the gipsying vine, scraped every bough,
Nipped back the shadowing leaves, thinned out the bunches,
And carried into the house for dinners and lunches.
Had we come here then, had we as guests walked round
To praise the gardener, hear a host expound
August usually dry if July be wet
Our disowning going would have been sans regret.
We'd barely have liked it then, could not have loved
As at first sight we did when the vine had shoved
Its wanton garlanded head out into the opening air,
Ramping out like a cat escaping, without a care
For its weakling, undersized cluster, its one last
Derisive pledge of duteous fertility past.

'FIE ON THE HEART ILL-SWEPT...'

Fie on the heart ill-swept
Where sorrows over-kept
Sodden with tears and foul
Lie mouldering cheek by jowl
With mildewed revenges
Grown tasteless with time's changes,
Limp wraths and mumbled visions,
Fly-blown into derisions,
Delights jellied to slime
And tag-ends of rhyme.

Life! Grant me a harder
Housewifery in my larder,
And if I may not eat
Fresh-killed meat,
Crisp joy and dewy loathing,
Let me have done with loving.
Aye, though philosophy's

25

Wan pulse my palate freeze
Ere I to carrion swerve
Carrion-like, let me starve.

A MAN IN A LANDSCAPE

Looking from where on the hill I sit
nine ricks I count,
three fields with stooks past counting,
twelve shorn pastures and two-score cattle browsing,
one barton below me, and on the skyline another,
and the shepherd's hut, bleached with winter and summer.
Narrow along the valley the road travels
with its ten telegraph poles, and out of it ravels
the stony track, mounting to the high fields of harvest
and the thistledown-cloud-scattered mute sky of mid-august.
Three hundred acres, may be, of the farm's eight hundred
lie in my sight as lies in my lap to be squandered
this hour of waiting, of willy-nilly patience;
and so I reckon up ricks and cattle, guess at the battalions
of sheaved corn, and all the landscape con and re-con.
Ah! How wearily it hangs from the shoulders of one man!

Minute on the opposite hillside, I saw him not
till the partridge brood, rousing at his slow foot,
flew up like a handful of ashes, and vanishing
designated him left alone, a labourer hoeing.
There he moiled, his fixed plover-flash of stripped-
to-shirt among the arrogant green of the turnip;
and sight brought sound with it, for now on the wind
from a mile away I heard his hoe clatter on the flint.
But at this spark of man kindled on the immense
landscape how the face of nature changed countenance,
how, at his tiny coming, the field receded, enlarged
its borders, drew away from him, and the horizon arched
its crest, developed the huge contours and implacable
of a wave about to fall.

I dare not turn my eyes from him, I dare not relinquish
that threated pinpoint of being lest it should vanish
out of the field where all day the long sun

has lit him crawling to and fro alone.
I strain my ears for the assurance that he still lives,
still turns the flints along the turnip grooves,
slow, slow . . . Ah, how slow to go,
who with each step drags after him this vast
mantle of landscape, this once-velvet now threadbare and
      trailing to waste!

THAELMAON

Early in the morning, late in the evening
Through this quiet valley where sheep are feeding
A man goes by and a man follows.
And all things heed them though no one sees them,
Whether they walk in clear or cloudy season,
Whether eastward or westward stretch their shadows.

He who goes first is bruised and wan-featured,
Limps with slow step as though he had been fettered,
Looks long and carefully, a grave beholder;
And he who follows is alertly footed,
And in black is ceremonially suited,
And tilts a headsman's sword over his shoulder.

After they are gone the empty valley
Fills with a long sigh, with a profound query,
As though the earth's timeless breast with its brief grasses
Stirred at some thought traversing its insentience,
Came to the brink of awakening with the question
'Will he come back again, the man who passes?'

VALE

When I was young
I wore a reefer coat,
A sailor's bonnet.
It had a ribbon on it
Saying *Antigone* or *Inflexible*.

27

As a mariner
I took my inland walks.
The long south-wester
Bowled my hoop the faster,
The north wind blew down acorns and chestnuts.

Roxeth and Kenton,
Greenford and Mutton Lane,
The gasworks and the canal:
These were my ports of call
Between the autumnal and the vernal equinox.

Sometimes my nurse
Stayed gossiping so long
That we, benighted,
Finished our voyage lighted
By Cassiopea, Orion, and Polaris.

But all these routes,
These islands and these havens,
Now lost and undone,
Are part of Greater London.
Nothing is left but a photo of Tib as a sailor.

'I SAID, FORBODING, . . .'

I said, forboding,
How shall my autumn furnish forth your spring?
How from my smouldered green,
And slaked, shall you replenish and preen?

But you, bestowing
On my dust your sun, take wing;
And risen with you, my care
Aims surer your flight, being heavier than air.

Oh then, thanksgiving
Take from this ground that you have taught to sing.

'WHEN I BEHELD YOUR HATRED...'

When I beheld your hatred glance
Off my unvisored countenance,
And through your mantraps one by one
Myself unscathed as water run;
And saw your well-appointed dart
Smirk like a posy on my heart,
I was abashed as though I had
Cheated at cards—for I was dead.

'DRAWING YOU, HEAVY WITH SLEEP...'

Drawing you, heavy with sleep to lie closer,
Staying your poppy head upon my shoulder,
It was as though I pulled the glide
Of a full river to my side.

Heavy with sleep and with sleep pliable
You rolled at a touch towards me. Your arm fell
Across me as a river throws
An arm of flood across meadows.

And as the careless water its mirroring sanction
Grants to him at the river's brim long stationed,
Long drowned in thought, that yet he lives
Since in that mirroring tide he moves,

Your body lying by mine to mine responded:
Your hair stirred on my mouth, my image was dandled
Deep in your sleep that flowed unstained
On from the image entertained.

'AH, SLEEP, YOU COME NOT...'

Ah, Sleep, you come not, and I do not chide you.
You the ever-young, the sleek and the supple,
How should I bride you
Who am so harsh with care, so grimed with trouble?

29

You to the child's cot and the lover's pillow,
You to the careless creation in field and steading,
And to my roof-mate swallow
Come with goodwill, who come not to my dull bidding.

Like lies down with like. If I am to woo you
I must disguise myself, and in youth's green
Habit pursue you,
Or imagine myself to what I never have been:

Or you in pity put on death's leaden likeness
To follow my weariness.

MODO AND ALCIPHRON

In the Lybian desert I
Saw a hermit's carcass lie,
And a melancholy fiend
Over the battered bosom leaned.

Black as a widow dead for love,
Motionless he drooped above;
Only his tail from side to side
Switched the sand with narrow stride.

'Grievest thou, imp, to see thy spoil
Lie thus quenched on burning soil?
Rinsed the brain, and the loin's lust
Safely reconciled with dust?

'Or perchance thy mournful hide
Dreads how well the lash will chide
When Pope Satan makes thee skip
For a negligent stewardship?'

With a sullen silence he
Raised his head, and looked at me,
Looked me through, and looked away,
Nor for all that I could say

Looked again. Quoth I, I've matched
Patience with yours; and so I watched

The slow, sun-swollen daytime through
To mark what this strange fiend would do.

Cramped and cold I woke from sleep
To hear the fiend begin to weep.
Twinkling in starlight the tears ran
Along his beard, and he began:

'Dead is the holy Alciphron!
Modo's occupation's gone.
All my pretty joys are sped,
Gentle Alciphron is dead!

'Never was there saint so mild
And so easily beguiled;
'Twas pure pleasure to torment
Anything so innocent.

'Danced I, gleaming in a dress
Of nimble maiden nakedness,
His prompt heart with hastening beat
Drummed the measure for my feet,

'And his glances whipped me round,
Till toppling in a dizzy swound
With long recovery I would twine
About him like the conjugal vine,

'While my forked and flickering tongue,
Constant as summer lightening, hung
On the scant flesh that wrapped his bones,
Till sighs long-husbanded, chuckling groans,

'Vouched for the pleasures he endured;
By thorns such pleasures must be cured,
And when most thick the thin blood fell
I knew that I had pleased him well.

'Then at other times I'd sit
Praising his spiritual wit,
Assuring him how deftly he
Could comprehend the Trinity,

'Flesh Christ, with never a trespassing glide
To error on this or 'tother side,
Show how original sin doth breed
Inherent in the genital seed,

'And every tinkling sophist quell,
Who questions that the troops of hell
Pester the saint upon his knees,
Actual and numerous as his fleas.

'But most of all 'twas my delight
To cajole him from the elected night
Wherewith the christian cowls his sense
From the allurement and offence

'Of a lost planet. I would be
Damnation swinging from a tree
With voice more wildly ravishing
For being damned, or in a spring

'With chill adulteries surprise
Him parched; often I thieved his eyes
To love me in a lizard, or in braid
Of sun begetting from a shade

'A spawn of dancing babies—all
Accursed as their original.
In many a salad I laid a snare
Of joy that he on such poor fare

'Fared well, or else on wafts of thyme
Into the warded brain would climb
Unchallenged, or tweaked him by the nose
With the remembrance of a rose.

'Thus did we wrestle, and never chaste
Turtles did rarer dalliance taste,
Thus mixed our opposites, as true
As plighted dock and nettle do,

'Thus to all time's example gave
Of the mutual comfort saint should have
With devil, devil with saint, and thus
I clean forgot how envious

'In his unmated splendour sits
He, the Tyrant—'
          As oak splits
Before the axe, and falls with a loud
Indignant groan, so groaned, so bowed,

The fiend, and lay in silence long;
But once or twice against the throng
Of stars raised up a blackening fist;
Then mourned, as mourning from a mist:

'Alas, how faithless man can be
To a fiend's eternity!
Into untiring malice doomed
Virtue as long-breathed I presumed;

'With never a care save which art next
To ply I looked on time unvexed,
Nor, in this plenty of sand, did doubt
The tale of his was running out.

'So Alciphron grew old, though I
Knew it not. This gew-gawed sky
Its virgin hood of grey had on,
And light was scarce, when Alciphron

'Awoke, and laid his hand on me,
And stared east. *Haec dies*, said he,
Quem fecit Dominus. I too
Looked east, and saw a path run through

'The kindling cloud. It bruised my gaze
To meet the intolerable blaze,
The ostentatious Rose, the blare
And uproar of light which threatened there;

'But Alciphron beheld and smiled,
Crowing for pleasure like a child
Who views its promised sugarplum:
Then, with a crash which has left dumb

'All thunder since, about us came
A simpering angel in a flame,

Who seized upon redemption's prey,
And bore him, like a child, away.

'Thus, O woe, I'm left alone
With this unanswering flesh and bone.
All my pretty joys are sped,
Gentle Alciphron is dead!

'Nothing is left me of my joy
But this contemptuous broken toy.
Modo's occupation's gone,
Dead is the holy Alciphron!'

'I HAD A WORD ON MY TONGUE . . .'

I had a word on my tongue
and a journey to go,
but they waylaid me
with love because I was young.

Love brought lullabies to sing
and a house to hold,
and they gainsayed me
with praise because I was strong.

Now I sit, cold hearth's crony,
while the word is told.
And they forsake me
who hear it and go on my journey.

SOME MAKE THIS ANSWER

Unfortunately, said he, I have lost my manners,
That old civil twitch of visage and the retreat
Courteous of threatened blood to heart, I cannot
Produce them now, or rig up their counterfeit.
Thrust muzzle of flesh, master, or metal, you are no longer
Terrible as an army with banners.

Admittedly on your red face or your metal proxy's
I read death, I decipher a gluttony to subdue
All that is free and fine, to savage it, knock it

About, taunt it to stupor, prison it life-through;
Moreover, I see you garnished with whips, gas-bombs,
    electric barbed wire,
And affable with church and state as with doxies.

But from other brows than yours I have felt a stronger
Voltage of death; walking among my fellow men
I have seen the free and the fine wasted with cold and
    hunger,
Diseased, maddened, death-in-life-doomed, and the ten
Thousand this death can brag have reckoned against your
    thousand.
Shoddy king of terrors, you impress me no longer.

BENICASIM

Here for a little we pause.
The air is heavy with sun and salt and colour.
On palm and lemon-tree, on cactus and oleander
a dust of dust and salt and pollen lies.
And the bright villas
sit in a row like perched macaws,
and rigid and immediate yonder
the mountains rise.

And it seems to me we have come
into a bright-painted landscape of Acheron.
For along the strand
in bleached cotton pyjamas, on rope-soled tread,
wander the risen-from-the-dead,
the wounded, the maimed, the halt.
Or they lay bare their hazarded flesh to the salt
air, the recaptured sun,
or bathe in the tideless sea, or sit fingering the sand.

But narrow is this place, narrow is this space
of garlanded sun and leisure and colour, of return
to life and release from living. Turn
(Turn not!) sight inland:
there, rigid as death and unforgiving, stand
the mountains—and close at hand.

EL HEROE

Nobody knew his name.
Pen nor paper will tell it.

We saw him rise up singing
Where the freshet leaps and falls.
With a gun at his shoulder;
Among the briars and brambles
His blue overalls
Were like a taunt sent ringing
Out to the eyes of the rebels.

The mountain wind arising
Keened all night for woe;
Midnight laid on his face
A handkerchief of snow;
Dawn came with a handful
Of woodland flowers to strow;
Like mourners through the hills
The freshets began to flow.

Nobody knew his name.
Pen nor paper will tell it.

WAITING AT CERBERE

And on the hillside
That is the colour of peasant's bread,
Is the rectangular
White village of the dead.

No one stirs in those streets,
Out of those dark doorways no one comes,
At the tavern of the Black Cross
Only the cicada strums.

And below, where the headland
Strips into rock, the white mane
Of foam like a quickened breath
Rises and falls again;

And above, the road
Zigzagging tier on tier
Above the terraced vineyards,
Goes on to the frontier.

JOURNEY TO BARCELONA

In that country pallor was from the ground,
darkness from the sky.
As the train took us by
we debated if it were mountain we saw or cloud.

The bleached fields are pallid as truth might be.
Men move on them like clouds.
Dwellings like hempen shrouds
wrap up squalor with a grave dignity.

Pale is that country like a country of bone.
Dry is the river-bed.
Darkness is overhead,
threatening with the fruitfulness implicit in storm.

The willows blanch, and catch their breath . . .
It rains in the hills!
The parched river-bed fills,
the sky thunders down fruitfulness.

Faithful to that earth the clouds are gathered again.
If the profile unknown
were cloud, it will be stone
before long. Rain from the red cloud, come to Spain!

PORT BOU

Through these ruined walls
the unflawed sea.
And to the smell of sunned
earth and of salt
sea is added a third

smell that cries: Halt!
I am what will be

familiar to you
by this journey's end.
I am, stale, the smell
of the fire that quenched
the fire on this hearth, that brought
down these walls, that wrenched
this wound in the ground.

I am the smell
on all the winds of Spain.
I am the stink in the nostrils
of the men of Spain.
I have taken the place
of the incense at the burial,
I have usurped the breath
of the rose plucked for the bridal,
I am the odour of the wreath
that is held out for heroes
to behold and breathe.
I cordial the heart,
I refresh the brain,
I strengthen the resolved fury
of those who fight for Spain.

'WALKING THROUGH THE MEADOWS . . .'

Walking through the meadows, to the sound of my tread
Words march through my head.
To a hundred hearts they are gone, and the hearers are
        won,
And march with me confident through this evening of
        summer begun,
And their thronging footsteps and mine are as one.

But a man comes here, and around me shadowless
Stretches the wide grass.
My own shadow I see and the shadow of a tree,
Million-flecked field flowers and a gull wheeling to the sea,
And the man from his work coming on to me.

Out of his day's loneliness he sights me friendly . . .
All my words are ended.
'The weather holds,' say I, and he answers me, 'Aye,
We are in surely for another drought. Ther's no rain in that
     sky
And the mid-May pasture is no more than ankle-high.'

What words can I find for him, what deeds declare
That his heart will hear?
The breaking of chains will not loosen the locked rain,
And a world however new-made must cringe when winter
     comes again,
And the wind blows to men's bones the old pain.

Through his sky the sickle moves to reap but the dark,
And his heel the spark
Hammers from the senseless flint where the cart-ruts print
Unchanging over changeless slopes the curves of least dint.
What words like new-come summer can re-mint

His stoic grey to green, summon his sap forth
To change the look of earth?
What deeds his hope retrieve that he may believe
Man also on a May-day shall rouse to blossom and leaf,
And bear to autumn's barn his full sheave?

Whence the word? He it is must prompt me to it.
His trudging foot
Hammer my heart till shaped and known the plough-share
     purpose be shown,
The field cloven, the seed strewn, the handsome harvest
     full-grown.
He coming with a sickle shall reap his own.

THE WINTER ROAD

A morning of black frost
iron in every tuft
of grass, and roadway roughed,
and every tree a ghost.

Every tree a ghost,
from the injured root
rising up mute
the traveller to accost;

and the mid-day air
dusky like a swoon,
and the afternoon
closing like a snare.

Winter's look of wan
over landscape strowed,
and the clanging road,
and a tramping man,

who does not turn his head,
who goes with rigid gait
lest he should be too late
for a workhouse bed.

Post or pale is nigh;
he sees his breath hang;
he hears his footing clang;
he feels the cars go by;

and the ghostly trees
with anguish at the root
sentinel his route . . .
Ah! but one of these

while unheeding he
went onward stirred, and cried
with summer voice: Abide,
O loved one, with me!

The blinding cars go past,
he stands through dazzle and dim
and sees his shadow limn
the shape of one who's lost

his dearest thing, and yet,
between frenzy and stupor swung,
must ask himself what's wrong,
40   how lost, and where, and what.

But vain to turn back sight.
Vain, vain to interrogate those
on whose stiff ranks now close
the iron veils of night.

THE TRAMP

The cloud has shed its snow.
Now it is bleached and pale
above the rigid hill . . .
How many miles to go?

The blackbird and the crow
like bouncing coffins go
across the sheeted snow.

Well may they move so light,
for they are empty all.
A vaster burial
she needs, who lies so white,

so stern, so motionless,
with a tree like a black tress—
the hill that I must cross.

For the hill along the west
like a dead woman lies;
and I must tread those thighs,
and stamp that icy breast.

The turnpike drags me on
towards my plighted one.
I look . . . and she is gone!

And rising into air,
with every breath more full,
more apt, more bountiful,
a living woman is there;

rounded and warm and white,
and lingering . . . and the sleight
of steam yet soothes my sight;

though now I see the train
running below the hill,
with shrewish voice and shrill
whistling me back again

to truth in a world of snow.
How fast go they! How slow
go I! How many miles to go!

PLUM TREE FROM CHINA

In the narrow garden,
Where I lay in the sun
Looking towards London,
A plum tree from China grew.

A few stammering blossoms
It put out in spring:
An idle hour's reckoning
Could have told all its leaves.

But with autumn emerging
The uncomforted tree
Reprinted unchangingly
Its Chinese Alas! upon air.

Once, and once only,
Where canker had rent
Its black bole, transparent
Oozings of amber came.

Jewels of frozen honey,
Distillation of crass
Sweet plum-flesh to topaz—
I bit and tasted one.

To this day I remember
How my dashed sense
Admitted with prescience
The taste of sterilised grief.

That phoenix-fruit long-guarded
Of the tree in distress

Had not even the bitterness
To tincture its flat wanhope.

O child well-warned, know passion
From passion's pure doll!
Dread that dewy alcohol
Of tears sublimed past salt!

'IN A FOREIGN COUNTRY . . .'

In a foreign country travellers who come to stay
But not to settle, after the first day
Or two of floating buy with pleasure sophisticate
Something regional, a hat of grass or a fur hat—
A dated seizin, an acclimatisation to borrow,
Wear for a while and cast away;
But I in a strange continent bought a sorrow,
And wore it for a half-year's stay.

Being more tractable a texture than grass or fur
As time went by my sorrow became embroidered
With roads and trees, quilted with mountains, dyed
With the colours of sumach and Joe-Pye-weed.
The hulking hillsides, shaggy with hemlock and pine
And rambling like bears along the horizon,
Were my sorrow's hem:
When I walked they wallowed after me, when I swam
They swam with me, their treetop stir
Silenced in the tepid lake-water.
The rocky pasture, echoing under my footfall,
Affirmed how weighty the garment I must trail,
The fox-grape and the sweetfern chafed by the midday
Sun, and the accomplished perfection of decay
That evening from the alembic forest distilled
Were the odours shaken out as my sorrow rustled
From one day to another day,
And my heels in desolate idleness tapping the road
In permanence of granite were shod.

Sometimes as a breast-pin I wore a poplar-tree,
And in its boughs a cat-bird complained,
And in its shade my friends sat reasoning with me.   *43*

At other times I let a river twist
Itself into a braclet round my wrist:
Thus sweetly (saying) might a neck be noosed
In a crystal halter,
Thus streamingly salvation come by water
And all your cares be at an end.
But breast-pin I pulled out and bracelet I let fall.
There would be other trees and other rivers,
And southward a heavier mantle I trailed
Into a poor land.
There was my sorrow embroidered with patched pastures,
With a scorched hillside sagging like a drained breast,
With the ghostly regiment of the felled forest,
With the gaunt water-course, with the forsaken avenue
Beseeching the witless mansion, with the tattered
        advertisement
Of the snuff that wards off the fever and dulls the ague.
There through the counterfeit rose-acres
I groped onward after the cotton pickers,
Hauling my sorrow after me like a gunny-sack;
There idle and desolate amid idleness and desolation
My heels dinting the red sand or the white sand
With the silence of negation were answered back.

Sorrow in one's own country is something familiar.
Wear it or tear it, it is a homespun wear:
It is the bus route and the grocer's doorway and the scent
Of the March dust under the April rain.
It is unbought, casual, climatic, dateless, an inherited
        garment,
The shawl one's mother and one's grandmother wore,
Easy to put on and easy to mislay:
Now I can scarcely believe that I wore and called my own
Anything so magnificent
As the sorrow I bought in a strange continent
And wore for every day.

In mid-Atlantic foundered the island of Atlantis.
There toll the bronze bells of the city of Ys.
There driftingly dance upon the unvexed tides
Drowned sailors with their Atlantidean brides
(But the head being heaviest they dance heels uppermost).
And there, midway between one coast and the other coast,

Dimming, submerging, falling from the light of day,
Past colour sombred and past texture sodden,
Wallowing downward towards the lost, the foundered, the
    forgotten,
Down, down to the innocence of legend it recedes—
My sorrow, embossed with mountains, darkened with
    forests, laced
With summer lightening, quilted with rivers and dirt
    roads—
My sorrow, stately as a cope, vast as a basilica—
My sorrow, embroidered all over with America,
That at a word from you in mid-Atlantic I threw away.

'UNDER THE SUDDEN BLUE . . .'

Under the sudden blue, under the embrace
of the relenting air, under the restored shadow
of the bird flying over the sunny meadow,
the garden ground
preserves an unconvinced and sullen face;
as though
it yet remembered the smite of frost, the wound of snow.
Automatically and without grace
it puts forth monosyllables of green,
answers Yes, or No,
with a muddy daisy, or one celandine,
or in ravel of last year's weeds lies winter-wound.
Poor cadet earth, so clumsy and so slow,
how, labouring with clods, can she keep pace
with Air, the firstborn element, tossing clouds to and fro?

And yet she answers with a spurt
of crocus, and makes light
of snow with snowdrops, and her celandine
is burnished to reflect the sun.

How like your absence and this winter have been!
Long vapours stretched between
me and your light, I saw you bright
beyond them, but your shine
fondled a field not mine.

There was the illumination and there the flight
of shadows black as night;
but I looked round
ever on the same november clear-obscure of dun
and grey and sallow and ash-colour and sere;
even my snows were white
not long, and melted into dirt.
Put out your hand. Feel me. Though the spring is here
I am still cold.

Because of this, because of the winter's hurt,
because I am of the earth element,
dusky, stubborn, retentive, slow to take hold, slow to
      loose hold,
because even to my hair's ends I carry the scent
of peat and of wood-smoke and of leaf-mould,
and because I have been
so long your tillage, so deeply your well-worked ground,
you must be patient;
forgiving my lack of green, my lack of grace,
my stammering blossoms one by one
shoved out, and my face doubtful under the sudden blue,
      under the embrace
of the relenting, of the returning sun.

'NOW IN THIS LONG-DEFERRED SPRING ...'

Now in this long-
deferred spring,
Blackthorn bush by the wayside what do you say?

Summer was a burning fever,
Winter a cold fever.
I was spared by neither.

But yet your cramped boughs
are pricked with flowers.

By rote, by rote,
These blossoms I put out.

They have not anything
to do with this spring.

They are but the badge
of an old pledge.
Farewell, and overlook
these white ashes among the black.

'SUMMER IS GOING . . .'

Summer is going,
Summer is gone.
Her green and yellow petticoats
Hang in the tobacco barn.

Naked she came,
Naked she must go.
Her rustling scalloped petticoats
Are ripe and lifeless now.

First they will tarnish,
Then they will brown.
Soon they will only be fit
To bundle up and burn.

AN ACROSTICAL ALMANACK, 1940

Virtue had a lovely face
Till a mirror showed it to her;
Now she brandishes the glass
In the face of every wooer;
And he sees a haggard elf
Scolding him, holding out to him
A cold copy of himself.

* * *

Alacoque, Alacoque,
Rumpled her maiden smock:

Thinking of the Sacred Heart
She would quiver and smart,
Each drop of its blood
Fell on her with a thud,
Pierced her like a dart.

Alacoque, Alacoque,
Swarmed up the Petrine Rock:
Not clash of keys nor frown
Under the triple crown,
Not syrup, nor scoff
Could keep the girl off,
Could keep the girl down.

Alacoque, Alacoque,
Now in a stony smock
Quietly you kneel
In the side aisle.
Under alabaster wimple
That no heartbeat can rumple
How does victory feel?

* * *

Lavender, who will buy
My sweet scented lavender?—
That ripened in July
And took so long to dry.
Oh smell it, it is sweet
Sewn in its winding-sheet
As though it did itself remember.

* * *

Envy to the counting-house
Ran, and pulled the Banker's sleeve.
Dreamy Banker, don't you grieve
These small deposits are not yours?

Do you think me poor? the Banker said.

Am I one of those whose round
Brings them here on market-day

Paying in with anxious joy
Penny as endeared as pound?

Oh, I am undone! the Banker said.

* * *

Necessity, Necessity,
Drives her wild caravan
Wherever she pleases.
Fences nor leases,
Uncles nor nieces,
Edict nor prayer,
Monk nor man,
Nothing can stay her!

Onward she drives her
Piebald stallion
Over hedges and ditches,
Cricket pitches,
Kings in their riches,
And the charcoal-burner:
On, on, on!
Nothing can turn her.

Paying no licences,
Speaking only romany,
No hand has ever
Crossed hers with silver,
Though futures she'll cypher
In every paw:
Gipsy Necessity
Who knows no law.

* * *

Timon, who had
A fig-tree in his garden growing,
Walked out at the cock-crowing
And found an Athenian lad
Had hanged himself thereon, and so was dead.

And as one fruit
Duly after another ripens
Old men, boys, and maidens
Took the same leafy route
To death from Timon's tree, grief driving them to it.

Timon at last
Sent heralds crying through the city
His fig-tree would shortly
Be felled, so as their host
He begged those who'd make use of it make haste.

Too late, too late,
O Timon, to recall the sally
That proved you not wholly
Impeccable in hate
Of man, thus to man's grief compassionate.

    * * *

Innocence lived on the heath,
Cracking stolen nuts with her white teeth:
Cast off by her virtuous kin
At Holy Christmas she got drunk on gin.

Innocence was no kitten:
Her memory went back to Troy and Eden;
But she was clean and hale,
With an eye like a falcon's and a tongue like a flail.

Then came a lawyer, who said:
Madam, you are no more disinherited.
England has need of you.
Old Habeas Corpus is dead, so make no ado.

He pulled off her coarse cleiding,
He dressed her all in white like a whore at a wedding;
In her cheek he drove a dimple,
And starved her till she was as small as Shirley Temple.

Now to the rich man's door
She drudges brazen-faced to beg for the poor:
She who *Arms for Spain!*
Shouted, now lisps coaxingly: *Aid for Britain.*

* * *

Naiad, whose sliding lips were mine
No longer than the nightingale
Paused between one song and another,
Where sit you now the willow throws
Her last gold to the sullen river?

Do you among your sisters tell
Yet of a kiss so weighed with woe,
So mute, so cold, you doubt the giver
Still walks about the wintry earth,
But in some deep pool drowned soon after?

* * *

Esther came to the court
Of the Eternal.
Her good deeds followed her
Like menservants and maidservants;
The tears of her children
Sparkled on her like emeralds,
The sighs of her husband
Billowed out her garments.

When Esther beheld
In the sackcloth of a widow
With a sword across her knee
Judith of Bethuliah,
She cast off her ornaments,
She bowed herself low,
Down to the foot that had arched
Over the blood of the tyrant.

* * *

Trumpeter of midday,
With a rickety grace
You step out to play
Above the market-place:
And in the clock-face
The minute hand slips free—
Tan-tan-taree!
The hour hand sets off on another chase.

Trumpeter of midnight,
With a clanking pace
You step out to affright
The echoing market-place:
And in the clock-face
The minute-hand slips free—
Memento mori:
The hour hand sets off on another chase.

Quia pulvis est—
Tan-tan-taray!
*Magister adest
Et vocat te.*
And over the clock-face
That's gilded broad as day
The cloud shadows play,
Catching and clearing in an endless chase.

* * *

Industry, your flax is spun,
Your linen loomed,
Your sheets hemmed,
Your washing sweetens in the sun.

Industry, your house is swept,
Your table scrubbed,
Your mirrors rubbed,
And all the while your Angel slept.

For while you did what should be done,
He wrote no word
Of your good deeds,
But like a white cat lay curled up in the sun.

* * *

Broceliande, dans ton hault forest
Gist Merlin le Graunt ki etoit Fay.

There he lies, hearing the wind blow;
Like grey moss his beard prickles the snow.

There he lies, wrapped in a furred cloak;
His hands are tangled in the roots of an oak.

The squirrels drop down acorns on his head;
He lies there quietly, pretending to be dead!

The swineherd and the old forester
Sit by his grave to eat their provender:

He hears them talking of the fate of England;
He lies there, holding the oak root in his hand.

Broceliande, dans ton hault forest
Gist Merlin le Graunt ki moult est Fay.

THE STORY OF A GARDEN

Three years ago
Newly-married my neighbours came to the new bungalow.
Hidden by lace
Curtains, their indoor life was their own business,
But I knew them when
They walked in their Adam and Eve aspect of rearing a
    young garden.

All was to do:
The raw hillside to dig, the tenured brambles to hack
    through,
The soil to turn
And sift and lime and rake level, the weeds to burn,
Paths to ram hard,
And tenderly the young fruit-trees to be settled in the new
    orchard.

And I could hear
Late through the April dusk their voices floating
    bird-clear;
He steadily

Counting the paced plan of where lawn and plot should be,
And she to him
Retailing her gay gazette of lilac-bud and transplanted
    lupin.

Now in this third
April the winter trimness of earth and branch is blurred
With imminent
Green thrust from sap and seed well-cared-for and
    confident;
And Adam goes
Slowly round his garden dressed as a soldier and Eve follows.

In careful and few
Words (for time is short) he counsels her what she must do
As summer comes on.
She nods, and stares at his boots, and promises that all
    shall be done.
With babbled cries
Answering back the thrushes, the two-year child trots
    about Paradise.

RECOGNITION

But this child was not of wax.
Life was under the mute skin
And still showed red through the cracks.
It is well known that the children of Spain

Were carved cheaply out of wood,
The children of China but yellow leaves on the wind:
This was an English child that lay in the road.
They told me to weep once more, but I found

No tears, and though the mourners then
Threw stones at me in grief's and God's name
I had no blood to quicken for God or man.
For I remembered how to my childhood had come

Hearsay of Justice. Now, overhead,
Rang the inflexible music of her sword;
Blindfold she went over with sure tread.
I knew, and acknowledged her, and adored.

THE VISIT

On Sunday evenings,
When the good folks have taken
Themselves to the sermon
I visit you.

I bring you a present:
Plums, it may be, or apples
Grown in my garden;
For that is due.

I bring my children
And talk about their doings.
You give them pennies,
And that is due.

I tell my troubles,
The price of food, the air-raids.
Kindly you listen
For that is due.

Past times we speak of,
Old scandals and dead neighbours.
You praise my husband
And that is due.

I stay my welcome
No longer than is civil
And from your doorway
You bid me adieu.

The organ is playing;
Homeward unused I carry
In hate and wont I bury
The love that drives me
To visit you.

from 12 POEMS IN THE MANNER OF BEWICK

Since they burned the olive yeards
Where shall the dove find
A leaf to comfort sailing Noah's mind?

Spain, Italy, Thessaly:
Steer where you will, scan,
Poor Noah, the coast-line of the Mediterranean,

The powdered bloom on the mountain-side
Thins sourly away:
Leafless returns the dove at the close of day.

* * *

Home again without a leg,
The village hero's home again!
Boy no more, nor half a man,
He lounges with the older men
Who sun against the churchyard wall.
Borrowing his crutch the sexton gay
Points out arisen left and right
New hillocks since he marched away.

* * *

There was life in this house not long ago.
A dog in the kennel,
A child in the cradle;
But a wind shook them and they had to go.

Your hand was cold in mine as we turned to go
From what, tear-blinded,
They saw in mind's-eye:
The wintry twilight falling stern and slow,
The casement lightless,
The chimney lifeless,
The broken bucket filling up with snow.

    * * *

This midnight sky,
Spangled with gay Finity,
Seems unlikely to supply
Even temporary accommodation for the Trinity.

DEATH OF MISS GREEN'S COTTAGE

The little snub-nosed squat victorian house
That preened in the sun through so many decades of peace,
Grey as a dove, and its slated salt-box roof
Sloped like the tail-feathers of a sitting dove,
All in a summer night scattered and gone
As a dove at a thunder-clap is flown!

At the blast it rose up from its foundation,
With a fluster it spread its wings of grey stone,
And went its piecemeal way into the dark, and is gone.

Not for years had it watched such a forward spring:
The birds had mated and hatched, and already the young
Were flying, flying, and the cuckoo had
Broken the sober pattern of its minor third
And called with a midsummer voice from the hawthorns
Shining like snow-mountains at the meadows' horizons

And there, solid among the foaming hawthorns,
It sat, and sober among the birds' orisons;
And its paint cracked a little in the sun.

And to us among other hawthorns that were as white
But rooted in unwandered meadows, she wrote:
Today as I went by your house, the garden was full
Of poets' narcissus, the windows open, I felt you were still
At home there, and everything as it was
In those years when we lived in security and with happiness.

The white iris, the scented lupins, the flocks of narcissus,
The shadow of the new-fledged ash tree like a caress
Fingering the shining garden and the little house.

And on the night of that same day it was gone.
Those who ran to the place stumbled on stones,
Trampled a chimney, tripped on unaccountable rocks
Of masonry scattered like chips from the blow of an axe;
Only by a thicker dust could they know they were there,
And the sighing ash boughs embraced their thighs where
      there had been a door.

The little house, so harmless and demure . . .
I am glad to think that on its last day it wore
Its laundered garden, its loved look, as when in love we
      were there.

IN EAST ANGLIA

Because it is a fine Easter bank-holiday,
With a blue sky and crisp waves flouncing the blonde
Beach and like a heart the bell-buoy chiming
And the larks singing over sea and over land,

Across the dunes and brushing through the marram
Grass the holiday strangers loiter,
Happy and idle and a little solemn,
Sobered by so deep a sky and so straight a horizon;

And the black dog barking for joy
Casts himself again and again on the subsiding
Wave, and the lover spreads out his overcoat
58   And lies down with his young lady beside him.

I pretend
That I too am come here on holiday
And have left my cares behind
In the pall of smoke that hangs over the city.

Like a visitor I stray
Hither and thither as the wind turns me,
And my heart is soft and light as a feather
Pretending that at the day's ending the wind will have
　　　blown me away.

SONG FROM A MASQUE

You shall wear
Spring like a garland on your hair,
Summer like a rose behind your ear;
And the autumn wood
Shall be your riding-hood.

You shall gather
The bearded mountain to be your father,
And for your wedded love the weather;
And the inland waters
Shall dandle your sons and daughters.

But where will you go
When the north winds do blow,
When the skies are black with snow?
I pray you, begone
From us before our winter comes on!

I SAID TO THE TREES

Superb in your last plumage—I said to the trees—
Your pomp is dated. Already the knife is whetted
In heaven to let-blood your scarlet to the lees.
The moon has tried its edge, the stars have abetted
The plot against your pride. To-night it will freeze.

Too rashly you have outfaced the heavens, I said.
Shall immortal azure brook that a six-months measure
Of green shall colour to death as the sun sets red?
Envious eternity waits to foreclose on each treasure
Of time: the knife is whetted and hangs overhead.

So I farewelled them, who stood in the rigid air
Already fettered. All night I heard the unuttered
Onslaught, my dreams were traversed by boughs bled bare,
My feet waded through leaves cast-off and cluttered.
I woke. Impassive the unaltered glory was there.

Not yet—said the trees—not yet. We choose our own time.
With armour undinted be another sunrise confronted.
We disarm on our own terms. Not till the rime
Had gone from the grass, not till the air was blunted
With noon did the first leaf fall like a chime

Beginning, like a music's first full note well-placed.
No rout imperilled it led with the step of a herald
But as one leading a procession it paced
Leisurely forth down air, and after it the berylled,
The gilded, the coralled marchers came without haste.

Grass was not green enough to receive them, day
Too brief a stander-by to behold them squander
A minted summer as they went on their way.
Slow they fell, as though in their passage they'd ponder
Ripely the final stratagem of decay.

True to the tree's foot they fell, they aimed
Themselves in piety to the parental deity
Which fostered them and in hour of death reclaimed;
To the father slumbering below in commanding velleity
They carried their tribute, the salt of the untamed

And wary sap which receding at winter's tread
Becked them to follow, to heap on the year's fallow
Their reinforcement of warmth, their succour to spread
Quilting the cold vigil to Candlemas from All-Hallow,
With the filldyke rains to rot back to the leaf-mould bed.

How greedy these trees in their autumn death, thought I.
Their summer recounted they stand absorbed and delighted
In husbandry of self-ruin. So, so to die,
With winter so outwitted and time despited
With unhurried gesture of summer worn and laid by!

And whether my riches replenish root, and the store
Of a life's rapture rise up to flourish my stature,
Or whether these fall from me for evermore,
With peace and insolence be my departure,
And proudly cast off the dated splendour I wore.

WE ACCUSE

Open the prison gates, let them come out—
Those who have endured insult, torture, the long
Warfare of mind against the armoured brute.
After a while there shuffled forth a throng
Of goblins, peering round for something to eat.

Speak to them of freedom, tell them their blood
Ran not only down gutters but to our hearts
Pipe-lined fuelled the spark of all we did.
Whimpering like apes they fought in fits and starts
For turnip-peelings trampled in the mud.

Take them by the hand, let flesh to flesh convey
The humble comradeship of mortal make.
Coldly they suffered us to lead them away,
But one or two glanced back as they forsook
The forfeited shelter of captivity.

EXILE

Trotsky was not
At Lenin's funeral,
And in the deep
Murmur of sorrow he had no voice,
And in the common lot
Of concern was impartial.
They that sow not, neither shall they reap,

They that did not weep
Shall not rejoice.

In the red cell,
Visited and alone,
And as in a profound
Trance of reflection the body lies,
Centred and peaceable,
Well-bedded a foundation-stone.
They that root not, neither shall they abound,
Out of the self-bound
Shall no harvest arise.

But hither and thither
As an anxious spider scurries
To choose a tenement
Among darkness and dust and mould,
Through the old world the other
Hastens and worries,
Grieving to set up his personal brief tent,
To see it rent,
To dangle for a new foothold.

TRIAL OF MARSHAL PETAIN

By, by, hushaby,
It is August that was July.
Summers shorten, arteries harden,
Pears in the Luxembourg garden
Ripen in paper chemises—
Bons Chrétiens and Marie Louises;
A pear for every senator,
A senator for every pear,
So it was in times that were,
Times that were are times no more.

Do, do, fais dodo,
It is Perhaps that was No.
Bugles mumble, honours tarnish,
Old acquaintance bob and vanish
Like apples in a wishing-bowl—

It was Weygand that is Laval.
A fig for every old acquaintance!
As good a cat for every rat,
For every flood an Ararat,
For every chance another chance.

By, by, hushaby,
It was spider that is fly.
Windows dazzle, ear-drums tabour,
Dead men speak from the sepulchre.
When the angry ghosts arise
All good children shut their eyes.
For all good children a sweet sop,
A sop for every Judas,
So it was in time to pass,
Time to pass is time forgot.

Do, do, fais dodo,
It is now that was ago.
Owlets cry and eyelids smoulder,
Dews round shuttered house fall colder,
En attendant sur mes genoux
Beau Maréchal, dormez-vous.
For every debt a due quittance,
For every child a nurse's knee.
Obdurate and bedraggled he
Drowses on the stern lap of France.

HYMN FOR HOLY DECONSECRATION

The Church's own detergent
Infallibly prevails
When Industry grows urgent
And mass devotion fails.
A single application
Removes th'inherent soil
Of previous consecration—
No need to scrub or boil.

O mystical emulsion!
O supervenient Tide!

63

It ousts the harsh compulsion
Of rape or suicide.
Outmoding all exertion
With candle, bell and book,
Its bubbling bland coercion
Pervades each hallowed nook.

Unchanged in outward seeming
But inwardly renewed,
Behold the fabric gleaming,
Disblest and disempewed!
Released from every rubric,
From every grace set free,
It soars as though of new brick
To Secularity.

To-day, though few in number
In purpose firmly shod,
We join to disencumber
This edifice of God.
Convinced th'Eternal Father
Who chose this His abode
By now would really rather
Move further up the road.

PORTRAIT

Down these dull lanes where men and cattle plod
Cycles the man of God.
With scant greeting and scant reply he hurries,
A man covered with worries.

At the vicarage, they say, the dust of seven mills
Lies on the unpaid bills.
His servants have left, his wife threatens to leave him,
His very terriers deceive him.

And in vain he toadies the squire, and the squire's like,
For soon the scandal will break;
No more tennis then, nor bridge, nor proffered cigars,
Nor ladies to open his bazaars.

Christ at his beggarly picnic could satisfy ten
Thousand on the lunch of two working-men;
Christ, too, said: Forgive us our sins as we forgive our
    debtors.
Christ knew nothing about his betters.

from FIVE BRITISH WATER COLOURS

Mr Gradgrind's Country

There was a dining-room, there was a drawing-room,
There was a billiard-room, there was a morning-room,
There were bedrooms for guests and bedrooms for sons
    and daughters,
In attic and basement there were ample servants' quarters,
There was a modern bathroom, a strong-room, and a
    conservatory.
In the days of England's glory.

There were Turkish carpets, there were Axminster carpets,
There were oil paintings of Vesuvius and family portraits,
There were mirrors, ottomans, wash-hand-stands and
    tantaluses,
There were port, sherry, claret, liqueur, and champagne
    glasses,
There was a solid brass gong, a grand piano, antlers,
    decanters, and a gentlemen's lavatory,
In the days of England's glory.

There was marqueterie and there was mahogany,
There was a cast of the Dying Gladiator in his agony,
There was the 'Encyclopædia Britannica' in a revolving
    bookcase,
There were finger-bowls, asparagus-tongs, and inlets of
    real lace:
They stood in their own grounds and were called Chats-
    worth, Elgin, or Tobermory,
In the days of England's glory.

But now these substantial gentlemen's establishments
Are like a perspective of disused elephants,
And the current Rajahs of industry flash past their wide
    frontages
Far, far away to the latest things in labour-saving cottages,
Where with Russell lupins, jade ash-trays, some Sealyham
    terriers, and a migratory
Cook they continue the story.

John Craske's Country

You cannot love here as you can love inland
Where love grows easy as a pig or a south-wall fruit.
Love on this coast is something you must dispute
With a wind blowing from the North Pole and only salt
    water between.

You cannot build here as you can build inland
With a thatch roof sprawling or with smart gables.
Here we build box-ways out of brick or flint cobbles
For a wind blowing from the North Pole and only salt
    water between.

You cannot eat here as you can eat inland.
A man can't do with less than six herring for breakfast
And something stronger than tea if he is to hold fast
Against a wind blowing from the North Pole and only
    salt water between.

And you cannot grieve here as you can grieve inland
Where the dead lie sweetly labelled like jams in the grocer's
    store.
You must blink at the sea till your face is scarlet and your
    eyes sore
With a wind blowing from the North Pole and only salt
    water between.

Thomas the Rhymer's Country

Time in its douce predestinating way
Manifests called and reprobate together.

Cacrahead and the Catrail were always grassed,
Craig Hill was always heather;
And there has always been the sheep on the one
And on the other the adder.

Clear as the word of God the March Burn
Runs between them. There I would paddle and ponder
Through the secure solitude of a child's afternoon
Were the choice set me whether
I would choose the velvet composure of the one
Or the besotting honey scent of the other.

Being predestined to grow up indifferent
To free-will, scarcely my own right hand neither
The right hand of God distinguishing from its left,
Now I would ask no better
Than on Craig or Cacra let fall, so there to lie
For ever and for ever.

'CAPTAIN JOHN SMITH . . .'

Captain John Smith, that wayfaring, seafaring, lovefaring
    man,
Sighted a profiled headland, that glimmering through the
    murky
Sad sea-mist recalled a lady he'd loved in Turkey.
Mapping the coast, he mementoed his fair Circassian.
Later advices from home re-named Cape Tragabigzanda,
    Cape Ann.

There is this much in a name that a high-minded Puritan—
Anxious John Winthrop, for instance—might have thought
    twice ere he ventured
Himself, frail vessel of virtue, into a land thus indentured
To Venus by evocation of a trousered Courtezan;
But there can be no wantonness between Cape Cod and
    Cape Ann.

How oddly, too, might have developed the Republican
Party under the spell of that relaxing nomenclature,

Sages and astronomers endorsed for the Presidential
    Candidature
By senators lolling with Hafiz on the silken divan:
The scions of Tragabigzanda, not the stern sons of Ann.

Tragabigzanda Tragabigzanda
Foiled is the travelled amorist, recalling his Amanda,
Lost, lost to New England is Cape Tragabigzanda.

from SEVEN CONJECTURAL READINGS

The Wife of King Keleos

Never was such a servant.
Nothing was too much for her to do,
She could card and spin, bake and brew,
She could watch untired the whole night through,
She was modest, prudent, observant,
She knew unfailingly where all lost things were,
She was abundant as a Lammas Fair . . .
Everything throve while she was there.

Everything but my heart:
She troubled my dreaming and my waking hours,
She dulled my embroideries and sapped my flowers,
The babe upon her knee was no longer ours.
But for all her deity and her art
She could not inveigle a mother's wit;
Before I stole to the hearth and saw her sit
Dipping the child in fire I was sure of it.

Trust no gods, I say.
I have had one in my house, I should know:
Here are my crooked hands to show
How narrowly and with what piercing woe
I rescued the child. But to this day
My mind misgives me, and must, till I spread
The bridal blankets, and with the maidenhead
The last tincture of deity is shed.

Monsieur de Grignan

There are too many doves!
Forever, forever arriving, their wings have cloven
My olive screens and my grooved cypresses;
Forever alighting, they lay on my roof a burden of
      whiteness,
A burden of softness,
Their alighting weighs on my roof like a burden of snow.

Roo-cooing, roo-cooing . . .
I have no chamber that is not filled with their clamour;
With strut and flutter they oust me hither and thither,
Their wings bewilder my blazon, and darken my
      forefathers,
My coffers are stuffed up with their cast feathers;
Among them I have mislaid the man that I am.

Into my wife's lap they are flown.
Bosom and wrist and shoulders, she is doves all over
And looks at me with strange eyes through a trellis of
      wings.
She does not heed me, for I am becoming already
What time will make me:
A letterback cypher, the man of her mother's daughter,
The man who unloosed the doves, and remembered
      for that alone.

A Leper

Narrower grew the cell
In which I dwelt,
Less and less light
Oozed through the window slit.

My pains had grown
To something I once had known,
Silvered in my snail shell
I was almost at peace.

Then came one whose shrill
Love beat on my face,
And tore me with his bill.

I know not where he has gone,
Who dealt me that kiss
And left me live-alone.
May God's worst pain be his!

'THROUGH ALL THE MEADOWS . . .'

Through all the meadows they are flowing,
To all the hilltops they are climbing:
Hedgerow and hedgerow and hedgerow.
Solemn and processional and shining,
In white garments they go.

To what intention are they plighted?
Where did they wash their festal apparel
So white, and so white, and so white?
What summoned out this maymonth nonpareil?
My despair, I say, and my delight.

From my astonished heart these votive
Hawthorns have come forth in procession,
Hedgerow after hedgerow after hedgerow!
In token of my release and my ransom
In thank-offering they go.

ASTRO-PHYSICS

i

As a poor clerk sums up, exact to pence,
A king's expenditure, nor wonders where,
Why, when, on whom disbursed, so he may fare
Unblamed down column and trudge homeward thence,
Astronomers compute with diligence
The spilth of light, check pulse of shaken air,
Audit the stars, this wealth with that compare,
But not this wealth with their own indigence.

Tied in its fivefold fetter, the duped mind
Amasses zeros, studies to detail
The enrichment of its lack; then unrepined
Turns back to strum the puny sensual scale,
Deaf to the ruby's steadfast note, and blind
To all the colours of the nightingale.

ii

Nought, nought, nought, nought . . . O wise Arabian!
Who, cyphering first, the primal zero wrought—
Thyself commemorating in thy nought,
Imposed on time an absence for a man
Circling around the dust thy finger ran,
And delved the sign with such enlargement fraught
That henceforth humankind beholds all thought,
All speculation, captive in its span.

Tagged to the sum of knowledge is this terse
Nought, nought, nought, nought; is, in its quiddity,
The hollow vocative O! that cries through verse;
An O ends God; and man's brief scrutiny,
From the round world rounding the universe,
Plots out its arc upon infinity.

iii

To no believable blue I turn my eyes,
Blinded with sapphire, watchet, gentian,
Shadow on snow, Mediterranean,
Midsummer or midwinter-moonlight skies.

Unstained by sight, unravished by surmise,
And uttering into the void her ban,
Her boast, her being—*I know not a man!*
Out of all thought the virgin colour flies.

After her, soul! Have in unhaving, peace,
Let thy lacklight lighten upon thee, read
So well thy sentence that it spells release.
Explore thy chain, importune suns to cede
News of thy dark—joyed with thy doom's increase,
And only by distinction of fetters freed.

   iv
I heard them say, Henceforth few stars, or none,
Shall whirl to being in galactic space.
The heavens are waxed old, and the embrace
Spent that begot the kindred of the sun.
Time quits his youth. The giants one by one
Husband the prodigal light that streamed apace
From squandered atoms, and the stellar race
More soberly to their extinction run.

Annihilation noosed them, and with fell
Contraction teaches prudence, but relents
Never, nor can, nor ever they rebel
Against self-waste until, grizzled insolvents,
They barter death for petrifaction, dwell
Onward but as his trophies and monuments.

'ACROSS TWO PASTURES . . .'

Across two pastures went the track.
Some lime trees made it half-way avenue.
The house was made of stone, and at the back
There was a well, and a lean-to.

It was a westward-facing house:
At the day's end I'd see the windows shine
As though it watched me nearing under the boughs,
And I was glad that it was mine.

One August afternoon I found
Three summer strangers sweating at my door.
I offered them a drink as duty bound
Seeing them sweltering and footsore.

Water, said they. From my cool well
What I drew up was water, but transformed
Somehow to wine as they began to swill;
Drunken as lords they swarmed

Indoors and outdoors, high and low.
One leaning from an attic window sent
Down tidings of a beam, and from below
Was answered with a pediment.

Here was a thing unique, and here
The replica of something famous they knew
Elsewhere. Blithe as three apes turned auctioneer
They searched my dwelling through

Before they went, saying I was
The owner of a jewel beyond price.
I watched them go, and turned back to my house
But could not look it in the face.

The thought pressed in: Of two things one,
My house like any wife had worn a mask,
Or I too dull a clod such graces to own.
Who lives there now I do not ask.

'HOW FARE MY ASH-TREES NOW? . . .'

How fare my ash-trees now?
Do my fruit-trees bear?
The gnarled apple and the stately pear—
How do they grow, and I not there, not there?

Neither more nor less
Than when you walked below.
Apple and pear tree fruit, and ash-trees grow,
And the ripe fruit falls, and the leaves begin to snow.

Yes, I remember well
The plunge of apple and pear,
The whirled whisper of ash-leaves flocking down air—
But is it all as when I was there, was there?

Yes and no.
Nettles and weeds grow tall
Muffle each fruit fall:
Unsought-for lie apple and pear, and rot one and all.

'THE BIRDS ARE MUTED . . .'

The birds are muted in the bosom of midsummer.
The wind has hidden itself under her green shawl.
There it nestles and lies slumbering:
She pulls her woods over all.

O breast, too deep in peace for song or sighing,
Lean over me in the solemn sycamore bough;
Shelter me from the echoes of an old crying,
Enfold me in here and now.

'BUBBLES RISE . . .'

Bubbles rise from the water and are domes,
Admiration burnishes them, Time tarnishes.
On a fine morning they seem to be there for ever.
Venice! Do you remember Byzantium?

THE ESPALIER
(1925)

QUIET NEIGHBOURS

Sitting alone at night
Careless of time,
From the house next door
I hear the clock chime.

Ten, eleven, twelve;
One, two, three—
It is all the same to the clock,
And much the same to me.

But to-night more than sense heard it:
I opened my eyes wide
To look at the wall and wonder
What lay on the other side.

They are quiet people
That live next door;
I never hear them scrape
Their chairs along the floor,

They do not laugh loud, or sing,
Or scratch in the grate,
I have never seen a taxi
Drawn up at their gate;

And though their back-garden
Is always neat and trim
It has a humbled look,
And no one walks therein.

So did not their chiming clock
Imply some hand to wind it,
I might doubt if the wall between us
Had any life behind it.

London neighbours are such
That I may never know more
Than this of the people
Who live next door.

While they for their part
Should they hazard a guess

At me on my side of the wall
Will know as little, or less;

For my life has grown quiet,
As quiet as theirs;
And the clock has been silent on my chimney-piece
For years and for years.

LONDON CHURCHYARD

As I walked through London
To ease my care,
I snuffed amid the houses
A greener air;

And behind iron railings
I saw branches wave,
Tossing their wild arms
Over, O! many a grave.

Such a sight as this
Pleased me very well.
I peered through the railings
That had a rusty smell—

All of a sudden
I heard a cry;
And saw a dark something
Crouched a new stone near-by.

It seemed lorn and witless
As sea-weed on a beach;
But it lamented
With a woman's speech.

'Woe's me, my lover!
Cold-hearted you are grown.
The breast where I laid my head
Lies beneath a stone.

I thought I held you fast
My kind arms between

But now you are gone from me
As if you'd never been.

'Falsely have you dealt with me,
Falsely have you beguiled.
Dead and buried with you
Lies my child.'

Piteously, piteously,
Thus did she rave,
And wrung her hands
And scratched on the grave.

COUNTRY CHURCHYARD

'Awake, good neighbours all,
That wake not for the day.
The church yews won't spread the news—
No tales tell they.
Awake, good neighbours, scramble out of your sepulchres,
    Cold lying is clay:'
'No,' mumbled they, 'No, no.
Suppose the golden cock should crow.'

'You loved a merry life—
For one more jaunt uprouse.
The moonlit stones above your bones
Show where you house:
Benjamin Harris, John French late of this parish,
    Mary his spouse:'
'No,' mumbled they, 'No, no.
Suppose the golden cock should crow.'

'Awake for time is short,
Your hour will soon be told.
Link bony hands, and dance in bands,
Nor dint the mould.
You'll caper limberly with no flesh to cumber ye—
    Better than of old:'
'No,' mumbled they, 'No, no.
Suppose the golden cock should crow.'

'Let friends and neighbours meet
With curtsey, beck, and bow.
When back in bed, if a maidenhead
Or a marriage vow
Doesn't tally exactly with who's under which blanket,
    'Twon't matter now:'
'No,' mumbled they, 'No, no.
Suppose the golden cock should crow.'

'Faint-hearted you are grown,
Neighbours, by lying dead.
This cock, your bane, is a weather-vane
With gilt overspread;
A trumpery figure, put up by the new vicar—
    Nothing to dread:'
'No,' mumbled they, 'No, no.
Suppose the golden cock should CROW.'

IN THE PARLOUR

    (i)

Come away from the door.
It has grown late;
The air is chill and frore,
And those whom you await
Will not pass by any more.

Close the shutters aright
And make all fast.
We shall have rain belike,
The sky is overcast:
No one will come here to-night.

Sit you down by my side,
Sing an old song.
Since you have been my bride
How well I like these long
Quiet evenings in Advent-tide.

(ii)

He How unobtrusively the snow
Comes down beyond the crimson blind!
I see it not, but through my mind
Sieve the large flakes, both soft and slow,
Warding us in from humankind.

She My nimble needle forth and back
Goes twanging through the tambour-frame
To stitch a bird without a name.
If an indifferent heart should crack
'Twould sound, I fancy, much the same.

He A cruel night for beast or man
To be abroad. But we might doubt
By this warm hearth the snow shut out,
Save for a denser silence than
Is wont to compass us about.

She The needle and the web, how fine!
The silks no thicker than a hair!
Each choice of tint calls forth my care,
And slowly goes the great design.
No matter. I have time to spare.

He 'Twill soon be time to go to bed—
Sweet bed, but cold! Drowsed though I be
I'll sit it out until I see
The wooden bird put forth his head,
And beck, and cry Cuckoo! to me.

She With every length of gliding floss
Wrought in to make my sampler gay
So much life's thread I stitch away.
But this bright wing will flaunt the gloss
Of life when I am dull as clay.

He Cuckoo! Cuckoo! My dear, you heard
The clock? Another evening gone!
She Asleep?
He   Not quite.
She   You've scarcely stirred.

81

He   In grave consideration
My thoughts upon that silly bird
Were fixed.
She   And mine on this.
He   Absurd!
We even think in unison.

TUDOR CHURCH MUSIC

Here in the minster tower
I sit alone,
While to mind's ear old books
Mumble and drone;
And the warm sun slants in
Over the cold stone.

Through the long afternoon
I hear the clock
Preach to the empty church:
Tick-tock. Tick-tock.
O, a rare text to expound
To a sleeping flock!

The patient organist
Who scrolled this clef;
The boy who drew him horned
On Gibbons in F;
Singers and hearers all
Are dumb and deaf—

'Dumb and deaf, dead and dust,'
Confirms the clock.
And life seems so far off
That at the shock
I see my calm hand start,
When footsteps knock

Upon stair. Holiday-makers
Out on a trip
To whom the verger propounds

Each trusty quip,
While, mute, they fidget together
In uneasy fellowship.

And only when they are gone
Do I doff the mask
Of the scholar deep in his book:
'Did they see me?' I ask,
'Or am I, too, a ghost?' and so
Turn once more to my task.

AN AFTERNOON CALL

To shelter from the thunder-drench
A scorched and sorefoot tramping wench
Came to my door and proffered me
Lilac, that I had viewed her wrench
Out of my neighbour's tree.

I bade her in. With glances keen
She eyed my well-found kitchen, scene
Of kind domestic arts;
Like one who curious and serene
Looks round on foreign parts.

She talked of winds and wayside fruits,
Seas, cities, fair-times, landmarks, routes
Of journeys past and gone.
I gave her an old pair of boots
That she might wander on.

WISH IN SPRING

To-day I wish that I were a tree,
And not myself,
Confronting spring with a neat little row of poems
Like cups and saucers on a shelf.

For then I should have poems innumerable,
One kissing the other;
Authentic, perfect in shape and lovely variety,
And all of the same tireless green colour.

No one would think it unnatural
Or question my right;
All day I would wave them above the heads of the people,
And sing them to myself all night.

But as I am only a woman
And not a tree,
With piteous human care I have made this poem,
And set it now on the shelf with the rest to be.

THE VIRGIN AND THE SCALES

This is a public park;
You may not pick the flowers,
Or loiter after hours,
Or kiss too deep in the dark.
Yet here is green, and sweet
Forgetfulness of the street;
Deep walks of chestnut and lime
Where the old may pass away time,
Pleasant picnicing places
For children with shabby faces,
Lawns blowing in the sun
Where dogs may roll and run,
And the patient grass
For lover and lass.
Is this then not enough?
No, not enough for one
I met there.
            Who?
                A nun.
(And yet, God knows, so old,
So battered with untold
Heavenly housewifery,
So vowed to poverty,

You would not think to find

Ambition in her mind.)
In wintry woollen stuff
Of abstinence was she dressed,
And winter was on her breast;
But midsummer's most complete
Honey-coloured, honey-sweet
Plenteousness was her plunder,
Standing the lime-tree under.

No housewife shelling peas,
No Saint upon her knees
Telling God's praises over,
Slip-finger, nor bees in clover,
Nor girl-child gathering
Cowslips in the spring
Showed with more innocence
Delight in diligence
Than she, cramming her bag
With golden handfuls of swag.
Love knit my heart to her:
I approached; but at the stir
Of footfall she glanced round,
Loosed her rich branch, and frowned
With such an air of doubt
As children show found out
In fault, till seeing that I
Smiled, she in turn looked sly
And faster than before
Plucked on. Said I: 'Here's more
Than you can lessen, though you
Should gather the whole day through
For your lime-blossom tea.'
'It is God's gift,' said she,
'And pleasant for the sick.
It grows so clean and thick
'Twere shame to let it waste.
Aye, gathered it *should* be.
But I must work in haste
Lest the Keeper come along
And tell me I do wrong.'

I looked up overhead
And saw the lime-tree spread

Above us like a tent;
Like a green and golden pavilion
Of some Arabian Night,
Murmuring as with consent,
And gleaming as though alight
With a million, with a million
Loops and tassels of scent.

I thought then: Who could grudge
Blooms to this holy drudge,
Or stay her wrinkled, deft
Old hands from their kind theft?
She thief, lawbreaker? She?
As well accuse the tree,
That day-long with sweet skill
Steals sap, steals chlorophyl;
That from earth, from dew, from air
Thieves that it may be fair
And show its works to men,
Who beholding it then
May glorify their Father
In heaven.
        No, but look farther.
I touch not blossom nor leaf,
And I, I am the Thief!
Thief so cunning and fell
That I am Keeper as well.
Good cause had she to frown
At my shadow blackening down;
For every joy I take
Becomes an iron grate,
And my innocent delights
Plant rows of iron spikes;
Worst, self-denying, this trick
Of integrity—not to pick
Blossom, bruise leaf, destroy
Aught from the common joy—
Binds in an iron band
My heart and prompts my hand,
Now lifted up to bless
In scrupulous emptiness,
To write these words of hate

THOU SHALT NOT on every gate.

Yet here is solace, and sweet
Redemption from the street;
A pause, a look of pity
For the begrimed city,
Green almsgiving, a lake
Of green where men may slake
Parched senses, wash off care.
Ah, if it only were
Not so precious, so deadly dear,
So dearly defrayed a delight
That whosoever comes here
Must come as Thief outright,
Or cloaking his envious mind
With love of humankind,
And with caution and mistrust
Walking among the just
Grow Thief so cunning and fell
That perforce he's Keeper as well.
Poor drudge, you had reason to start,
When with love in my heart
I approached you, as though you saw
In me the offended law.
Truly, to-day I must be
Offended because of thee.
For every blossom you pick
Must wound me to the quick,
And by that bag you've crammed
With mercies I am damned;
Worst, worst, your innocence,
Your happy, happy love,
Your hand, so hand in glove
With the tree's consenting,
Is a sword to drive me hence,
Lamenting, lamenting;
Is a flame brandished to fright
Me from a forfeited delight,
Repenting, repenting;
Is a key in the unrelenting
Hand of the uncreate,
Locking the garden gate.

O why must my spirit pine
For a few handfuls of lime

Plucked by a poor old nun,
Whose cares are all in one
Concern so summed up and shriven
That were I to tell her but half
Of the coil through which she's driven
My thoughts, she must either laugh
As a nurse laughs at a child,
Or with a sigh, maybe a frown
For one so devil-wiled,
Brush all my vain-wit down?
And yet I linger, I delay,
Hankering, as though some clue
She had hold of, answer knew.
As though, should I say:
'No, dear, you may not pick
Lime-blossom for the sick;
For know you not, since the Fall
Not one tree but all, all
Must bear forbidden fruit,
And are poisoned at the root
By man's repentant tears?'—
She might reply: 'Yet here's
Good warrant for what I do.
When he was walking through
The harvest he plucked the ears
Of corn and shared them among
Those with him, for they were anhungered, and so was he.
Thus his disciples he taught
How to steal as they ought,
In joy and peace of heart;
Thus he took the sinner's part;
So much to thieves a friend
That he had them with him till the end;
Thus, thus, he would set us free.
But till everyone believes
In him we must all be thieves.'

I BRING HER A FLOWER

Sweet faith
Such looks of quiet hath
That those on whom she's smiled
Lie down to sleep as easy as a child.

No night,
However dark, can fright
Them, no, nor day
To come, however bleak and fell, dismay.

But sound
Sleep they in prison-bound
As when at liberty
And if they wake, they wake in charity;

Like her,
Who rousing at the jar
Of weary foot in the rain
Pitied the wakeful sentry for his pain.

[Like her: *Rosa Luxemburg.*]

THE LENTEN OFFERING

Christ, here's a thorn
More poison-fanged than any that you knew:
On the north side of the churchyard it grew,
Where lie the suicides and babes chance-born.

Christ, here are nails,
Once driven in, will never lose their hold:
Forged at Krupp's, Creusot's, Vickers', and tipped with gold
Pen-nibs that signed the treaty of Versailles.

Christ, here's a sharp
Spear, can wound deeper than all other spears:
In baths of human blood and human tears
Tempered, and whetted on the human heart.

CAVES OF HARMONY

Play, dark musician, play—
How almost human sounds your saxophone!
(Somewhere in Africa
An angry lion tosses up a bone.)

Sambo's a ready scholar
And hides his black skin under a black coat.
Although he wears a collar
Adam's own apple yet sticks in his throat.

Play, dark musician, play—
I see your imitation diamond flash.
(Once in America
Your fathers howled and writhed beneath the lash.)

How leers the blackamoor,
Exhaling his melodious delight!
Music's his paramour;
And yours, and mine, since we dance here tonight.

Play, dark musician, play—
Outdo the beast's roar and the scourged slave's moan.
Ambassador from the U.S.A.,
How almost human sounds your saxophone!

OLD MAN

Reading in bawdy books
The old man sits.
De Sade plays Abishag
To his cold wits.

Under his bushy brows
His eyes are mild—
There's no more harm in him
Than in a child.

SONG FROM THE BRIDE OF SMITHFIELD

A thousand guileless sheep have bled,
A thousand bullocks knelt in fear,
To daub my Henry's cheek with red
And round the curl above his ear.

And wounded calves hung up to drip
Have in slow sweats distilled for him
The dew that polishes his lip,
The inward balm that oils each limb.

In vain I spread my maiden arts,
In vain for Henry's love I pine.
He is too skilled in bleeding hearts
To turn this way and pity mine.

LET ME GO!

Any wind but this—
That with remembrance of rain
Grown soft and pitiful, embraced me
As I walked homeward.

And any other look
Than the full-moon sheds to-night—
As though she bent like a mother
Above her sleeping children.

Not to be denied
The wind gropes over the house;
And now it has brushed aside the curtains
And walks about the room.

Too well, too well I know
Whence you have journeyed, O Wind!
And what the landscape of nestling hill and valley
That the moon eyes so lovingly.

COUNTRY THOUGHT FROM A TOWN

(i)

Averted from myself
I walk up and down—
I see how in the light of the arc-lamps
The trees look stricken and brown.
Autumn is an unkindly thing
In a town.

The leaves fall aimlessly;
Frustrated in their decay,
With scraps of paper and bus-tickets
They will be swept away.

All the mortality in me
Yearns to go
Somewhere alone into the country,
Where elms stand in the hedgerow;
Through fields completed and contented
To walk to and fro—

To hear leaves falling
Like a quiet breath;
To be a partaker
In their death.

(ii)

Cold, is it cold?
Blows there a wind
All night through?
Does a frozen dew
Lie on the wold?

Dark, is it dark?
Blotted from being
Cottage and garth?
Has the last hearth
Quenched its spark?

Still, is it still?
Wakes the wind only?
Sunk in a deep
Midwinter sleep
Valley and hill?

No, not all cold,
Nor yet all dark,
Nor yet quite still.
Such is not God's will.
In the sheepfold,

Warm in the ewe's fleece,
Lies the lamb newborn.
To and fro all night
The shepherd bears a light,
Telling his flock's increase.

THE GREEN VALLEY

Here in the green scooped valley I walk to and fro.
In all my journeyings I have not seen
A place so tranquil, so green;
And yet I think I have seen it long ago,
The grassy slopes, and the cart-track winding, so.

O now I remember it well, now all is plain,
Why twitched my memory like a dowser's rod
At waters hidden under sod.
When I was a child they told me of Charlemagne,
Of Gan the traitor, and Roland outmarched and slain.

Weeping for Roland then, I scooped in my spirit
A scant green Roncesvalles, a holy ground,
Which here in Dorset I've found:
But finding, I knew it not. The years disinherit
Their children. The horn is blown, but I do not hear it.

Hush, my dear, hush!
Who are these that pass
Up shady lane?
Their feet don't brush
Any dew from the grass
And they are silent, too.

Hand in kind hand
Go some, and closelier linked
Another twain;
And others stand
As a-drouse, indistinct
Beneath the darkening boughs.

Ghosts, ghosts are these!—
Long-dead maidens, each
Beside her swain—
Between the trees
Pacing slow, without speech,
As they were wont to go.

Strange, some should choose
Thus their mouldered dears
To meet again,
Whom long misuse
Of marriage, taunts and tears,
And the slow grudge of age

Warped and estranged;
Sure, this place above
All others fain
They'd leave unranged,
Lest a gaunt dead love
Them, like a dead child, haunt.

Ah, but not so
These who in true-love-knot
Their arms enchain.
Dead long ago
Are they all, and forgot
The life that held them thrall.

Nought now exists
Save fancies nursed apart.
And of all this train
Scarce one that trysts
With a seeming sweetheart
But walks beside a dream.

THE TRAVELLER ENCOUNTERED

The highroad runs plain
Between Thaxted and Dunmow,
But I had chosen to go
By bridle-path and lane;
To see the champaign,
And the stooks a-row—
There I met an old fellow
Standing in the rain.

He was bowed and lean;
But clear was his eye
As a rift of March sky,
His face like a quarrendine.
'You must have seen
Many changes,' said I.
'Changes, lady? Aye!
Four times I have been

'Forced to lie abed;
Once I had the ague,
And thrice did I spew
Up my blood so red.
'Twas my lungs, Doctor said,
And the most I could do
To last a week or two—
Ten years he's been dead.

'My wife died.
And then after her
My eldest daughter.
Eight years come Whitsuntide
The house where we did bide

Was pulled down. It stood yonder,
Just by the tall fir
With the rick alongside.'

Thus did he talk,
Twisting the while
A sprig of camomile
Or a corn-stalk.
'Follow the grassy baulk
Till you come to the stile.'
So, mile by mile,
He told over my walk.

Musing on country folk
I bade him good-day.
And going on my way
To myself I spoke:
As well might I invoke
These hedges to say
Who passed by yesterday;
Or question yonder oak,

Bidding it declare
What changes it had seen.
'In summer I was green,
Acorns did I bear.
Come winter, I was bare.
For years full eighteen
This meadow has not been
Under the ploughshare.'

But Labour-in-Vain
Was the epitome
Of changes sighed to me
By the doomed champaign.
And turning once again,
Far off did I see
The man and the tree
Standing in the rain.

THE REPOSE

At Bradwell in the marshes
There is an inn.
Few are the travellers
Have rested therein.

The folk that sit there
Have but little to say;
They sit looking out of the window
At the churchyard across the way.

Growing among the graves
Is a green weeping willow.
The graves are all green
And peaceful as a pillow.

The bar-parlour is shaded
With a green gloom,
As if the willow-branches
Were waving in the room.

Churchyard and church and inn—
They are all very old.
Even the beer they draw there
Seems to taste of the mould.

THE TRAVELLER BENIGHTED

On through the quiet country-side
The road runs small and white,
The trees stand still on either side
As if to watch me there—
But stilled, stilled is the air
At the oncome of night.

And see, behind my back the moon
Eyes me with steadfast gaze;
I did not think she'd spill so soon
Her silver in the brook—
But calm, calm is her look
As she mounts through the haze.

As though I'd shed it like a husk,
My body casts no shade;
I walk suspended in the dusk
Just as a spirit might,
For yet, yet there is light
In the west—but 'twill fade.

Yes, fade it will, and I shall trace
My bobbing shadow spread
Before me on the whitened face
Of the road where I must go.
And then, then I shall know
What it is that I dread.

THE HAPPY DAY

All day long
I purpose in yonder
Green meadows to wander
And think of a song.

I shall take
Provision of berries,
Black treacle cherries,
And possibly cake.

Where the boughs
Of gliding willows
Freckle green pillows
I shall drowse,

Or wander blithe
Through scented acres
Where haymakers
Sharpen the scythe.

I shall not lack,
I shall not trouble;
Through fields of stubble
I shall come back

While dusk is spread,
While twilight lingers—
With purple fingers,
A song in my head.

NELLY TRIM

'Like men riding,
The mist from the sea
Drives down the valley
And baffles me.'
'Enter, traveller,
Whoever you be.'

By lamplight confronted
He staggered and peered;
Like a wet bramble
Was his beard.
'Sit down, stranger,
You look a-feared.'

Shudders rent him
To the bone,
The wet ran off him
And speckled the stone.
'Dost bide here alone, maid?'
'Yes, alone.'

As he sat down
In the chimney-nook
Over his shoulder
He cast a look,
As if the night
Were pursuing; she took

A handful of brash
To mend the fire,
He eyed her close
As the flame shot higher;
He spoke—and the cattle
Moved in the byre.

'Though you should heap
Your fire with wood,
'Twouldn't warm me,
Nor do no good,
Unless you first warm me
As a maiden should.'

With looks unwavering,
With breath unstirred,
She took off her clothes
Without a word;
And stood up naked
And white as a curd.

He breathed her to him
With famished sighs,
Against her bosom
He sheltered his eyes,
And warmed his hands
Between her thighs.

Strangely assembled
In the quiet room,
Alone alight
Amidst leagues of gloom,
So brave a bride,
So sad a groom;

And strange love-traffic
Between these two;
Nor mean, nor shamefaced—
As though they'd do
Something more solemn
Than they knew:

As though by this greeting
Which chance had willed
'Twixt him so silent
And her so stilled,
Some pledge or compact
Were fulfilled.

Made for all time
In times unknown,

'Twixt man and woman
Standing alone
In mirk night
By a tall stone.

His wayfaring terrors
All cast aside,
Brave now the bridegroom
Quitted the bride;
As he came, departing—
Undenied.

But once from darkness
Turned back his sight
To where in the doorway
She held a light:
'Goodbye to you, maiden,'
'Stranger, good night.'

Long time has this woman
Been bedded alone.
The house where she dwelt
Lies stone on stone:
She'd not know her ash-tree,
So warped has it grown.

But yet this story
Is told of her
As a memorial;
And some aver
She'd comfort thus any
Poor traveller.

A wanton, you say—
Yet where's the spouse,
However true
To her marriage-vows,
To whom the lot
Of the earth-born allows

More than this?—
To comfort the care
Of a stranger, bound

She knows not where,
And afraid of the dark,
As his fathers were.

EPITAPHS

(i)
Here lies Melissa Mary Thorn
Together with her son, still-born;
Whose loss her husband doth lament.
He has a large estate in Kent.

(ii)
After long thirty years re-met
I, William Clarke, and I, Jeanette
His wife, lie side by side once more;
But quieter than we lay before.

(iii)
A widowed mother reared this stone
To Annott Clare, aged twenty-one.
Seven live sons have I, but she
Was dearer than them all to me.

(iv)
Here lies the body of Tom Fool,
Who died, a little boy, at school
Oft did he bleed and oft did weep,
And whimpering, now has fallen asleep.

(v)
John Bird, a labourer, lies here,
Who served the earth for sixty years
With spade and mattock, drill and plough;
But never found it kind till now.

THE SAILOR

I have a young love—
A landward lass is she—
And thus she entreated:

'O tell me of the sea,
That on thy next voyage
My thoughts may follow thee.'

I took her up a hill
And showed her hills green,
One after other
With valleys between:
So green and gentle, I said,
Are the waves I've seen.

I led her by the hand
Down the grassy way,
And showed her the hedgerows
That were white with may:
So white and fleeting, I said,
Is the salt sea-spray.

I bade her lean her head
Down against my side,
Rising and falling
On my breath to ride:
Thus rode the vessel, I said,
On the rocking tide.

For she so young is, and tender,
I would not have her know
What it is that I go to
When to sea I must go,
Lest she should lie awake and tremble
When the great storm-winds blow.

THE IMAGE

'Why do you look so pale, my son William?
    Where have you been so long?'
'I've been to my sweetheart, Mother,
    As it says in the song.'

'Though you be pledged and cried to the parish
    'Tis not fitting or right

To visit a young maiden
    At this hour of the night.'

'I went not for her sweet company,
    I meant not any sin,
But only to walk around her house
    And think she was within.

'Unbeknown I looked in at the window;
    And there I saw my bride
Sitting lonesome in the chimney-nook,
    With the cat alongside.

'Slowly she drew out from under her apron
    An image made of wax,
Shaped like a man and all stuck over
    With pins and with tacks.

'Hair it had, hanging down to its shoulders,
    Straight as any tow—
Just such a lock she begged of me
    But three days ago.

'She set it down to stand in the embers—
    The wax began to run.
Mother! Mother! That waxen image,
    I think it was your son!'

''Twas but a piece of maiden foolishness,
    Never think more of it.
I warrant that when she's a wife
    She'll have a better wit.'

'Maybe, maybe, Mother.
    I pray you, mend the fire,
For I am cold to the knees
    With walking through the mire.

'The snow is melting under the rain,
    The ways are full of mud;
The cold has crept into my bones,
    And glides along my blood.

'Take out, take out my winding sheet
    From the press where it lies,
And borrow two pennies from my money-box
    To put upon my eyes;

'For now the cold creeps up to my heart,
    My ears go Ding, go Dong:
I shall be dead long before day,
    For winter nights are long.'

'Cursèd, cursèd be that Devil's vixen
    To rob you of your life!
And cursèd be the day you left me
    To go after a wife!'

'Why do you speak so loud, Mother?
    I was almost asleep.
I thought the churchbells were ringing
    And the snow lay deep.

'Over the white fields we trod to our wedding,
    She leant upon my arm—
What have I done to her that she
    Should do me this harm?'

GREEN PASTURES

'O, I could lean
And look for ever
At such a scene!—
And bless the Giver,
Who beauty gave, and best of all,
Sameness, unwearied and perpetual.

'Let such a sight
Brim up my seeing,
And with delight
Renew my being,
Until the prospect calm and kind
Seem the reflection of my mind!'

Said t'other: 'At most
This field you're praising
Has but the boast
Of being good grazing.
You're easy pleased if what you like
Best be a green field and a stone dyke.'

THE SOLDIER'S RETURN

Jump through the hedge, lass!
Run down the lane!
Here's your soldier-laddie
Come back again.

Coming over the hill
With the sunset at his back—
Never be feared, lass,
Though he look black;

Coming through the meadow
And leaping the watercourse—
Never be feared, lass,
Though his voice be hoarse;

Belike he's out of breath
With walking from the town.
He will speak better
When the sun's gone down.

BLACK EYES

Long Molly Samways
Went by just then.
Strange, how that girl
Gets off with the men!

With her head wig-waggling
On her long neck,
And her hair straggling
Down her back.

Past ten of the clock
She'll get up in a daze,
And spend the morning
Lacing her stays.

She wouldn't go
To the Whitsun Fair
Because of the trouble
Of getting there;

And if she be common
To half the town,
'Tis to please her back
That she lies her down.

Such a long, lazy
Slug-a-bed
Won't have her sleep out
Until she's dead.

And the Judgement Trump
May split the skies—
Though it should wake her
I doubt if she'll rise.

BLUE EYES

Barbara Cushion
Weeps in the lane,
And vows she will never
Go brambling again.

Down her fat face
Fat teardrops run,
And splash on her bosom,
One by one.

With sobs and cries
She shakes like a shape—
What is the matter,
Is it a rape?

Oh no! It's her feelings,
Poor girl, that smart;
And Jem's unkindness
Has broken her heart.

For months she has had
A mind to Jem,
So when she was out
She smiled at him;

Down the green lane
She watched him come—
But all he did
Was to pinch her bum.

FARMER MAW

Who's he you saw,
Stranger, among the stooks?—
'Tis Farmer Maw
Scaring away the rooks.

Once, stout and tall,
He had no peer to plough;
But this is all
Poor Farmer's fit for now.

On Lammas Eve
He hoed the Seven Acre,
And taking leave
Looked round like God the Maker:

His hay well ricked—
His fields secure and small—
With a most strict
Eye he surveyed them all;

And finding less
Than usual to offend
His carefulness,
Went home, and made an end.

After she saw
Hired bailiff reap and bind,
Poor Widow Maw
Sat down and called to mind

How oft her Dear
Exclaimed with scornful oaths
At waste of gear
Unthrift. His working clothes

She fetched, and laid
Them out upon a table;
Though patched and frayed
They yet were serviceable—

Aye, in such worn
Apparel, and bemired,
As men might scorn,
Scarecrow were well-attired.

Thus, stuffed with straw,
As large as life he stands—
A shape of awe—
And overlooks his lands,

His flocks and herds:
But sore, poor soul! beshit;
For those bold birds
Don't honour him a whit.

MRS SUMMERBEE GROWN OLD

As tall as the church tower,
And as stark,
The churchyard elm
Rears into the dark.

And many's the evening
I've walked in dread
To think that its boughs
Were overhead;

And many's the midnight
I've walked in fear
To think that its branches
Were drawing near.

For we live here alone—
The Rector and I,
Both of us grown old,
And unwilling to die;

And the churchyard elm
Has arms like a fiend:
Many's the dark night
I've thought they leaned

Downward, downward—
As though they'd claw
Us into the churchyard
Like things of straw.

But thanks to the rulers
Of the realm
We were delivered
From the elm.

For the Inspector
Chanced this way.
He wrote in his book,
And had his say

Of regulations
And bye-laws—
Then came the woodman
And cut its claws.

Harmless and glum
The monster stands
And holds to heaven
Its baffled hands.

The Rector and I
Can walk beneath,
Untroubled by
The fear of death.

And on still nights
When no one's about
I dance round the elm,
And thus do I flout:

Coffin-tree, coffin-tree,
You shall get neither him nor me!
Your branches are lopped,
Your games are all stopped.

STOCK

Farmer Hood's wife
Was brought to bed.
'Look at the baby!'
The midwife said.

Scantly he glanced
At the babe she bore.
He had seen plenty
Like it before;

And 'Troubles,' quoth he,
'Never come by half,
For the Guernsey heifer
Has slipped her calf.'

THE OLD SQUIRE

Squire England has grown old:
Too stiff to ride to hounds,
Too blind to shoot his coverts,
He takes up his great stick
And potters about the grounds.

The meadows and the pond,
The fig-tree on the south wall,

The plantation of young spruces,
The yew hedge twelve foot thick—
He stares at them all;

And grumbling as he goes,
He stops here and there
To spud up a dandelion.
His mind is full of doubt,
For a stranger is his heir.

House, meadows, walks and trees,
Although his sight be dim
He sees them very plainly;
He prays that none may flout
The things so dear to him.

MOPING CASTLE

'Why have you planted firs
About your dwelling,
Of trees created
Choosing the most adverse
To mortal cheer?
Whose breasts uncouth, both song
And spring repelling,
With endless sighs are freighted;
Foreboding every year
A deeper wrong.

'Or have you planted firs
About your dwelling
That they in proxy
Might all your sighs rehearse?
Ill-starred one! doomed
To mourn your frustrate prime,
Your sons rebelling,
Your Dear another doxy,
Your mouldered heart entombed
In waste of time.'

'No, Friend. I planted firs
About my dwelling;
But, I protest, meant
No clue so apt for verse
As you conceive
These sombre groves to give.
Soon ripe for felling,
Firs are good investment;
And though I live to grieve,
Yet I must live.'

THE SICK MAN'S GARDEN

He has been ill so long
    On whom it depended,
    That the garden untended
Is beginning to go wrong.

The gate has fallen awry,
    The tools are half rusted—
    They will be encrusted
All over, by and by.

The rose has broken loose
    From the arch where he trained it;
    Dead petal on petal has stained it
With its own juice.

Walks and plots are unkempt—
    It is all dishevelled;
    Like a skein unravelled,
Like a forgotten thing dream'd.

And peering through the gate,
    And closing in around it,
    The thickets that bound it
Seem to be lying in wait.

My heart foretells the day
    Toward which it moulders,
    When men with bowed shoulders
Shall carry him away.

Herb-border and flower-bed
 Underfoot they shall trample,
 And briar and bramble
Make slower their slow tread.

The mourners as they pass
 Will stumble and shuffle,
 Their steps shall be muffled
With the swishing of long grass.

Departed the last black form
 And the last black shadow,
 From thicket and meadow
Shall clamber in a swarm

Of wildings and weeds out-cast,
 By exile eagered
 For the garden beleaguered
Which has fallen at last.

By those remorseless, dumb
 Spoilers invaded,
 The flowers unaided
Shall all be overcome;

Save only those at need's
 Touch who turn traitors,
 Changing their natures
And reverting again to weeds.

Thus shall wild earth be paid
 The debt so long owing;
 Whilst he, unknowing,
Deep in wild earth is laid.

WHITE MAGIC

Young man, be warned by me,
 And shun the hour
 When the full moon has power
114 To sway men like the sea.

I with my love kept tryst
   One moonlight night.
   Something did us affright—
And she went home unkissed.

We saw as clear as day
   The thing we knew;
   Only the sky more blue
Seemed, and the grass grown grey.

Round us the orchard trees
   Like spirits stood—
   When she threw back her hood,
She looked like one of these;

So blanched the face I knew
   It seemed estranged:
   Its moonlight aspect changed
My eager blood to dew.

Disheartened, we returned;
   Nor met again.
   I have grown old since then,
But I have never learned

By what mysterious art
   The moonlight thieves
   Colour from the young leaves,
And passion from the heart.

AS I WAS A-WALKING

Sweetly fell the rain on the springing grass,
The birds sang all with voices as clear as glass;
   To greet the blackthorn I turned aside—
   A presence too lovely to pass—
But as with worship I neared it, a man I espied
Asleep in the rain beneath the blossoming tree.

I forgot to look at the tree, I looked instead
At the man who lay so still with averted head.

Because I could not see his face
I wondered if he were dead.
My mind was full of doubt as I left the place—
But dead or alive he was a stranger to me.

IN THE COTSWOLDS

All day the rain
Fell on the wheat
And dripped from the gable
On to the stone;
And all day long
I sat alone
Save for the dog
Who slept at my feet.

Slept—till a-sudden
He roused in fear,
And snuffed at the door,
And would not be quelled.
I opened—and there
An old crone I beheld,
And round about her
The dusk drawn near.

Something she said—
But her voice was hollow,
And chill was the hand
She laid on mine.
Her words were a riddle
I could not untwine;
And when she turned onward
I knew I must follow.

I felt the watery
Stubble souse
My ankles, and round me
Saw corn-shocks blurred.
And faint and fainter
Yet I heard
The dog bark on
116 In the empty house.

THE LITTLE DEATH

What voice is this
Sings so, rings so
Within my head?
Not mine, for I am dead,

And a deep peace
Wraps me, haps me
From head to feet
Like a smooth winding-sheet.

Before my eyes
Reeling, wheeling,
Leaf-green stars
Have changed to purple bars

And flickered out;
Spinning, thinning,
Up the wall,
That has grown very tall.

Only that voice—
Distant, insistent;
Like the high
Stroked glass's airy cry;

Echoing on,
Winds me, binds me
As with a thread
Spun from my own head.

O speak not yet!
Forget me, let me
Lie here as calm
As saints that nurse their palm;

Whilst like a tide
Turning, returning,
Silence and gloom
Flow in and fill the room.

THE DIVER

Self-loving I strayed
Through leagues of fir-wood—
Dream-like as woods
In water suspended,
So hushed was the shade,
So cool the silence;

Nor stayed, till I saw
My watery woodlands
In a deep tarn
Hanging head-downward,
As though they would draw
The soul down after them.

I thought: How sweet
To bathe in those waters!
I stripped myself bare;
On the pine-needles
I settled my feet,
And dived in fearless

To greet with the glow
Of an ardent lover
That limpid depth,
That bride-bed of stillness
Which far below.
Awaited my coming.

O, but beneath
The rocky cornice,
Ready to pounce
There lurked a Nixy!
With ice-cold teeth
She bit and tore me,

And wreathed her fierce
Embraces about me
In coil on coil
Of anguish unspeakable,
And snarled in my ears
With a voice of darkness.

In fear of my life
I fought the Nixy
Till back to her den
At last I drove her;
To whet her knife
And await the next-comer.

Dry-footed on shore
I scrunched the pine-needles,
And watched the tarn
And its basking tree-tops
Resume once more
Their lovely stillness:

All, all like a charm
Inveigled the spirit;
Prompted: How sweet
To bathe in these waters
Here is no harm—

But I knew better.

UPON A GENTLEMAN FALLING
SERIOUSLY IN LOVE

Who loves his kind, loves bone,
Flesh, play of sinew, shoot
Of sense, the turn of a head,
A voice answering his own:
Who loves a house, loves stone,
Iron, plaster, brick, glass, lead,
Timber hewn off and mute—
            And these alone.

Who wins his kind, wins store
Of joys, griefs, memories, brain's
Diligence, heart's ease, a share
Of life not his before:
Who gains a house, a core
Of blank and senseless air
Cased up on matter gains—
            And nothing more.

Sun may warm stone, awaken
Casement, with farewell kiss
Flush thatch—'tis all a show.
Though man a more unshaken
Diurnal love bestow—
He gains not even this.

And blest are they whose thrall
Hearts can endure this passion,
Hopeless, uncompromised
By aught reciprocal;
Yea, saints emparadised
May love God after this fashion.

THE CAPRICIOUS LADY

No, no, I do not choose
Commonplace flowers like these!
Such artless pinks and blues—
Forget-me-not, maiden's blush—
Are tedious to my sight.
But give me, if you'd please,
Blossoms more recondite:
Cocks-combs of crimson plush,
Large, spider-speckled, rare
Orchids, or tulips whose
Smooth flesh has learnt to wear
The colour of a bruise.

THEODORIC

Praise the great Goth, Theodoric!
Who, a true patriot, led
His northern hordes into Italy,
Where he'd be better fed.

Sturgeon, peacock, assafœtida—
Nought came amiss to him
(Though Peter Vischer of Nuremberg
Makes him out to be slim.)

Once only did his appetite
Quail at a new dish;
When they served up an aged senator
In the shape of a large fish.

The dead eyes glared reproachfully—
Fear spawned in his blood
Agueish pangs innumerable
As fishes in the flood.

Not furs of marmot and zibeline,
Nor a great fire near-by,
Could warm the wretched Theodoric
As he lay waiting to die;

Chattering about old Symmachus,
And Boëthius his friend,
Who with no consolation but philosophy
Made a far braver end.

HONEY FOR TEA

I've sat in the sun
From three to five
Watching the bees
About the hive.
They are horribly alive!

From white to red,
From red to white,
They weave Euclidean
Tangles of flight,
And nowhere find delight:

But them a maniac
Industry eggs
Onward; they grapple
With hairy legs,
Methodical to the dregs.

The blossom rifled,
With laden thighs

Further each willing
Eunuch plies:
A dull way to fertilize.

And back to their cells
They come at last;
Armed, incurious,
Sailing past
Me where I sit aghast.

Oh, horrible
That aught can be
So sufficient, yet
So unlike me!
I shall go in to tea.

There in the parlour
I shall find
Things to restore
My peace of mind;
By man for man designed.

The rat-tail spoons,
The china dishes,
Smooth as sequined
Sides of fishes,
Obedient to my wishes;

The sturdy table
So plain and whole,
The meek sweet
Of the sugar-bowl;
These shall confirm my soul

Till I, emboldened,
Lift down from the shelf
The hoarded treasure,
Taken by stealth
From that inimical Commonwealth.

BODLEY'S LIBRARY

Chained to their shelves
Sit Origen,
Aquinas, Gregory
Nazianzen,
Bede, Alcuin, Scotus—
All the wise men
Of golden mouth
And faithful pen.

Falcons once
Of piercing flight,
Chained they must needs be
Or out of sight
They'd soar. But now
They blink at the light,
Like old brown owls
Awaiting the night.

A SONG ABOUT A LAMB

'O God, the Sure Defence
    Of Jacob's race,
Lover of innocence
    And a smooth face,
Accept my sacrifice—
A little lamb, bought at the market price.

'With fleece so soft and clean
    And horns not yet
A-bud, the creature's been
    The children's pet.
And sore they wept to see
Their snub-nosed friend come trotting after me.'

God heard: the lightnings brake
    Forth in his honour;
But by some slight mistake
    Consumed the donor.
The lamb fell in a muse—
But soon took heart, and leaped among the pews.   *123*

HYMN FOR A CHILD

Flocking to the Temple
See the priests assemble
Where a child expounds
What the wise confounds.

All the scribes and sages
Quit their dog's-eared pages;
Spell-bound by his sense
And his eloquence.

Speaking without bias,
He reviewed Elias;
Said the dogs did well,
Eating Jezebel.

Just as he disposes
Of the Law and Moses,
Mary came in haste—
Caught him to her breast:

'We have sought thee' saying—
Chid him for delaying.
Then without demur
He went back with her.

Those he was amazing
Straightway broke out praising;
Calling him a mild,
Nicely brought-up child.

Teach me, gentle Saviour,
Such discreet behaviour
That my elders be
Always pleased with me.

THE SCAPEGOAT

See the scapegoat, happy beast,
From every personal sin released,
And in the desert hidden apart,
Dancing with a careless heart.

'Lightly weigh the sins of others.'
See him skip! 'Am I my brother's
Keeper? O never, no, no, no!
Lightly come and lightly go!'

In the town from sin made free,
Righteous men hold jubilee.
In the desert all alone
The scapegoat dances on and on.

BYRON 1924

Much as they all deplored his morals
Our fathers left the bard his laurels.
But in these more precisian days
We shake our young heads over the lays.

GRACE AND GOOD WORKS

Blest are the poor, whose needs enable
The rich but timely charitable
To take the Kingdom of Heaven by force.
The poor are also saved, of course.

MORNING

The long, long-looked-for night has sped.
'Tis time we should arise
Out of this tossed and blood-stained bed
Where a dead woman lies.

FAITHFUL CROSS

Strange, that his sorrow should
Only be understood
By two rough pieces of wood.

The friends that lingered there,
However true they were,
Had grief of their own to bear.

They stood and mourned apart:
With but half a heart
For his sorrow and smart;

They mourned, and went their way
Into Heaven to be gay.
The Cross is faithful to this day.

O Tree of Life, that root
Hast not, nor hope of shoot,
Nor but this one sad fruit—

Thou, not Mary or John—
Thou, that he died upon
He chose for his eidolon.

Though he by a word or two
Or a look, men's hearts could woo
And knit, as none else could do;

Not one of the brotherhood
To whom he did good,
But two rough pieces of wood,

Hewn-off, exanimate,
Could carry and constate
His and his sorrow's weight.

THE MAID'S TRAGEDY

I kept two singing birds
In a cage of bone—
Hatched-out on the same day;
But since one flew away,
T'other's alone.

I spoke him gentle words
And bade him sing.

But he hung down his head
As if discomforted,
And drooped his wing.

My mood was turned to rage;
I stinted his seed,
Opened the cage-door wide—
Starve, or begone! I cried.
He did not heed.

Silent within his cage
I see him mope
Like any turtle-dove.
The dumb bird I called Love,
The flown bird, Hope.

COMMON ENTRY

I hate my neighbour with bitter hate—
Night and morning, early and late,
Her and her works to the Fiend I commend;
For she's had it mended the garden gate.

For every comer 'twould grind and squeak;
But when One came here who had most to seek
It would cry aloud at his hasty shove,
'Here, here's your lover!' and redden my cheek.

Oh yes, he still comes, though the gate doesn't tell—
But I wish my neighbour were deep in Hell.
How dare she the least of my joys estrange,
Or threat me with changes when all's so well?

THE ALARUM

With its rat's tooth the clock
Gnaws away delight.
Piece by piece, piece by piece
It will gnaw away to-night,

Till the coiled spring released
Rouses me with a hiss
To a day, to another night
Less happy than this.

And yet my own hands wound it
To keep watch while I slept;
For though they be with sorrow,
Appointments must be kept.

MATCH ME, O ROSE!

A red rose shining in the sun
Told me of summer new-begun.
I smoothed each petal, and kissed each petal,
And counted them one by one.

Eighteen—and I had two years more.
'Match me, O rose!' I said; and tore
In half two petals, two crimson petals,
To bring them to a score.

Just at that moment the wind blew—
Petal by petal away I threw,
And turned to the rose-bush, the lovely rose-bush,
Where other roses grew.

THE ONLY CHILD

When I was small
My mother had an Indian shawl,
Spun from the friendliest kind of goat
And dyed a comfortable red.
And when I had a pain in my throat
I used to take the shawl to bed.

So soft it was
That through her wedding-ring 'twould pass;
So warm, it nursed all care aside;

So wide, a covey of babes might be
Happed up in it—soft, warm and wide
As sleep, that shawl was lent to me.

THE BURNING-GLASS

All day the Sun looked down
On England; heath and town,
Cornland and woodland, mountain and champaign,
And the bright tangled skein

Of Thames, Avon, Severn, Trent—
Everywhere his beams went.
They lighted upon ships far out to sea,
And sifted every tree.

And few, and dull, were they
Abroad in England that day,
But looking up at the blue heavens overhead,
'Fine harvest weather,' said.

Turning him to his rest
Within the patient West—
As though he kept the primal law in mind
To multiply his kind—

Throughout the land his rays
Set windows in a blaze;
But nowhere, save at Wells in Somerset,
Did a live Sun beget.

There, under cottage brows,
Glittered intact the spouse
Whose steadfast welcome the steadfast greeting could match,
And fired a neighbour's thatch.

Strange chance! (Enough to undo
Man's wit, might he look through
Seeing, and know the Sun an enormous spark
In caves of endless dark;

And, like ourselves, condemned
His little light to expend
By rote. But our imaginations deck
The heaven's hideous black.)

Strange chance! meeting well-met!
Chance more wild-faring yet
I woo, that with long hope and true intent
My burning-glass present

To that unmeasured, un-
surmisable incendiary of suns—
Life—that some beam of it, matched by my art,
May fire a stranger's heart.

PEEPING TOM

TO T. F. POWYS

Out of the land
He grew as grows the weed,
But had no land
For his own need.

He to a farmer
His crafty sinews hired,
Rising up early
And going home tired

For six days of the week—
Poor Tom!—and said on Sunday,
Leaning over a gate:
'To-morrow be Monday.'

Few were his thoughts,
Devious, and unexpressed;
Yet one strong yearning
Swelled in his breast

Through rain and shine,
Through months of earthly labour;
Till at last he spoke
His thought to a neighbour.

'I should like well
To have some land of my own,
To be my land
And mine alone:

'Say, half an acre—
More would outdo my means—
To grow potatoes
And a few beans.'

Up at the Inn
His neighbour made it known
How Tom wished
For land of his own.

About the village
To all men's ears it ran;
The farmer heard it,
Who was a rich man.

Green water-meadows,
Large barns, deep fields he had;
His servant's wish
Made his heart glad,

For he in plenty
Was rooted like an oak;
And Tom's half-acre
Seemed a good joke.

He gave the ground
And all men said of him
He could well afford
To have his whim.

The plot of ground which the farmer gave
        Did not cost him dear.
All unfenced and untilled it lay,
        And far away
        From cottage and inland tree;
Where the rolling down rears up like a great slow wave
        And then falls sheer
        Four hundred feet to the sea.

Thither poor Tom,
His day's toil over, would walk;
And marked, and swaled,
And scratched on the chalk—

Too much intent
To note the oncome of night
Till to ease his back
He stood upright.

And plodding homeward
Through nurtured fields, his mind
Still delved in the patch
He had left behind.

Sea-winds blew there,
Sea-birds flew there,
Nothing grew there

Save the inherent tares of barren ground;
Grasses shrivelled and stiff,
And frantic thistles scattering their seed.
Claw-rooted was each necessitous weed
And salt to the taste,
For the blown rack groped over the waste,
And evermore the sea with a trampling sound
Beleaguered the cliff.

A row of beans
Was the first thing Tom set.
Most died: the rest
The rabbits ate.

He gave up beer
And saved to buy a fence.
His wife blamed him
For having no sense;

And all his friends
That saw him study and grieve—
Landless themselves—
Laughed in their sleeve.

Tom heard them out;
He did not say them Nay,
But still to his patch
Went day by day,

Disheartened, perhaps,
But redeless to forego
The dogged dream
He had cherished so.

And little thought
His straitened brain-pan knew
Save only that
There was much to do.

From the beginning
The weeds had been his bane,
And tilling the ground
Made them as bad again.

He groaned aloud
To see how they would thrive
Where nothing he planted
Could keep alive;

And fresh weeds grew
That had not grown before;
For each he spudded
There sprang ten more,

That bloomed in his face
As if from very spite.
It chanced, such a blossom
Caught his sight

Just as he struck work.
His back was aching so
That he was half-minded
To let it go,

But from long habit,
With look indifferent,
Above the invader
Wearily he bent

To root it up:
His face by slow degrees
Awakened
He went on his knees—

There is no beauty like the beauty of the wild,
That blossoms suddenly out of the bare hillside.
It is the barren woman that goes with child,
It is the clenched knot of necessity untied,
Eternity waylaid, and labouring creation
Into forgetfulness and laughter beguiled:
A relenting, a reconciliation, a glimpse of the bride,
Nature, hidden under her dark veils of Time and Space and
  Causation.
                    Out of the hillside a word:
'Lo, here I am! Quick, gather my secret, cried—
Had you not come—to the waste, from pole to pole
To echo forever unheard. Had I died, had I died,
Perished had with me, unguessed, the clue of the whole.
But now are the heavens opened, and Salvation
Is sprung up like a flower out of the earth.
Look! I am newly-made, the dew of my birth
Is of the womb of the morning; I hold in my wide-
open petals the epitome of that blue
In seas drowned, in distance secluded, in air enskied:
                    And all, all is for you.
Come! Kneel beside me and unlearn your soul.'

Ah, not for man the message, the revelation!
On hillsides desolate and bare, by paths untravelled,
In swamps, and skyey wastes the tokens are spilled.
Wild beauty like a bird flits here and there,
Homes not to hand nor snare, and nowhere settles.
Who's he shall augur from her flight? And who shall dare
Unravel the plain speech of five blue petals?
Not man's mind, that chooseth a good
Obsequious to the God his proud heart hath chosen,
That parteth light from darkness and right from wrong,
                    Nor brooketh the unfulfilled.
Let him tread out the blossom and ignore the song
                    And go upon his way.

But some there are who hearken, who stay,
Who kneel and worship before the undesigned,
And all their strength relinquish to obey
A voice that seeks not to be understood—
No, nor yet purpose has enough to mock.
Awhile they feed on brightness; but ere long
They find their hearts astray, and their blood frozen,
And know themselves averted from their kind.
Extremity of light has made them blind.
With look so vacant as to seem serene,
They wander towards darkness, and as they go
Idly a few belated berries glean,
Or darnel and the clammy nightshade wreathe,
                    Or to themselves speak low;
And in the end lie down upon the rock,
And to the heedless air their last loud groan bequeath.

Darkness rose up out of the deep;
Headland by headland along the coast
Lost colour, shape, identity, stole from sight,
Folded in darkness like a flock of sheep.
                    Up on the height
The flower ebbed from his vision like a ghost,
                    And Tom went home to sleep.

Changed henceforward was his mood.
All he'd endeavoured, all he'd planned
Forgetting, his mind at ease, he would sit awhile
To watch the gulls, or stretch full-length would brood;
                    And camomile,
Chance-plucked, chafed for its savour in his hand,
                    And thyme or fennel chewed.

Mildly now he could behold
Thistle and coney flourish unchecked.
The unequal combat relinquishing he let fall
His spade, or only dug to smell the mould;
                    But joys past all
Former surmise he harvested from neglect,
                    That joyed nor reaped of old.

Sweetness had pierced him like a dart.
Careless of duty, afield he ranged,
And spared with fostering hand the weeds amid
The farmer's crops, such wonder was in his heart.
                    The farmer chid—
And swore the politicians were deranged
                    To take the labourer's part.

Christmas came, and quarter-day;
'Goodwill to all men' chanted the choir,
'And on earth, peace.' The earth in a riveted black
Frost fast bound like a cataleptic lay.
                    The times were slack.
The farmer said to Tom: 'I don't require
                    Servants not worth their pay.'

Household shipwreck disposing as best
He could, since none near by would employ
Such a half-wit, on a tramp for work he set out;
Of more than land and livelihood dispossessed,
                    For care and doubt
Sat plotting deep in his heart that his secret joy
                    Might vade with all the rest.

Everywhere rejected, he turned
Onward by darkening ways and grim
Gaunt woodlands where yet would kindle from bough to
                                          bough
The irresistible wildfire of spring for which he had yearned.
                    Small difference now
'Twixt leaves unborn or dead underfoot to him
                    Whom spring no more concerned.

Lengthening days would but strengthen his care,
Nor spring be even what once it had been—
A dazzle in dull eyes, chance heart-thrust of a bird's song,
Hint of a covenanted joy all creatures share;
                    For he too long
Had watched a wildflower's visage, and had seen
                    No hope, no purpose there.

Whither he went,
And what the welcome he found,

Or if he yet
Were above ground,

Came never word.
His name was clean forgot;
Unless folk said
Tom was a bad lot.

Many years after,
His tale was told to me.
I for a whim
Went off to see

Tom's patch, but might
Have sought in vain for it
Had not my foot
Caught in a bit

Of galvanised netting—
Good heartless shop-stuff, wrought
To outlast man
And man's thought.

I gave it a kick;
And after one more look,
Moved off to find
Some sheltered nook

Where I might sit
And watch the seagulls fly.
All that afternoon
No one came by,

Save one old man
Scarcely more human than they—
And he, I think,
Had lost his way.

For as he went
He'd stop and look about,
And shake his head,
As if in doubt

Of where he was;
And once, as though he'd read
The answer there,
Pulled up a weed

And peered at it
Full steadfastly—and then
Throwing it down,
Limped on again.

TIME IMPORTUNED
(1928)

THE ARRIVAL

When I set out I did not know
Whether an ash tree or an elm
With branches waving slow
And a soft summer voice would overwhelm
My questing thoughts with the certainty of arrival;

But now on the dusky lawn I stand
And neither ash tree nor elm tree greet:
A deeper plumage is fanned,
The air wanders enchanted with one sweet,
And in the lime tree a nightingale is singing.

THE LOAD OF FERN

Now I am sure
That the year is come to the turn, though Summer delay,
Sitting drowsily in the mute shade of the sycamore,
Waiting for moonrise, for one last moonrise more
To pour its floating silver over the stooks
That kneel all night and pray,
Motionless, like saints in heaven who kneel and adore;
Yes, now I am sure, though Summer delay, her dear,
Her last looks taking, her looks of leave-taking,
That the year is come to the turn;
For lumbering down from the moor
The farm carts creak and sway with their load of fern,
With their load of fern, a wilder load than hay.

So thunder-still is the air
That while they are yet far off I can hear
The axles whine and the horses snort,
And the long ring of shouted speech,
As solemnly wain follows wain, and each in turn
Delays awhile, shifting with slow care
Under that bronze bulk, under that vast rustling and
        toppling freight,
To steer true through the gate.
And now they plough
Onward through meadow grasses that cleave and cling   *141*

To spokes and felloes
As ripples cleave dividing about the prow
Of the ship who comes slowly, slowly into port.
Steady she keeps on her way, and her sail bellies
As near she passes and nearer, and you can hear
Her canvas thud and her blocks complain, men's voices,
     and the ring
Of chains and winches and pulleys and all her gear,
Till for love of her, unknown, and unknown her seafaring,
The heart stands up to cheer her.

O now I think how the year
With all her freight of harvest, with all her gear
Of seed and blossom, of berry and bracken frond,
Puts into port.
But here she cannot stay:
She must put forth again, she must away,
Steer for the equinox, hold out her sail
Taut to the buffeting wind, wince under hail,
On, on, into the winter seas that lie beyond,
Into the deep nights, into the sheer
Darkness, into fog and storm and snow,
Into the grinding frost, into the shortest day . . .
O the long voyaging ere she can return
With her load of fern!

But you, last freight, and emblem of the close,
Last-garnered, furthest-fetched, and most her own,
Sweet breath of the wild, harvest untended and unsown,
Tawny with long regards of the sun on solitude,
Wise-rooted, nurtured with natural sap alone,
Strong gipsy child of an earth virgin and unsubdued,
Come in and house
Your warmth and scent of summer, come in, come in!
Here in a drowsy twilight roofed with stone
Store your sweet breath with cattle breathing warm
Sweet sighs of quietude, espouse
To indoor dusk your rust and russet glows,
Bring warmth, scent, colour, bring the wild earth's
     well-being into shelter;
Ere the first trumpet of the gale be blown, or the storm
Beat like a distant drummer, or Winter begin,

When the winds arouse and the rains pelt
And helter-skelter the leaves scud off from the groaning
    boughs.

SAINT ANTONY ON THE HILLSIDE

Short sleep, brief waking,
Dawn like a bird flown by,
The swollen sun forsaking
His dark bower of cloud
And sinking beneath the mountain;
My slender rill of time
Still bubbling from the fountain
With voice not loud,
But loud enough to chime
Me to my meditations;
Years making and unmaking
The net of constellations;
Winter, a look of rime,
And Spring, a blossom falling,
And Summer, a blade of corn,
Soon ripened, soon bowed;
These Lord, with patience
I glean, and wait thy cry,
Thy word recalling
Me from these fields where I
Am, even as Ruth, forlorn.

Long sleep, eternal waking . . .

WALKING AND SINGING AT NIGHT

Darkened the hedge, and dimmed the wold,
We sang then as we trudged along.
The heart grown hot, the heart grown cold,
Are simple things in a song.

The lover comes, the lover goes,
On the same drooping interval,
Easy as from the ripened rose
The loosened petals fall.

Between one stanza and the next
A heart's unprospered hopes are sighed
To death as lovely and unvexed
As 'twere a swan that died.

Alas, my dear, Farewell's a word
Pleasant to sing but ill to say,
And Hope a vermin that dies hard;
As you will find, one day.

SEXTON AND PARSON

'Sir, what shall we do?
Here's Edward Buckland found dead,
Edward Buckland the gipsy man,
And Paradice his wife is dead too;
Both dead of fever in their caravan.
They must have died before the storm began,
For the wind has blown open the door,
And the snow lies drifted on the floor
With never a footprint thereon.'

'What shall we do, sexton, what shall we do?—
We will bury them together, the two
In the one deep grave shall lie together,
Safe put away from their journeying, from storm and
        winter weather.'

'Sir, what shall we do then?
I will dig them a nice grave;
But after I shall be put to shame,
With register before me and vestry pen
And nothing to write but death and a wayfaring name—
Neither age nor walk in life nor whence they came.
As I live, Sir, the proverb is just:
In hoar-frost and gipsies put no trust,
For come noontide they are gone.'

'What shall we do then, sexton, do then?—
We will enter their names in the book, and when
They died, and *Travellers* we will call them:
Travellers they, ay, and all men till sweet rest befall them.'

COUNTRY MEASURES

'That tune, child, which swayed you and buoyed out your
    frills
Till you looked like a blossom that wafts to the ground
Must have come a long journey, thus to set twirling round
The shepherds and nymphs of the Vauxhall quadrilles.

'To such country measures the haymaker swings
His scythe as he paces the meadow alone;
As though to their requiem are the tall grasses mown,
And the moon rises over the wood as he sings.

'The traveller hears him, and pays him a sigh
(Or 'tis paid to the *lacrimae rerum*, maybe);
For these airs have a voice of such lorn sincerity
That the soul must assent ere the reason knows why.

'Young Careless has one that would make the tears start,
Of a girl that's deserted and grieves for her case:
'Twas sung by a milkmaid down on his father's place,
And before he forsook her he'd got it by heart.'

WILLOW

Catkins, by village folk
'Tis called, and after, palm;
Whose pewter fur rose-flushed
Sprays gold-dust and smells balm;

Lovely on countryside—
First hatched of all the brood
Spring mothers on the brown
Nest of the English wood;

And lovely in London too,
A greeting seeming beyond all
That envoy flowers have brought
Authentic and personal

(As we, should one beloved
Offer a keepsake, choose
No rarity but what's most
Made by his wont to use);

For man has untaught the flowers
Their first obedience,
But in a willow branch
There can be no pretence.

I with such word of Spring
By the old brown man was plied,
Who with slouched hat, and stick,
And tousled and sad-eyed

Dog at his slow heels,
Wanders through streets and squares,
With kingcups sometimes, or groundsel,
Or russet wild pears.

Said I, close to my breath
Holding the willow wands:
'In sheltered woodlands now,
Or growing beside ponds,

There must be boughs a-plenty
With their catkins putting out.'
And as I spoke I was glad;
For it seemed beyond doubt

That Spring, the swallow, was come,
And that under her sky
All men would be happy, though none
Should taste such joy as I.

Me narrow-hearted, how
His honest answer chid!
'Yes, it's too common now
To fetch the price it did.'

THE MORTAL MAID

As a fish swimming through the water's glimmer
I wooed you first,
When to the wishing well you stooped your visage
And slaked your thirst.

With a hair plundered from the white beard of Merlin
You shall be tied;
With a grass ring plighted you shall come at nightfall
To be my bride.

The straight rain falling shall be the church walls,
And you shall pace
To where an old sheep waits like a hedge-priest
In a hollow place.

In his inheritance of the kingdom of Elfin
Your son shall be born,
And you shall christen him in the dew that glistens
On the holy thorn.

THE HOUSE GROWN SILENT

After he had gone the wind rose,
Buffeting the house and rumbling in the chimney,
And I thought: It will roar against him like a lion
As onward he goes.

Seven miles before him, all told—
Chilled will be the lips I kissed so warm at parting,
Kissed in vain; for he's forth in the wind, and kisses
Won't keep out the cold.

Closer should I have kissed, and fondlier prayed:
Pleasant is the room in the wakeful firelight,
And within is the bed, arrayed with peace and safety.
Would he had stayed!

THE ESPOUSAL

Such silence was on the woods and on the meadows where
    none
Walked save the departing sun,
Where nothing breathed save the warm sweet of
    midsummers past
In quiet hayrick housed fast,
That I thought: Perhaps for no other end was I born
Than with step deliberate and unaware
To wander my way to this wood-encompassed pasture
    where
Stands one ash tree, all green and lorn.

Long while in silence as by a friend I sat by the tree,
Whose shadow moving over me
And lovingly lengthening such sheltering joy shed into my
    soul
That ere I turned homeward, its bole,
Large and austere, I twined my arm's half-hoop to embrace,
And laid my eyelids and my lips along
Its braided weather-silky bark, and looked up into the
    throng
Of boughs as looking up into a husband's face.

JUST AS THE TIDE WAS FLOWING

It had grown late
And I had turned inland
When one with rolling gait
Came down toward the strand:
It was a drownèd sailor.

'Greeting, poor ghost!
I do not fear you much.
On this cruel coast
There must be many such
Wandering, could we but see them.

'And wander well you may
On such a night as this,

When the smell of the mown hay
Comes like a kiss
From the earth, our quiet mother.'

'Greeting, my kind
Lass-alive,' said he.
'Turn back if you've a mind
To come walking with me;
For 'tis seaward I'm going.'

'Seaward, sailor? No!
Elsewhere let us rove.
But half an hour ago
I was down in the cove:
There is nothing there, nothing—

'Only the endless chide
Of waves furled and unfurled;
Only a making tide,
And an ebbing world.'
'Ay, is the tide making?

''Tis even as I guessed;
For where I lay underground
Something troubled my rest,
A tremor and a sound
Under the green fields travelling;

'Coming nearer and more near,
And searching me out
Till at last 'twas so clear
That with a great shout
I remembered, and came forth.'

'Remembered? Ah, poor soul,
Have you remembered all—
The ship past control,
In the icy squall
Like a maimed beast struggling;

'Rearing at every shock,
Blind in blinding night,
And hounded toward the rock

By the unchanging spite
Of the sea, man's old enemy?

'Turn back, my friend,
Turn inland once more.
At the voyage end
'Tis best to sleep ashore,
In a safe bed, and a holy;

'Or should you wakeful lie
You need not be dismayed,
For resting near by
Are many of your trade
Who have gone down into deep waters:

'Kind company for you,
Who the long night long
Shall tell old yarns through,
And roar out the old songs,
With *Adieu to you, Spanish Ladies!*'

But he as I spoke thus
Brushed by me, with the Nay!
Of one whose imperious
Need can brook no delay;
And in a moment, vanished.

THE RIVER OUSE

Through his broad lands the river goes,
Rolling and plentiful as they;
The willow blossom he bears away
And bears away the winter snows.

Anon to the darkening bridge he comes
And heaves his shoulder against the piers;
His own full voice is all he hears,
He does not hear the sound of drums,

The soldiers marching overhead
For sea and foreign service bound—

High in the air a martial sound,
A passage athwart his passage shed.

On flows the river and on go they;
Left! Left! drums the heart in my bosom.
More sad than snow, more dear than blossom,
My peace of mind they bear away.

I followed the river in my pain
And heard him say, secure and grave:
The tears you shed upon the wave
No tide shall ever bring again.

While yet upon your visage shine
And scald their tracks, while yet in me
You wring your hands, they haste to be
Absolved into a larger brine:

Therein, a nameless salt, they'll weigh
The flood that bears to distant shores
Lovers as dearly lost as yours,
Or sting an unkissed check with spray.

You will not know, and though you should
(Since strangers these) you would not care
How they commerce with your despair—
Launch on your tears, it does you good,

Weep to encounters chance shall bid—
By then this grief may seem as strange:
Let sorrow in the water range,
Be sighs in air forever hid.

Others, more rash than you, leap down—
With every tear, with every breath,
You shred your moment's self to death:
My dear, what need is there to drown?

IN THE VALLEY

On this first evening of April
Things look wintry still:

Not a leaf on the tree,
Not a cloud in the sky,
Only a young moon high above the clear green west
And a few stars by and by.

Yet Spring inhabits round like a spirit.
I am sure of it
By the swoon on the sense,
By the dazzle on the eye,
By the long, long sigh that traverses my breast
And yet no reason why.

O lovely Quiet, am I never to be blest?
Time, even now you haste.
Between the lamb's bleat and the ewe's reply
A star has come into the sky.

A PATTERN OF TIME

Still in the shining garden
Where once in time long gone
I walked alone, a maiden,
A maiden walks alone.

She halts before the rosebush
As though she could not tell
What thoughts now press upon her—
I know her thoughts full well.

Red, red are the roses;
But yet there is something more;
And through the garden she wanders
As though she would implore

Blossom or leaf to reveal it;
They are silent every one:
I, only I, could tell her
What she shall tell to none.

But rapt and heedless walks she,
And furtive I hurry by;
For it would spoil her dreaming
To look on such as I:

ELIZABETH

'Elizabeth the Beloved'—
So much says the stone,
That is all with weather defaced,
With moss overgrown.

But if to husband or child,
Brother or sire, most dear
Is past deciphering;
This only is clear:

That once she was beloved,
Was Elizabeth,
And now is beloved no longer,
If it be not of Death.

THE RED DRESS

Dress, you are braver than I.
Red in grain, you'll not fade
Though you should be laid
In an oak chest, by and by.

Others shall lift you thence
To the patter and stir
Of shrivelled lavender,
With female reverence

Murmuring in awed tone:
'So rare the web, so rich
The broiderer's stitch on stitch,
See, it will stand alone!'

Good dress, I charge you, be
In other time, other place,
To some woman of my race
True as you were to me.

In the warfare of sex
Be at eye's onset

Like the ring of a trumpet,
To challenge and perplex;

When souls clash in the fray,
To the breast at stake a shield
Whose scarlet shall not yield
Nor leak of blood betray;

And in that hour surprising
When the heart's garrison
Know themselves undone,
A flag still flying.

THE REQUIEM

Walk cautiously round Love
Who thrown and spent lies here;
Raise not your voice above
A whisper lest he hear you—
Hush, for fear!

Rouse not those furious plumes
Whose wrath so far and fast
Pursued you to these glooms,
That have from everlasting
Waited to cast

Their shadow on this end:
This demi-god in dust,
This dust that could contend,
And a slave's courage mustered
Up for that thrust—

Not to Love's heart (that, none
Can pierce) but to his own;
Which violence being done,
The victor stands up lonely,
And Love lies prone.

Look not too long on him
(Speak soft, and warily tread)
Lest viewing him harmless dim

Your memory of him dreadful;
Lift not that head,

Seek not that hidden face,
Lest dying should restore
Those looks of childish grace
Which in Love's innocent morning
First Love wore.

THE JET CHANDELIER

Sunset, sunrise,
Are but surmise;
All change of changing days is safely hid,
And light sifts through the laurel screen,
Mute and submarine.

Here comes no wind to stir,
No sun to fade:
Here in this northward-facing room
Is a sure shade
For one who is afraid.

No colour at all
On hanging or wall—
And slowly in unshaken fires consume
The candles rising tier on tier
In the jet chandelier.

Here comes no hope to hound,
No love to smite:
Only a midnight sun illumes
This world as white
As snow, as still as night.

TRIUMPHS OF SENSIBILITY

   (i)
Above my own distress I hear
Outcry of anguish, groans of fear,
As though the trees in yonder wood
Mourned for some vegetable good.

Foul thought! Creation's innocents,
Them but the rainy wind torments.
What, do you wail still? O, it's true!
Man, the Sick Beast, has been with you.

    (ii)
There is a fiend called Hug Me Tight
Who watches round me day and night.
Waxing and waning like a coal
His eyes look darkness into my soul.

I hear his loud and casual tread
Stalk through the disinhabited
House of my mind where he alone
Goes up and down, goes up and down.

He shoots no bolt, he turns no key,
He lets me sleep in the scullery;
Of my left ear he's made a trap
To catch the drips from the water-tap.

I am not chained, I am not tied,
But lest I run on suicide,
Or harm myself in my self-rage,
He keeps me in a glassy cage.

Sometimes my friends and lovers come
Like trippers to the Aquarium;
They peer, they tap upon the pane,
And presently they're gone again.

I know they are alive, because
I see their breath besmirch the glass;
But be it sigh or be it scoff
It takes the same time to fade off.

And I am glad when they are gone;
For Hug Me Tight will come anon,
And all their looks and all their sighs
Dismember and anatomise

Till they as I are cold and vile,
Guttering friendship to beguile
An itch of self-complacency.
Only my fiend is true to me;

Only my fiend with supple tongue
Can lick my brain and heal the wrong
Which loving much and thinking more
Have wrought in fibres of one-score.

And then night comes, and he and I
Together in one darkness lie.
He holds me in a close embrace
And bites off my nose to spite my face.

   (iii)
'Tiger strolling at my side,
Why have you unbound the zone
Of your individual pride?
Why so meek did you come sneaking
After me as I walked alone?

Since the goat and since the deer
Wait the shattering death you wield
In a constancy of fear,
By your stripes, my strange disciple,
Am I also to be healed?'

'Woman, it was your tender heart
Did my bloody heart compel.
Master-mistress of my art,
Past my wit of wrath your pity,
Ruthless and inexorable.

'I hunt flesh by fallible sense;
You a more exquisite prey pursue
With a finer prescience,
And lap up another's unhappiness:
Woman, let me learn of you.'

AT THE MID HOUR OF NIGHT

Between twelve and one,
Between one and two,
While I sit here alone
As I often do,

With a resolved rhyme,
With an emptied glass,
At the nadir of time
Strange things come to pass.

Many fantastic shapes
Before me detail—
A brown garland of apes,
An Indian with a flail,

A fair woman clad
In rustling shocks of corn,
An aeronaut run mad,
A little unicorn

That sings shrill and clear
With a trembling throat,
A man who flees in fear
Holding an artichoke,

A priest wearing a mask,
Tumbling acrobats,
A negress with a basket
Of avadavats—

They troop by me then,
But nothing say to me;
These dreams of sleeping men
Which waking I see.

SAD GREEN

The glass falls lower,
And lowers the wet sky,
And by a fire sit I
Hearing the lawn-mower

Nearing and waning—
Howbeit out of tune
The essential voice of June
Patient and uncomplaining;

For though by frost and thunder
Summer be overthrown,
The grass plat must be mown
And the daisies kept under.

KILL JOY

I watched the lambs at play
Within a meadow;
And watched there, too, a grey
Unhappy wolf that lay
Still as a shadow.

As though to lure him in
The lambs were prancing;
He slobbered at the chin,
And said that only sin
Could come of dancing.

Thus saying, he nearer crept
On his empty stomach;
Marked his bright spoil, and leapt—
O, like a love-adept
How he could mammock!

'Thwart his shag breast the slender
Booty brandished,
Off loped the greyfoot then,
And crunched it in his den
With howls of anguish.

But back he came anon
To his old covert,
Still lank, still woe-begone;
And still the lambs played on,
Careless as ever.

'Wolf! Wolf! His sleep is a sham.
Fell he'll awaken.
And will you dance till he cram
You all?' Said the youngest lamb:
'Friend, you're mistaken.

'Foul looks the creature wears;
Evil you deem him;
Yet with our lily airs
From all his craft and cares
We will redeem him;

'For much he longs to play
But dares not venture,
And wearier every day
Grows of his tasteless prey
And his mate the vulture;

'So hither must he creep,
And suffer hunger,
Till with one surpassing leap
He jump in among the sheep,
And be wolf no longer.

'Then from all bonds of right
And wrong unfettered,
He'll dance with us in white
Array till at fall of night
Wat, our good shepherd,

'Come, and the tale being told
Of our full number,
With joy he shall behold,
And latch us in the fold
Of innocent slumber.'

COUNTRY THOUGHT

Idbury bells are ringing,
And Westcote has just begun,
And down in the valley
Ring the bells of Bledington.

To hear all these church bells
Ring-ringing together—
Chiming so pleasantly,
As if nothing were the matter—

The notion might come
To some religious thinker
That the Lord God Almighty
Is a travelling tinker,

Who sits retired
In some grassy shade,
With a pipe—a clay one—
And plies his trade,

A-tinkling and a-tinkering
To mend up the souls
That weekday wickedness
Has worn into holes:

And yet there is not
One Tinker, but Three
One at Westcote, one at Bledington,
And one at Idbury.

THE DEAR GIRL

'Pretty, say when
You will have tied your posies?
Pinks for the men,
And for the maids, moss-roses.'

'I've told my score;
And yet I would apparcl
One posy more
For leave-take and nonpareil;

'And when 'tis done
I will myself bestow it
On the breast of one
To whom I think I owe it:

'A quiet breast,
Which nothing now amazes,
Wearing a fancy vest
Of green sprigged o'er with daisies.

'Yes, 'tis for Dick;
I never had a fellow
With head so thick,
Nor curls so crisp and yellow.

'He sued in vain;
I counselled him with laughter
To end his pain
With a rope's-end and a rafter;

'And in despair
He perished at my bidding.
He too must wear
A breast-knot at my wedding.'

THE RIVAL

The farmer's wife looked out of the dairy:
She saw her husband in the yard;
She said: 'A woman's lot is hard,
The chimney smokes, the churn's contrary.'
   She said:
'I of all women am the most ill-starred.

'Five sons I've borne and seven daughters,
And the last of them is on my knee.
Finer children you could not see.
Twelve times I've put my neck into the halter:
   You'd think
So much might knit my husband's love to me.

'But no! Though I should serve him double
He keeps another love outdoors,
Who thieves his strength, who drains his stores,
Who haunts his mind with fret and trouble;
   I pray
God's curse might light on such expensive whores.

'I am grown old before my season,
Weather and care have worn me down;
Each year delves deeper into my frown,
I've lost my shape, and for good reason;
    But she
Yearly puts on young looks like an Easter gown.

'And year by year she has betrayed him
With blight and mildew, rain and drought,
Smut, scab, murrain, all the rout;
But he forgets the tricks she's played him
    When first
The fields give a good smell and the leaves put out.

'Ay, come the Spring, and the gulls keening,
Over her strumpet lap he'll ride,
Watching those wasteful fields and wide,
Where the darkened tilth will soon be greening,
    With looks
Fond and severe, as looks the groom on bride.'

THE SAD SHEPHERD

Of a day's motoring, of half England left behind,
Why should this one sight be so clear in my mind?
A country churchyard crowded with tombs and trees,
And three or four foot reared by the deaths of centuries,
So that we from the road could view as on a stage
The congregation coming out after morning prayer.
With loitering alacrity they trooped out into the air,
Greeting and grouping anew, glad to disengage
Voice and limb from decorum of Sunday demean,
Content to be going home, and content to have been.
But privily along a pathway narrow and overgrown
With hooding cypress the priest went walking alone,
Counter to the sun hastening, and away from his kind:
A black gown he wore and carried a book,
And I thought: There works some torment in that man's
    mind
Which he would hide from all, but which I by chance have
    seen—
For his lips were pinched close, and frenzy was in his look.   163

SONG

She has left me, my pretty,
Like a fleeting of apple-blows
She has left her loving husband,
And who she has gone to
The Lord only knows.

She has left me, my pretty,
A needle in a shirt,
Her pink flannelette bedgown,
And a pair of pattens
Caked over with dirt.

I care not for the pattens,
Let 'em lie in the mould;
But the pretty pink bedgown
Will comfort my lumbago
When midnights are cold;

And the shirt, I will wear it,
And the needle may bide.
Let it prick, let it rankle,
Let my flesh remember
How she lay against my side!

SATURDAY EVENING

'Who's he that went by just then
In a glory of speed, in Hosanna of dust,
Riding his motor-bike as though he must?'
'He? That was Ben,
One of the village young men,
Off to the town in spite of our Member's strictures,
To buy some fags, and pick up a girl, and go to the pictures.'

'Well-informed Sir, you are wrong.
I do not impeach your knowledge of local
Gothic, but let me tell you how that same yokel
Was the heart of song;

And at his passage a throng
Of warriors blown from Troy to an English shire
Rose up to whirl after him, to hang on the air and admire.'

EPITAPHS

I, an unwedded wandering dame
For quiet into the country came.
Here, hailed it; but did not foretell
I'd stay so long and rest so well.

* * *

I, Richard Kent, beneath these stones
Sheltered my old and trembling bones;
But my best manhood, quick and brave,
Lies buries in another grave.

* * *

Her grieving parents cradled here
Ann Monk, a gracious child and dear.
Lord, let this epitaph suffice:
Early to Bed and Early to Rise.

* * *

Within this narrow cell is hived
The sweetness, wedded but unwived,
Of Mary Grove, whose loss I rue.
And here our babes lie buried too.

* * *

I, Sarah Delabole, espied
My daughter's daughter's child a bride.
They value yet my hard-won gear,
My lore not so, and that lies here.

* * *

As you are now so once was I,
And loved in churchyard nooks to pry;
But bolder sports would choose, I trow,
Were I again as you are now.

POTEMKIN'S FANCY

I salute thee, great Catherine,
With a strange device.
See how imperiously the torches shine
Through the walls of ice!

Steep are those walls, and thick,
And glister like tears.
Each with a torch, a seven-foot candlestick,
Stand the tall grenadiers.

Icicles are not more rigid
Than these stand to attention,
Nor heart of empress and statesman more frigid
Than this pleasure-house of my invention.

Within are the singers and trumpets,
Venice masquers and French wine,
The fairest virgins and the noblest strumpets
Of old Rurik's line,

And the English ambassador at sixes and sevens
How to sleep through such pomp:
Without is the wolfish gaze of the freezing heavens
And the frozen swamp.

Brandish your flambeaux, great Catherine!
Let all Europe admire
A palace hewn out of winter as from a mine
And streaming with fire.

But the clear walls stand fast:
They melt not, neither do we,
Inexorably bewintered in the blast
Of a measureless ennui.

ALLEGRA

'Child, it is late in the day and late in the year
For you to be lingering here.
Cold airs creep out of the churchyard clay,
The sun has gone down, the elms look hollow and sere:
This is no time, this is no place for play.'

'O, but I'm happy here, I play as I please;
And my companions are these
Tall stones and yew bushes, whence I peer
At the old brown man who grumbling upon his knees
Tends the hillocks, not recking a child is near.'

'But, dear, the daylight grows narrow, 'tis time you were
    sped
With warmth and kisses to bed;
For now are all good children of Harrow
Asleep save you, O truant, still stirring the dead
Leaves with your footfall, swift and light as a sparrow.'

'Alas, don't send me to bed, for I sleep alone,
Not daring to weep lest my own
Uncomforted voice be a thing to dread;
For my nursery walls are built of the echoing stone,
And cold is all underfoot, and dark overhead.'

Thus steadfast still to the same wild story clung she:
'I am always alone, for he,
The Boy who comes here, can't join in my game.
Look, yonder is where he comes, to the stone by the tree.
I pity him much, poor boy! because he is lame.

'There with a book lies he, or else he will raise
His handsome head, and gaze
Out over the plain with a look made free
At the westering sun, and the elm-tops afloat in the haze
Like shadowy islands remote in a golden sea.'

'The body is embarked . . . I wish it to be buried in Harrow
Church. There is a spot in the churchyard, near the footpath, on the
brow of the hill looking towards Windsor, and a tomb under a large
tree . . . where I used to sit for hours and hours when a boy.' Byron
to Murray, May 26, 1822.

Here might he crop the sweetest grass, and here
Be cooled by sweetest airs and here by right
Of those majestic horns which year by year
In solemn increase chronicled his reign

Might none resort but he: here he withdrew,
As to his setting draws the unquestioned sun,
Kingly enough to reign in private too.
Beneath him all his realm of pasture spread:

Unhasting flowed the river, and arrayed
In noon and summer both the land had peace.
All this his yellow eyes largely surveyed,
And mounting to his ears familiar notes,

Piece-meal ejaculations of content,
Told where his happy subjects to and fro
Strayed on the lower slopes. Up the ascent
Two strangers came, an old man and a boy.

No shadow of disquiet crossed his mind;
By smell and gait and garb he knew they were
But shepherds, human adjuncts of his kind.
They neared, and sat them down upon the sward.

Their voices lulled him; he began to doze,
For he was ancient, kingly cares he bore,
And his long day of power approached its close.
Calmly, as on the ripened landscape, he

O'erlooked the present prospect of past life:
Lordship by wax and wane of moons full-globed,
Rivals out-matched, vanquished cabals, the strife
Of fronts and the first challenge, and the ewes

Obeissant, and the warm fleece of his dam.
Forgotten fears of the wolf thronged up. He awoke—
A voice struck on his hearing: Lo, a ram
Caught in a thicket! By his spreading horns,

Token of sovereignty, he was betrayed.
Snorting and stamping his forehoof he stood
With brows entangled while the hawking blade
Flashed in the sun above the substitute.

THE LOUDEST LAY

In deep midnight of a deep
Midwinter's night I lay asleep,
And dream-awakened, seemed to be
Turning over drowsily
Pages brittle, brown and sere
As leaves blown into the new year.
Such a book it was as shrewd
Sir Thomas Browne by lamplight chewed;
Mumbling marvels, point-device
In the *Sic et Non* of lies,
And with bright clear-obscure of youth
Enchanting what it had of sooth.
But lullabied by tales that are,
Being fabulous, most familar,
I read unheeding, and only this
Recall:
      In India there is
A vale sequestered and serene
As that momentary green
Secluded in the breaking wave.
The aspen branch a Brahman gave
To Alexander, that with cold
And lisping leafy voice foretold
To him his ending, was, men say,
Out of this valley fetched away.
There may the parent trees be found
Whose roots, deep-questing underground,
Bathe in the river of the dead;
Thence are they always green, thence fed
With knowledge of all ends to come;
To them the young Phoenix flies, and dumb
With awe he folds his wing, and stays
To hear, through lapse of timeless days,
Their solemn converse, calm and slow,

Reverberate death's wave below.
Hither by mountain passes grooved
Where but the eagle's shadow moved
I, to discover if a frond
Yet grew those lifeless crags beyond,
Vocal from the prophetic root,
Came unattended and on foot.
All night long the vale I roved,
Seeing through mango turrets groved
Planets and constellations rise,
Pitiless as a serpent's eyes;
And many a branch plucked I and pled
With it to learn if I were led
So many dangerous continents through,
Here to make end, with but the dew
To anoint me for my burial
Beneath the tamarind blossom's fall.
Dumb were they, till the wind of morn
Gave them a murmuring voice forlorn,
Deepening round me as the day
Flowed down the hillside, sad and grey
As water flowing. On fared I,
Still seeking, though I knew not why;
For nought was here for me to find
Save a green valley that resigned
Itself unto a sunless sky . . .
And then a thing of light flew by;
So hued, and sang so clear, it seemed
A rainbow sang or music gleamed.
Not in vain had I come, not wholly
False the tale of something holy
Inhabiting among the wood;
Since here with ravished heart I stood
And watched the Phoenix, bird-alone,
Building his pyre upon a stone.

Thither in his beak brought he
Branches of the sandal tree,
And tear-shaped golden gums he prised
From the wounded, hoary side
Of balsam-pine and benjamin.
Swift he wrought, as though within
His breast he felt the implicit flame

Quicken, a force that overcame
All bird-like dalliance and delay;
By his own wing-strokes fanned halfway
Already to a thing of fire,
Deft and devout to frame his pyre
As that would be to undo it. Yet
New fire, true bird, were so well-met
In him that the conjunction showed
Only how warm a bird's heart glowed;
For having brought a bough and twined
It in the texture to his mind,
Perched on the stone, with innocent pride
He would cock his head a-side
To contemplate his work, and sing
Softly to himself, as Spring
It were, and he a nest would build.
Thus did he labour, and thus filled
With wonder I stood and watched him there,
Whilst all around watched too: the air,
Dedicate to his next flight, held
Its breath, the bubbling fountain welled
Like incense, and the woods as still
As woods in water hung, until
Having woven in some two or three
Long weeds of gleaming laurel he
Perched once more upon the stone,
And looked, and saw that all was done.
Then, then, he clapped his wings, and sang
So loud that all the valley rang,
Re-echoing his lonely joy;
So clear, his singing seemed to buoy
The heavens up, so thrillingly
That one by one each ancient tree
Lit up with blossom, flowed with sound,
And trembling like a merry-go-round,
Slowly with majestic yearning,
Turning, turning, turning, turning,
By that loudest lay absolved,
Slowly with solemn joy revolved.

　　Sweet! Sweet! O, sweet
　　Death is a lovely feat
　　For the rash self-consumed

Who in wide air entombed
Wander forever free.
Joy! O Joy, to be
Unwinged, so that I fly,
Disvoiced, that chant may I!
Though fine songs are sung
Flame has a shriller tongue,
And paints upon the wind
Thought's quickness unconfined.
All achievements claim
Their apotheosis of flame:
Tall towers burn higher,
Troy lives in a fire.
Time can never quench
Troy burned for a wench;
That smoke has unfurled
A banner over the world,
And many a bright spark
Flying through Time's dark
Shall kindle the unreckoned
Host of the unquickened;
Yea, continents yet drowned
Beneath Ocean's bound
Shall raise their heads to behold
Troy burning as of old.

Thus did he sing; and at the word
Burning a mightier plumage whirred
Invisible, and smote the pyre,
And the air was shaken with fire.

THE TREE UNLEAVED

Day after day melts by, so hushed is the season,
So crystal the mornings are, the evenings so wrapped in
    haze,
That we do not notice the passage of the days;
But coming in at the gate to-night I looked up for some
    reason,
    And saw overhead Time's theft;
For behold, not a leaf was left on the tree near by.

So it may chance, the passage of days abetting
My heedless assumption of life, my hands so careless to hold,
That glancing round I shall find myself grown old,
Forgotten my hopes and schemes, my friends forgotten
     and forgetting;
   But all I can think of now
Is the pattern of leafless boughs on the windless sky.

SONG FROM A MASQUE

Under these chestnuts and these elms
Shade is a kind of nunnery;
And here the elder nurses sit,
And tell their tale, and rock their prams,
And wind their wool and sew their hems.

They hear far off the city clocks
Speaking of noonday drowsily;
Lou crochets, Ann and Sarah knit,
And deep asleep the sooty flocks
Lie round the hawthorn roots like rocks.

Like a green wave the shade o'erwhelms
Their converse and their housewifery,
Like darting fish the sparrows flit;
The babes stare upwards from their prams
With eyes as senseless-bright as gems.

Full fathom five, among the rocks,
Mermaids, sea-cloistered virgins, sit.

WINTER MOON

Tycho, a mountain in the moon,
Has long ago put out his fires—
Or so astronomers avow—
And dark the crater, and cold, yet now
About my hand, about the quires
Where this night through my hand has strewn

Words unavailing, frustrate phrases,
Tycho's malignant bale-fire blazes.

A licking frost, a lambent chill,
It lights the unkindled sacrifice
And plays about me to benumb.
The words I wait for will not come,
And cowering down, as under ice
Dumb water cowers, my lost thought still
Shows me a tree upon the wold,
That stands, and cracks its heart for cold.

NARCISSUS

'Narcissus! Beautiful white narcissus!'
Morning and evening as I go by
I hear the man at the corner cry:
'Narcissus! Beautiful white narcissus!'

A peck of March dust blows over his basket,
The papery blossoms are nipped and dry.
As well throw money away as buy
Pavement stuff that is drooping already.

This street is used by practical people,
They jostle onward, and so do I.
But if by chance a poet went by
I think he might stop, and give the man sixpence—

Not for the flowers; for the dream's sake merely,
For the clear stream and the far sky,
And beauty lingering in the cry—
'Narcissus! Beautiful white narcissus!'

THE RECORD

On winter eves when you are grown
Tired of your household talk of this
Gone well and t'other gone amiss
You will put on the gramophone.

Then shall the faithful air remit
My singing self which now I must
Engrave on silence and entrust
To the unmemoried; then, quit

Of all but that one being, I
Shall bear your leaning souls along
Till voice and purport, songster and song,
Are fused into a single cry,

And you shall feel the authentic pang:
The traveller, pausing at the sound,
To see your listening looks around
Would think a living woman sang.

LINES TO A CAT IN A LONDON SUBURB

Quadruped on a bough,
Cat absolute, Cat behind
All cat-shows of your kind,
I see and salute you now:

Massive, tenacious, bland,
Sardonically surefooted,
Pacing along the sooty
Aspen branch, and fanned

By all the obsequious Spring
To ear fine-furred and strong
Squat nose conveys of song
Or scent wave-offering;

As pace in stealthy hope
Through incense cloud and *Tu
Es Petrus* hullabaloo
Cardinals into Pope.

But more compactly wise,
More serpentine in sin
(My more than Mazarin)
Your commerce with the skies;

While vacant and serene
Your eyes look down on me,
In all the wavering tree
The one unshaken green.

THE MAIDEN

If I were to give you
A knot of white violets,
Plucked from the nest
Beneath the warm hedgerow,
To wear on your breast,
You would shake your head and sigh
To think the poor blossoms must wither and die.

If I were to give you
A cage of sweet singing-birds,
In a cruel hour
Betrayed from the greenwood,
To hang in your bower,
You would bid them all fly free,
So sad to your ear would their meek music be.

But if I were to give you
The heart out of my bosom,
At your least whim
With joy to burn ruddy,
With anguish to dim,
O then you wouldn't say no,
But take it, and use it, and never let it go.

THE POSSESSION

Now sinks the winter moon,
And brightens as she goes,
And on the village street
A shadow throws:

The shadow of the house
Wherein I darkling sit
Watching that other house
That stands opposite.

There she, towards whom my mind,
My senses, and my will,
Like a compass-needle fixed,
Point trembling still;

She, towards whom the hushed
Tide of my blood is bound,
Lies in her maiden sleep,
Scornful and sound.

Wake not, reck not;
Sleep warm and smoothly dream
How your shut window-pane
Looks back a gleam

Which splinters in my sight
As merciless as they—
Those diamond looks of scorn
You brandish by day.

Wake not, reck not
My wealth of love can hire
The cold-blood moon herself
To abet my desire;

Nor how as I sit here,
Darkling within my shade,
Like some cool strategist
Whose plans are laid,

I watch my force advanced,
The unstirring shadow thrust
By her conniving hand
Over the ice-crust

Of the road, and up the wall
Until your window is won,
And from long watching I
And the shadow are one.

Then wake, then reckon,
Then hide your eyes for dread,
And know that more than shadow
Stands over your bed.

KIND FORTUNE

White hand in brown hand lay,
To ears where brilliants shone
Hoarse voice went mumbling on
Till White Hand turned away:

'Husband handsome and kind
And pretty babes and gold
To squander—I've been told
That story times out of mind!

'Good mother, be your next
Client some nursery-maid;
You'll drive a better trade
With such.' 'Ah, don't be vexed,

'Lady! I but declare
What is so smoothly writ
On this smooth palm. Come, sit
By me again, compare

'Our two hands side by side,
Till like unlike thus grooved
So deep in mine had proved
To you I have not lied.

'Here is a husband, too,
And handsome, but not kind;
Here, pretty babes, that pined
A weeping winter through

'Because I had not gold
Nor pence their wants to heal,
And was too weak to steal;
178 And here, down this long fold

'Of flesh, a life too long,
Frayed out with cares and crossed
With Lost, Lost, Lost . . .
Dearie, don't judge me wrong!

'Though outcast I and banned,
This once I have spoke true;
And many would envy you
What's in this happy hand.'

EVENSONG IN WINTER

A red light streams from windows and doors,
The flagstones crack and the organ roars,
And through the churchyard, silent and glum,
Figures darker than darkness come;
And a child says: 'Mother, I can tell!
It's the Devils trooping out of Hell.'

SELF HEAL

First at our meeting-place
As I practised patience
A flower looked out of the hedge
As though seeking acquaintance;
And I thought, when my dear one came
She should tell me its name.

For she boasted, there grew not a herb
In heath, meadow, or wood
That she couldn't clap name to as pat
As old Culpeper could;
And rather than own herself spent,
Why, a name she'd invent.

Many a time since then,
And in many a shire,
Has that flower looked up at me
As if to enquire:
Have you learned me yet? and below
My breath I say: No!

For my dear one but came to declare
That while scorning to flirt
A new love was more to her mind:
At the time I was hurt;
But I think (though the song it may mar)
Things are best as they are.

SWIFT THOUGHT AND SLOW THOUGHT

Out of the field two hoers raise
Their heads to watch the express go past,
And swift think I:
How stablished and secure their days,
But mine flit by too fast.

The lolling vapour thins away,
The air is sweet and silent again,
And they think slow:
Ah, to what happiness speed they,
The folk who go by train!

THE MILL IN THE VALLEY

Though for ten years and more the mill
Disused and tenantless has been,
A grey house and a hanging green
Dwell steadfast in their mirror still.

Where erst were waggons bringing wheat,
Were trampling hooves, were whistling boys,
The water with an idle voice
Goes brimming idly through the leat.

The roof is falling in, the door
Upon its crazy hinges grieves;
West winds autumnal drift the leaves
Over the empty granary floor:

And from all life it is estranged,
Unless a stranger come this way,
To lean upon the gate, and say:
180 ''Twas busy once, but times are changed.'

The miller was a careful man,
Thrifty and keen, a man of weight;
But thrift's a grass-work against fate,
And in his time the change began:

Until for waggons ten that crossed
His bridge there came but five, but two,
And he had nothing left to do
But close the mill, for all was lost.

To shun it ruined, once his boast,
He to a distant town did fare;
There, died: but thence the man of care
Returned anon a careless ghost.

Through the long winter-time he keeps
His comfortable grave, but when
The April dusks stretch out again,
When hawking swallow dips, and leaps

The fish all silver from a spool
Of spreading silver spreading still,
That sets the grey house and green hill
Rocking and deepening through the pool,

He comes—not now as once he trod,
Ownerly and deliberate,
But sauntering at a holiday gait;
And pauses to set up his rod

And knots the fly and having essayed
A whip or two creeps crafty near
The water's edge, as though the fear
That he, a shadow, should cast a shade

Were the one care he had in mind:
The very stones of his house-place
Cry out to him his old disgrace,
But he is deaf to them, and blind.

Others have seen him plain, but I
Him thus revisiting have traced
But by the surface silver-laced
Where the flung line has fallen awry,

Or when the chatter of the reel
Discovers at a cast well-sped
The millpond giving up its dead
Duly to the dead master's creel.

AWAKE FOR LOVE

They are all gone to bed;
But I for love of them am still awake,
Companioning the fire that falls a-drowse;
My spirit walks around the darkened house,
And feels the wind, and sees the heavens shake
Their diamond tresses overhead.

Love has extended it
Into the changing stature of a cloud;
My arms embrace the eaves, my bosom pressed
To the cold slates yearns warm above their rest,
Over their roof-tree my vast love is bowed,
As bowed before their hearth I sit.

My wakefulness includes
Their sleep, my compact kept with time and space
Vouches for them enfranchised, their dreams glide
Unchallenged through my being, as the tide
Of guarded life-blood on with even pace
Flows through the body's solitudes.

TOO EARLY SPRING

Has but half a day, or is it half a year
Gone by since to these rounded meadows and shy
Entangled willow copses I came with my dear?

Leaves were crowding prick-eared to the live air . . .
But when? That small red sun bewinters us again,
And round us the trees stand motionless and bare.

Come, let's away, my dear, let's away without noise.
Our Spring has stolen hence, and why do we linger
On this last year's grass? Ah, where are all our joys?

DEATH THE BRIDEGROOM

O Bride, why dost thou delay?
The Bridegroom waits, it is thy wedding day.
Now, while the sun has yet a stair to climb,
Now, while thy beauty yet foretells its prime,
    Arise and come away!
    Yet a while, said she.
    Wedded I would not be
Till I have trimmed my virgin coronet
With windflower, stitchwort, and white violet.
Once more a-blossoming let me go!
On my behalf the flowering roots were set,
And well, well do I know
Whereabouts in my Father's park they grow.

O Bride, why dost thou delay?
The Bridegroom waits, it is thy wedding day.
Now, while the sun his noonday splendour wields
Nor yet with lengthening shadow scythes the fields,
    Arise, and come away!
    Yet a while, said she.
    Wedded I cannot be
Till I have packed my bridal dower-box
With ermine, emeralds, gold, and the meek flocks
Of threaded pearls, and then fastened on
My cloak that's damasked like July hollyhocks—
For now Spring tints look wan,
And Summer's are the colours I would don.

O Bride, why dost thou delay?
Morning and summer both are fled away,
And now it is thy wedding night,
And out of the black sky the snow falls white.
    No longer mayest thou delay.
    Yet a while, said she.
    Though wedded I must be,
Suffer me yet to warm my hands before
The fire, old love-letters to read o'er,
And have one last look round;
Ay, and beneath God's rood I would implore
That mercy may abound,
For perilous is the journey whereon we are bound.   *183*

PAY WHAT THOU OWEST

Seven loud and lusty bells
Hang in our steeple;
Ancient they are, so Parson tells,
And have names like people:

Francis Philpot, Brother John,
Wenceslas Carey,
Bristol, Kirry Leison
And Gaudy Mary.

All have names save only one,
Deepest and slowest,
Him the ringers in their fun
Call Pay What Thou Owest;

All ring true save him alone,
Flawed in the casting,
Harsh and dull has been his tone
From everlasting.

Twice a week on winter nights
The ringers assemble,
Practising triples and such-like flights
Till the air's a-tremble.

Fleet and clear the echoes scud
From rafter to rafter,
And Pay What Thou Owest with a thud
Follows halting after.

The other bells so smooth of speech
Answer each other,
Sweetly answering each to each
Like sister and brother;

They laugh as merrily as elves,
Seeming to flout him;
You'd fancy they said amongst themselves:
'We could do without him.'

As when as a school-boy I for a while
Was feeling down-hearted
I've sat at the dark end of the aisle
Till the tears have started

To think that I and the bell alike
Were both unneeded;
Yes, and I've groaned aloud belike,
As harshly as he did.

Old year out and new year in—
Time's a rare songster,
And a man doesn't care as he sits at the inn
How he felt as a youngster.

A child in the cradle, a friend in the grave,
Getting and spending,
With the bells coming in at the end of the stave
Like a tol-de-rol ending;

Merry come sad and even come odd—
If you've an ear for
That song you don't stop to ask your God:
'What am I here for?'

Man on earth and bells on the wind—
Often I've said it—
Clash the same pattern time out of mind
To their Maker's credit;

Only the bells had this to boast;
They lasted longer:
'Here's the Long-Livers!' I called as a toast—
It seems I was wrong there.

For Pay What Thou Owest is cracked at last,
A crack that will flourish
Up through his singing side as fast
As this sore I nourish;

So it's a match between him and me:
I think he will win it,
For to run a noose from the bough of a tree
Is the work of a minute.

He to the foundry and I to clay—
Since we must sever,
One debt standing over I'd have him pay
Ere he's dumbed for ever:

Gaudy Mary and the rest
They can be merry all,
But Pay What Thou Owest is the best
When it comes to a burial.

THE VISIT

Last night it chanced that I, who dwell alone,
And am not much dismayed
To hear my solitary midnight said,
Nor wish for livelier company than my own,
Hearing the hour
Spelled slowly stroke by stroke from the church tower,

And gathering up myself for bed, my mind
Prepared to disarray
Itself of yet another dullish day
Yet somewhat pitying that which it resigned,
Became aware
Of a sigh, not my own, breathed on the air.

'You have guessed right,' said she. 'I am a ghost.
I will not haunt you long;
But I am weary, for the wind blows strong,
And looking in on you, you seemed almost
One such as I;
So I am come to bear you company.'

Right neighbourly beside my hearth she sat,
Full fluently conversed,
As one in England's decent topics versed—
Birds, beasts, the Royal Family, this and that;
But nothing told
Me of the dead, save that they feel the cold.

At length all things seemed said. A silence fell,
And in that silence we heard,

Loud as a trumpeter, a chirping bird
Greet the March morning; then quoth I: 'Well, well—
The days begin
To draw—' 'O no,' cried she. 'The nights draw in!'

SPARROW HALL

'Who lives in that house,
That is so old and grey,
Like a sleepy old nurse
Who at close of day
Sits watching with kind eyes
Children at their play?

'For frolicking in the wind
Blossom lilac and may,
Laburnum and guelder rose,
Tossing this way and that way;
And the young-voiced blackbirds
Sing on the blossomed spray.'

'No one lives there at all.
Ever since my day
The trees have bloomed untended,
Whilst wandering into decay
The house sleeps in their midst:
I have never heard say

'That ghost walked there,
Good men to affray.
It's a pity nobody takes it.
Perhaps, Sir, you may?
For standing so long empty
The rent would be little to pay.'

'No, friend; it is not for me;
I must hold on my way,
For life calls me, and love calls me,
And I must obey.
Perhaps I shall come back to it
When I am old and grey.'

THE DECOY

In these level fields
That still remember the sea
I have hollowed a creek,
I have planted a grove;
I have bidden the proud
Air-wandering birds that rove
Day-long from cloud to cloud
To shelter in me.

And I have tamed two birds,
Called Metre and Rhyme,
At whose sweet calling
All thoughts may be beguiled
To my prepared place;
Yet tamed, by blood they are wild,
Being on all-mothering Space
Begotten by Time.

RAINBOW
(1931)

RAINBOW

Rigid in heaven stands the bow
Above the thunder's overthrow;
Beneath it, washed to milk, a bough
Of this year's cherry is budding now.

Emerging from the storm's embrace
Sleekly winks the market place,
And lustred weather vanes one by one
Preen their tinsel in the sun.

Revived from shadow man and man
Step briskly forth and praise the plan
That with the lancing East unlooses
Adder-brood lightnings and sky-juices,

Since on March dust an April morrow
Of sun-slashed rain falls due to furrow,
And the dabbled blossom innocent
Smiles on a world survived; but bent

Is yet the crude unslackening bow
Whose primal blue and red and yellow
Outface with aristocratic stare
The hybrid hues of earthbound air.

Fade! Fade! Uncurtained Covenant,
Too naked truth of light and gaunt,
Revealed by twitch of weather-flaw;
Momentary menace of a law

(Howbeit sight's cozening scribble gloze)
Brandished immovable by those
Eternal arms outstretched beneath
Man's private remedy of death.

Not so the sanguine patriarch,
Congratulating round the ark,
To whom this sign ostended spelled
God's moody mind from man withheld.

Distance seemed safety then. God furled
In heaven bespoke all well with the world.
Retreating with his bow the archer
From farther off shoots deadlier.

Artillery mathematical,
Out of the void his arrows fall
And onward to the void are sped,
But we, our woe, distargeted,

Quivering void and void betwixt,
With each discovered shaft transfixed
Fester to feel the wound, and know
No animus behind the bow.

Rigid on air, as hung the smile
Of the absent cat, it looms awhile;
But will be gone before the bough
Discards the diamond drops where now,

Echoes of a threat unsaid,
The primal yellow and blue and red
Wink back from every water-flaw
The unrelenting look of law.

OPUS 7
(1931)

'Ere I descend into the grave,
let me a small house and large garden have.'
So Cowley wished; and if he could have seen
Rebecca Random's cottage at Love Green
he would have cried: "tis here!' Deep thatch it had,
large beams, small windows, all things such as glad
the hearts of those who dwell in town but would
spend weekends in the country; strangers stood
admiring it, cars stopped, Americans
levelled their cameras, and a painter once
sat for two days beside a pigsty wall
to take a picture of it, though as all
agreed who stole a passing squint, his view
was Bedlam-work, all daubs, red spots and blue,
mingling with white unearthly atomies
where drawers and nightgowns hung to better eyes.
   Nor did folk only gaze. Many enquired
how old Rebecca was, or if she hired
out furnished rooms in summer. Sure, they said,
so aged a woman only needs a bed
and a back-kitchen. She can cook, maybe;
our wants are few: breakfast, lunch, dinner, tea,
beds made, rooms cleaned, our laundry now and again
(we see she launders) . . . They enquired in vain;
Rebecca lodged nor let, nor would she hear
of sale—'twas freehold—though an auctioneer
came in his Austin Seven from the town
proffering fifty guineas, money down.
Neighbours discussing this across the fence
declared her foolish, but approved her sense;
for fifty guineas, though a weighty sum,
so headlong gained is bound to be *Light come,*
Light go, while fifty guineas safe refused
is yours for ever, virgin and unused,
a fortune none can filch, deny, or spend,
undimmable boast, and credit without end.
   Leave we the house and walk the garden round:—
a good half-acre, and old orchard ground;
in all Love Green the easiest soil—a mould
sweetened with ending of sweet lives untold.

Blossom and leaf and twig and windfall were
mixed in that gentle lap; time did inter
his summers there, and bade them rot in peace,
natural resurrection, due increase
promising, and continuance of green
out of their sere. But now few trees were seen,
and they, lopped back; as rare and circumscribed
as kings in Europe now those trees survived,
and to the spring a shrunken blooth put out,
by few bees visited, for all about
their feet a new democracy displayed
livelier assurances of richer trade.

Here at Old Christmas bloomed the Christmas rose,
true to her date however men dispose
the calendar; here velvet wallflowers bloomed,
and with attempting breath March gales perfumed
from their male chastity almost; snowdrops and squills
limned April skies below while yet the hills
rose into mist, while yet the shepherd blew
warm on the lamb beside the quaking ewe.
Here, when the lamb leaped gleaming in the sun,
was mustered such a garden garrison
as tale outnumbered, penny packet's show
outshone; but not, like Marvell's, ranked in row,
drilled under colours, marshalled for parade—
these a more unsophisticated fusillade
loosed off, hub-bub of shape and hue and scent,
a countrified militia, where intent
is to be foremost all, most willing each.
Rebecca was no Frederick, to teach
austerer discipline; they throve, said she,
as children do, by mixing company;
one countenanced another, and the soil
was plenty good enough for none to moil.
And should some wilding outlaw, long decreed
by due botanical consent a weed,
to her tilled ground come interloping back,
let it but bloom, she would not bid it pack.
Bloom did they all, the bond beside the free,
true clove carnation neighbouring succory,
Ishmaelite poppy with delphinium;
it seemed the Eden or Millennium
of flowers, how all at peace together grew:

the feckless, well-apparelled lily-crew,
yet gay in gospel since they chanced to please
Christ on his rambles, lived not more at ease.
Nor did their mistress labour overmuch.
Some skill she had, and, more than skill, a touch
that prospered all she set, as though there were
a chemical affinity 'twixt her
stuff and the stuff of plants—a pulse, a stroke,
implicit in her grubbing paws, that woke
the dreaming seed, and bade the root take hold;
an Open Sesame of the hand, that old
west-country parlance knows as 'a green thumb'.
    'Rebecca do have luck with flowers,' quoth some,
glancing across the hedge, while others mocked
to see so rich a ground so idly stocked.
But praise and blame had other fish to fry,
and aimed on their own cares went careless by.
It was the children who delayed. To them
Rebecca's garden was the diadem
of all Love Green; not even the churchyard,
with rivalry of elegiac jam-pots, hard-
frozen lilies and roses under glass,
and the new war memorial could surpass
it as a gazing-stock and raree-show.
More it was not—how much more, being so!
A prohibition in the first-devised
garden that paradise emparadised,
which slighted, all was common as elsewhere:
so here, to those unfallen without, there were
no weeds, no toil, no curse, save the well-known
shrill threat of 'Drat you, leave my gate alone!'
Over that gate they leaned in long survey,
and stared as though at India or Cathay.
There were the flowers; pampered, secure, and calm
as turbanned sultans underneath a palm,
they in their usurped territory reigned,
and with renewing pomps their pomp sustained,
flaunting their privacy, confederate
but with themselves; and there, with lumbering gait,
Rebecca, stooped and stout and red of face,
moved like the guardian goblin of their race—
herself no flower. Yet this disparity
seemed more contrivance than fortuity,

a stroke of art, a discord shrewdly set;
her foulness to their favour matched well-met,
as ogres elves corroborate in fables.
But where, you ask, where were the vegetables?—
The dues each rustic from however clenched
soil should extort—potatoes duly trenched,
the buxom cabbage, onions well-trod,
and marrows rounding to the glory of God
at harvest festival—you name not these.
They were not. Save those wizened apple-trees,
whose windfalls only wasp and ant found sweet,
this garden offered nothing one could eat.
Fie, fie, indeed! How wanton and perverse!
Grow only flowers?—as well write only verse!
And in so good a soil? Were but this realm
an honest Soviet, judgement would o'erwhelm
her and her trumpery, and the freehold give
to brisker hands. How did the woman live?
You called her stout. I'd like to see her thin,
then she'd find out if flowers pad bones from skin.
Rebecca lived on bread, and lived for gin.

   When grandees feasted have, to see the abhorred
heeltaps and damaged dainties to the board
come cringing back agrees not with their taste—
eat they will not, and yet they would not waste.
Then to the butler's or the cook's discreet
beck comes the charwoman on stealthy feet,
and in a bag receives, and bears away,
the spoiling relics of a splendid day.
Time bears (my Lord) just such a bag, and deft-
handed is he to pouch whatever's left
from bygone exploits when their glories fail.
I knew a time when Europe feasted well:
bodies were munched in thousands, vintage blood
so blithely flowed that even the dull mud
grew greedy, and ate men; and lest the gust
should flag, quick flesh no daintier taste than dust,
spirit was ransacked for whatever might
sharpen a sauce to drive on appetite.
From the mind's orient fetched all spices were—
honour, romance, magnanimous despair,
198 savagery, expiation, lechery,

skill, humour, spleen, fear, madness, pride, ennui. . . .
Long revel, but at last to loathing turned,
and through the after-dinner speeches yawned
those who still waked to hear them. No one claps.
Come, Time, 'tis time to bear away the scraps!
   Time came, and bent him to the priestlike task.
Once more Love Green beheld its farmers bask
in former ruin; home-come heroes, badged
with native mud, to native soil repledged
limbs that would lose their record, ten years hence,
whether they twinged for tillage or defence.
No longer was the church on week-days warmed
that special liturgies might be performed;
war-babies, too, now lost their pristine glamour,
and were as bastards bid to hold their clamour.
So Time despatched the feast; some items still
surpassed his pouch, though; one of these, the bill.
Many, for this, the hind who pinched and numb
faced the wet dawn, and thought of army rum;
many the mother, draggled from childbed,
who wept for grocer's port and prices fled;
and village Hampdens, gathered in the tap,
forsook their themes of bawdry and mishap
to curse a government which could so fleece
on spirits under proof, and call it Peace.
   And thus it was Rebecca came to grow
sweet flowers, and only flowers. War trod her low.
Her kin all dead, alas! too soon had died;
unpensioned, unallowanced, unsupplied
with pasteboard window-boast betokening
blood-money sent from a respectful king,
she on her freehold starved, the sullen bait
of every blithe philosopher on fate.
Dig she could not. Where was the farmer who
would hire her sodden limbs when well he knew
how shapely land-girls, high-bred wenches all,
would run in breeches at his beck and call?
To beg would be in vain. What patriot purse
would to a tippler open, when its terse
clarion call the *Daily Mail* displayed:
Buckingham Palace Drinking Lemonade?
So fared she worsening on, until the chimes
clashing out peace, renewal of old times—

but bettered—sent her stumbling to the inn.
No! No reduction in the price of gin.
    A crippled Anzac saw her. 'Here, I'll treat
the lady. What's your fancy? Take it neat?
Say, here's the lousy peace they talk about!'
The fire so long unfelt ran like a shout
of Alleluias all along her blood.
Reared out of her indignities she stood
weeping for joy. The soldier looked, and laughed,
and poured another, and again she quaffed,
and a third time. It was a rousing drink;
through weeks to come it did her good to think
it had been hers—long weeks of misery,
cold, influenza, charitable tea.
And in the spring he came once more; still lame,
not brown now, emptied of his mirth, he came,
and leaned across her gate. 'Those flowers you call
wallflowers . . . I'd like a few.' She gave him all.
    Mute and intent he turned them in his hand.
She watched them too, and could not understand
what charm held him thus steadfast to a thing
that just bloomed out by nature every spring.
At last he spoke, though not so much to her
as to all things around. 'My great-grandfer
was bred up hereabouts; and here he courted
his girl, and married her, and was transported
for firing ricks, and left the girl behind.
He picked a young she-convict to his mind,
and settled down, and got a family.
He told my grand-dad, he my dad, him me,
all about England. When I was a pup
I felt to come to England I'd give up
all I could ever have—and here I am,
her soldier. Now, I wouldn't give a damn
for England. She's as rotten as a cheese,
her women bitches, and her men C3's.
This silly sloppy landscape—what's the use
of all this beauty and no bloody juice?
Who'd fire a rick in these days?' 'Farmer Lee
fired his for the insurance once,' said she.
He heard not, and spoke on. 'I've come too late,
and stay too long. Ruin can fascinate
a man like staring in a cattle-hole;

that still, black water-look pulls down his soul.
England is getting hold of me. That's why
I asked you for those flowers. Good luck! Good-bye.'
He turned away, and turned again, and slid
a paper in her hand. When she undid
its crumples she was clutching a pound note.
The liquor seemed already in her throat.
Quick! to the inn! And yet she still delayed.
Strange thoughts worked in her mind. She watched them
      braid
themselves into an order, vivify
into a scheme, blossom, a policy.
As some on liquor, some on flowers were set;
would pay, too, witness this; each violet
crushed drop by drop into a glass would spill
its farthing, ha'penny, pennyworth, until
the glass brimmed to her stooping lips. Why, then,
grow flowers, sell flowers, buy liquor—so, Amen!
    Dull is despair. As well sharpen a knife
on lead, as wits on wanhope; the sole life-
blood of all cunning, spur of every plan
is hope; hope makes the Machiavellian.
Up at the inn Rebecca half-displayed,
half-hid, the miracle. 'Oh yes, I paid
twelve-and-six for the bottle, money down . . .
a wicked price!' She toyed with half-a-crown.
'This here king's head be pretty, don't you think?'
Nearer they drew, and hoped she'd stand a drink
(she did not), and, a thirstier hope than this,
hoped she'd tell more. 'They have not come amiss,
these warm spring days. My wallflowers are a show.
Were, I should say, for but an hour ago
I sold them to a foreign gentleman.
Soon the Co-operative will send their van
Tuesdays as well as Fridays, so I hear,
and Mrs. Bulley's other leg is queer.'
She rose, and left them gazing in their beer.

    Enough was said. Before the celandine
opened to the next sunrise, all Love Green
welcomed this wonder risen in their east,
and to amazement sat, as to a feast.
Two-headed monsters are the natural diet

of those pure minds which dwell in country quiet—
sustenance never lacked, where dullness sways
with earthy sceptre the farm labourer's days.
Blest fertile Dullness!—mothering surmise,
rumour, report, as stagnant water, flies,
whose happy votaries, stung by every hatch,
divinely itch, and more divinely scratch!
Nothing's too wild for credence, or too slight
for fancy to apparel it in light
fetched from the half-wit moon: a gate-post can,
if rightly studied, feed the mind of man
with a rich entertainment; an old goat
more plenteous bawdry than the French priest wrote
bequeath, sprat wag more waves than any whale;
but best of all, strangers deck out a tale.
    Trade on that morrow throve uncommonly.
Each housewife viewed her stores, and found that she
were instantly undone, did she not haste
for Empress washing blue, or salmon paste,
or postal orders, or canary seed.
They stayed at leisure who had come with speed.
The shop was thronged; unheard above the din
the door-bell rang as more came pushing in;
unmarked the painted ship rocked on the tide
of time still ebbing from the morning's pride,
while wet umbrellas, ranged in patience glum,
mixed sullen swamps on the linoleum.
Joy was it in that dawn to be alive;
like a queen bee escaping from the hive
a wonder was abroad. What though Miss Gale,
the sibyl priestess of the royal mail,
for all their offerings, knew no more than they,
or knew, but did not feel inclined to say?—
as devout scientists can from a tooth
enjoy a dinosaur, the quest for truth
scarce checked at this; since fate would not reveal
the stranger whole, they'd run him down piecemeal.
    One, it appeared, had seen him; another, heard
the thunder of his chariot wheels; a third,
scorning this mortal for more inward light,
had dreamed the whole affair last Tuesday night.
A handsome youth. He had a dog with him.
202 Two dogs. Three dogs. Gentry must have their whim.

Four dogs. His car stood by the vicarage.
No, no, he walked, poor soul, bowed down with age.
A bag he bore. Two bags. Three bags. No doubt
these white-slave traffickers do go about;
wenches he sought, no wallflowers. Not at all,
he bought the flowers for his wife's funeral,
and looked near death himself, so pale and wan.
A red-faced man. 'Twas pity he was gone.
　　So spoke each one her mind. More sparingly
they of Rebecca spoke, a topic she
past mark of mouth, a hackney whom for pride
no conversationalist would deign bestride,
not worth a word, and barely worth a sneer.
Was this the clod which fate chose out to rear
a headstone in the corner?—was her patch,
with its half-dozen listless hens a-scratch,
and rabble of weeds, fit place for chance to sow
and nurse a wonder up incognito?
Beneath few words they hid their discontent,
and a *nil admirari* sanction lent
to this wild thought of flowers exchanged for gold;
resolving inwardly that as they strolled
homeward, they'd pause with stealth and view the scene
where these same well-paid gillyflowers had been.
　　View it they did. There was not much to view—
a score of double-daffodils, a few
small, chilblain-coloured primroses, the dears
of some flower-fancying matron of past years,
and near them, drooping as abashed, their bright-
starred woodland kin, transplanted overnight.
No matter: it was none of these they eyed,
but the robbed wallflower stock, which testified
the wonder true. What next? The common itch
for relics, palpable tokens that enrich
hearsay to history, and Jack's master drape
in reassuring likeness to Jack's shape
—Shelley, rare soul!—I have his trousers here.
So every dame must have her souvenir;
beg it for choice, but if unbeggable, buy,
steal, have somehow, before the virtue fly
which contact had bestowed, or rival feel
like lust. They were not called upon to steal.
Rebecca, with an air of every day,

was well prepared to tell them what to pay,
mention, advisedly, another's bid,
and vow in the same breath to keep hers hid
who topped it, lest a spouse should grieve to hear
where money went that might have gone on beer;
thus, dealing with them subtly one by one,
made thirty pence. Her commerce was begun.
   Waving the last farewell with silver-crossed
blest hand, she stood in contemplation lost,
with pursed-up lip, and slow exacting gaze
eyeing her ground, as strategist surveys
the dedicated field of victory;
then searched, as for an omen, in the sky.
The day's long rain was past. Vanquished and cowed,
across the west staggered the rearguard cloud,
and paused awhile, and showed its bloodied flank;
then on to the death-looking north, and sank.
Twig, leaf and blade in the light's evening
dandled a diamond, faintly glittering,
while overhead some stars, distinct and small,
glittered like water-drops and did not fall.
   O Spring, O virgin of all virgins, how
silent thou art! I have pursued thee now
along so many winters, sought and snuffed
through last year's grass for thee, combing each tuft
to find thy tiny spears that I might prick
my heart on them; ice has not weighed so thick
but I have seen thy blue within its breast:
I have been sure of thee ere others guessed.
In the lean wood, watching, knee-deep in snow,
myself watching a redskin river flow
eastward to the Atlantic, I had yet
eyes to discover thy first ensign set
flickering on a hazel-bush. Gone then
redskin and river; I was home again
in thee, in thee! But when the long pursuit
expires in the achievement, thou art mute.
Each year I find thee as last year thou wert;
hushed, rapt, annunciate—a speechless hurt
trembling on the green sky and from the branch
that thou must bring to green. Oh, how to stanch
the sorrow welling from an April dusk,
204 that lifts the moon and buoys it like a husk

up the long dark?—how treat with this most dear,
most dolorous virgin-mother of the year?
Frustrate I stand before thee, dispossessed,
unaimed, and feel the quickening in my breast
fail, and sigh back again to clod. O Spring,
how silent thou art! I hear the water ring
shallow along the ford, I hear the birds
lancing the air with joy; thou hast no words
for me, and on my lips the question dies.
I know not why I sought thee, nor surmise
what was the ecstacy I could not snatch,
nor ever shall, though at the last I match
my silence against thine, and scatter down
the staff, the cockle shell, the pilgrim gown,
on my last wayfaring to thee waylaid.

    How long this winter night! How far I've strayed
out of its compass, and return how slow
to the sad self I left five hours ago!—
back from spoiled Saugatuck, back from my death.
The ashes on the hearth lift at my breath
but no spark follows them, my movements smite
the sleeping house. How long this winter night!
And down what leagues of darkness must I yet
trudge, stumble, reel, in the wrought mind's retreat;
then wake, remember, doubt, and with the day
the work which in the darkness shone survey,
and find it neither better nor much worse
than any other twentieth-century verse.
Oh, must I needs be disillusioned, there's
no need to wait for spring! Each day declares
yesterday's currency a few dead leaves;
and through all the sly nets poor technique weaves
the wind blows on, whilst I—new nets design,
a sister-soul to my slut heroine,
she to her dram enslaved, and I to mine.

    Nature in town a captive goddess dwells;
man guards, and grilles enclose, her miracles,
the devotees who through her temples pass
with reverence keep off the new-sown grass,
and not a waft of her green kerchief, spring
down sky-forgetting bus routes signalling,
but some heart greets it, some fidelity

205

awaited, and with love looks back reply.
　　This is her civic state. On countryside,
goddess too truly to be deified,
she a more real tribute entertains
of endless strategy, mistrust, and pains.
The farmer, slouching by his sodden shocks,
groans her a hymn, the vigilling shepherd knocks
his breast for cold, telling through every joint
a rosary of aches; hoers anoint
her floor with sweat, and the small-holder, sworn
lifelong the same sour clods to grub forlorn,
weighed with reiterated genuflexions, bows,
stiffens, warps earthward, effigy of his vows.
Them, unappeased, the immortal doxy flouts,
with floods in harvest capping seedtime droughts,
paying their toil with the derisive gold
of ragwort, tansy, and corn-marigold,
or, while their ewes breed not and their pigs die,
bidding the mole increase and multiply.
These are her common flouts; these she confers
impartially among her worshippers,
and can be borne; but hardly, when she wills
her absolute whim to manifest, and spills
foison on unlimed acres, comes a guest,
blowsily plenteous, to the harvest feast
of him whom every diligent neighbour mocks;
whose sheep stray with their scab to wholesome flocks,
whose dodders creep, whose seeding thistles are flown
to tended fields, and leers on him alone.
　　Vainly they rail, the righteous Esau tribe—
too wise, too witless to hold out the bribe
no woman can resist: incompetence.
Well for their peace of mind Rebecca's fence
warded sweet flowers, and only flowers, a gear
beneath their envy. With the growing year
a tide of green swept the brown earth and broke
in such a foam of colour as awoke
new being, new ambition, new delight
from the quotidian faculty of sight.
Not hers, but Nature's, was the artifice.
Do as she would, she could not do amiss.
Uprooted in full bloom (and as some said
out of the churchyard furtively conveyed,

for none knew certainly whence came the trove)
pansy and gold-laced polyanthus throve.
A dead geranium from the vicarage
rubbish-heap scavenged had but to engage
root in her mould to start again to life,
and a pot lily, from the farrier's wife
cajoled, speared up though planted upside down.
   There was a Woolworth's in the market town—
the Araby, Spice Island, Walsinghame
miraculous of every village dame,
who from its many-breasted mercies drew
the joys of spending and of saving too.
Thither Rebecca went and like a child
hung o'er the tray, believing and beguiled.
Each pictured packet held a sensible hope,
lisping and sliding in its envelope—
such colours, printed bright and sleek as flames,
such flouncing shapes, and starry, and such names!—
Sweet Sultan, Arabis, Virginia Stock,
Godetia, Clarkia, Alyssum, Hollyhock,
Nasturtium, Mignonette, Canary Vine,
and Everlasting Peas, and those, more fine,
which bore such titles as Miss Wilkinson,
Cora, Mnemosyne, and Gonfalon.
   Returning in the carrier's motor van
she sat nid-nod, while conversation ran
blithe as a freshet over ulcered legs,
murders, spring onions, and the price of eggs.
Hesperus, the kind star which bids all home,
lightened that company jolting through the gloam,
loosened each tongue, and mellowed each fatigue;
resolving friend and foe into a league
which in that narrow heaven close-housed should dwell
in idleness like saints to hear and tell,
sitting for ever filled and never tired
in the blest influence of that star attired.
Them, as though God's, the driver's countenance
out of his mirror overlooked with glance
immovable, while they whom he conveyed,
being mortal, but his hinder parts surveyed.
And like a God he, unpetitioned, knew
of each the ending and appointment due,
for each too soon arrived, when she must make

her bustle, and farewelling friends forsake.
But for those yet within, who felt the breath
of evening enter, it was but a death
that the door closed on, and the dusk estranged,
and but one hearer for more heard exchanged;
and loudlier talked the dwindling company,
and life reared up as at a funeral tea.

But now Rebecca, wont to chatter ding-
dong with the merriest, and when drunk to sing,
sat mute and pensive as a maid returned
from meeting love, whose lips have newly learned
silence beneath a kiss. No van saw she,
no burdened neighbours joggling knee to knee,
but a fenced garden where red faces loomed
lusty a peony bed, or eyeballs bloomed
flax or forget-me-not, or jessamine
muffled a grizzly beard and columbine
dangled its dovecote from a dirty ear.
Then in a flash all these would disappear,
and in a pantry rows of bottles, all
brimful, clinked cheek by jowl, both great and small.
Blest view, whichever way!—blest state to be
thus bearing home her own felicity,
feeling within her lap the future grope
stirring and swelling in its envelope,
foretasting in her soul draughts even now
on their long distillation sped. 'I vow
she's drunk as a lord again,' neighbours declared,
seeing with what a lost and lofty air
she scrambled out, waving them such adieux
as only emperors or drunks might use.

Quitting the company to become its theme
she reached her gate, still heavy with the dream,
and leaned there, spinning trophies in her mind
of blooms and bottles endlessly entwined.
The dusk had fallen, parenting the dew
under its cloak; uneasy a wind blew,
bidding mankind go in and lurk at ease . . .
Hence, ye profane, before Night's mysteries
out of an elder world that must be done
in the consenting absence of the sun.
Now ebbed the tide of waking from its shores:
about her was the sound of closing doors,

and hens shut in, and the last buckets filled,
and homing footsteps on their threshold stilled.
Now waxing on the air invisible
the wood-smoke hovered with a sharper smell
as fires were fed and kettles set to boil.
Unseeingly she watched the darkening soil
suck back the green, the red, the blue, unchild
itself of all the gaudy brood beguiled
out of its bosom by the clasp of day,
save whimpering white from its own being astray;
until at last she stirred, sighed, saw around
but night, and heard her sigh the only sound.

She lumbered up the path, stooped for the key
under its brick, went in; but presently
came forth again, bearing a lantern lit,
and smiled about to see its presence flit
by bush and tuft and tree with swinging stride,
waking a startled green on every side—
the painted emerald of a theatre bower;
then knelt, and fell to work with all her power.
To sow by lantern light—it was a scene
unpaired in all the annals of Love Green,
flat against nature and good usage, less
act of a wantwit than a sorceress.
Outlandish her vast shadow prowled and stayed—
a rooting bear, a ghoul about her trade—
beheaded, with her rising, into dark.
Birds scolded at her, dogs began to bark,
John Pigeon, reeling home to fight his wife,
checked at the glare, and bellowed out *The strife
is o'er, the battle done*, to scare the fiend;
while him forgetting, Mrs Pigeon leaned
out of the bedroom window in her nightgown,
rapt as a saint at gaze, to track the light down.

As when a single cackle bruits the hawk,
and straightway the whole henrun wakes asquawk,
word of this wildfire ran the village through.
Casement of casement asked, what was ado,
but stayed no answer, since each cared alone
to set on wing some theory of its own.
Those blest with most propinquity declared
Rebecca mad, or held that she prepared
unhallowed grave for an unlicensed birth,

or hoard of buried bottles would unearth.
Those midway souls, who but her shining saw,
propounded fire, or the offended law
arrived with handcuffs on a bicycle;
whilst those who nothing saw, but heard the swell
of hymns devout and holy psalms intoned
in such a voice as but one neighbour owned,
were perfectly convinced that Mr. Pigeon
had cut his consort's throat and found religion.
Danger! yelped dog to dog. At Limetree Farm
tin-voiced gallinies furthered the alarm,
and from their windy city roused, out-wheeled
the affronted parliament of rooks, and pealed
their backward-jangled tocsin overhead,
till Parson Drumble in his genial bed
dreamed of church robbers, woke, and slept once more.
    Meanwhile Rebecca, placid as the core
of jostling whirlpool, grubbed and grunted on,
bedding Sweet Sultan by Miss Wilkinson,
larkspur by mignonette and arabis.
No ears had she save for the sliding hiss
of seed released into her horny hand—
a drowsing multitudinous murmur, scanned
with tiny lapse and check—nor any care
for other life than that implicit there;
her being so much in future fixed that she
inhabited an anonymity
of time, an ambiguity of day
hollowed from midnight. And as dreams convey
their own penumbra of oblivion, so
she moving with her lantern to and fro
pulled darkness after her, and with such sleight
reshaped her wavering world elsewhere, one might
think 'twas her dream, not she, that walked the night.

    Odd, that upon the morrow, with no word
blabbed, or hint breathed, all knew what had occurred,
and saw the house unfired, the sinner unwrung,
the martyred wife alive and giving tongue,
with never a backward longing, never a sigh
for nobler prospects with the dark gone by.
Thus banded starlings, in an elder bush
a-babble, feel a pentecostal push,

rise like a handful of thrown dust, and sweep
mute along air as though they flew in sleep,
and veer as one, by some unbidden bid,
to a new feeding-place; but why they did
just so, just then, not even themselves could tell,
nor need they ask, since here, too, they feed well.
Now at this truth intuitively met,
gossip scarce greeted gossip thereon, but set
up a new calf by general consent,
to glister a religious ornament,
a beacon to all minds, a thing to swear by:
seed sown by night is bound to come up rarely.
Some praised Rebecca's cunning, some her lore;
all recollected well how once before
some other scientist, removed, or dead,
or aunt to a step-brother-in-law, or read
of in the paper, used the midnight hour so,
and gained a golden medal at the flower-show.
   In the long dusks, when maidens first delight
to stroll bare-armed, and the first midges bite
and swallows hawk them, it became the mode
to wander musingly along the road
and halt, by chance, beside the garden plot.
Maybe Rebecca with her watering-pot
stood there; if so, good manners bade one edge
How-do-you-do-ing nearer to the hedge,
casting a courteous sheep's-eye undeclared;
if not, one leaned upon the gate and stared.
By the next evening, having grown more bold,
and the latch somehow giving way, behold,
one stood within, admiring as was due
the way these night-sown seedlings always grew.
Then the same delicate combat was rehearsed,
whether fish fly, or angler fish, snap first—
so the wise gudgeon thinks, at any rate;
Rebecca, deftly twitching back the bait
with 'Oh, 'tis nothing. And besides, I believe
I promised it to another. I should grieve
to disappoint her, seeing her so set,
and these particular blooms so hard to get.'
'There, there,' quoth gudgeon, 'I won't spoil your trade,'
and twiddling in her pocket still delayed,
priced other nosegays, fancied she'd take none—

flowers do but die, when all is said and done;
a foolish ware. 'Yet some will pay for them,'
answered Rebecca, stroking down the stem
with a foreclosing gesture that stroked flame
from the poor fish's heart, and left her tame
to the taught melody as a violin.
This was a pleasant way of earning gin:
easy as kiss your hand, and seemly too;
for with her trade Rebecca's credit grew,
and those who lately saw her and disdained,
a sot athirst, more reverence entertained
for one who paid with such imperial airs
for her own liquor, and might pay for theirs.
    Close to the ground at first her commerce spread:
posies to take on Sunday to the dead,
a sixpenny knot to deck the mantelboard,
or the young breast of Joy, from her abhorred
black dress and apron freed to disembogue
one night a week in a silk blouse from Vogue.
But with the epiphany of her midnight seed
her light was from these grovelling bushels freed,
and waxing with their greenery upthrust
into a higher sphere, a more august
and profitable air. News wrought like barm
when Mrs Sankey of the Limetree Farm—
she who in winter wrapped herself in furs,
and walked out with two chasing terriers
like any Squire's lady—through the gate
loosing her imps to romp and ruinate,
said with her civilest show of teeth, 'I hear
you're selling flowers. I hope they are not dear.'
The flowers were hers, and hers extremely cheap.
What simple shepherd would begrudge a sheep
to Pan flockmaster?—and the sacrifice
was eased by knowing she could raise the price
to humbler customers henceforth, and so
recoup the loss from which such gains should flow.
    Drunkards, they say, however they may hap
to fall, earth takes them kindly in her lap;
rock's a down bed to them, and paving-stones
receive with deference their unbroken bones;
the sun by noonday, and the winter's night
scathe not, edged tools don't cut them, nor dogs bite,

but wandering unharmed they recreate,
fall as they will, unfallen Adam's state.
A like kind providence now brooded over
Rebecca's steps, even when she was sober.
Her ways were plenteousness, her paths were peace;
all summers, even wet ones, brought increase,
and markets matched themselves to her supply—
as in political economy.
None gave a tea-party or funeral
lacking her wares; she decked the village hall
for whist-drives, and the set bouquet supplied,
with fern bewhiskered, and with ribbon tied,
for Lady Lee who opened the bazaar.
The doctor, semi-centaur of a car
weather-and-way-worn, subtle and obdurate
as he, was never known to pass her gate
without the purchase of a buttonhole.
She filled the chimney vase, the silver bowl
whose bright undinted cheek looked back the rife
wrinkles of Fanny Grove, a virtuous wife
for five-and-twenty years, and polishing still,
and the cracked teapot on the window sill
of sluttish, sickly, smiling Jenny Prince,
of all save love of flowers deflowered long since.
Gentle and simple, shamed and proud, she served:
to her the wantwit's cumbered footsteps swerved,
and Mrs Hawley of The Bungalow—
who worshipped flowers, but couldn't make them grow—
bought week by week wellnigh a bottle's-worth.
Summering visitors, who found that earth
untutored but such simple toys purveyed
as died on being plucked, increased her trade
and spread her fame so far from coast to coast
that she was asked to send off flowers by post.
Her blossoms capped like foam the making tides
that heaved the graveyard mould, and went with brides
to church; pulpit and lectern, font and pew,
they trimmed for feasts, and the long week-days through,
on the unvisited close air that breaths
exhaling, kept Christ company with their deaths.
    All this for gin. Yes, as you say, all this
for ransom, ease, illusion, the sole kiss
lorn age can trust to, the last kindness done

bewintered flesh that has outgrown the sun.
O faithful bottle!—whose dispassionate lip
pours to the solitary fellowship,
whose borrowed blood abhors not nor disdains
to live awhile along the dullard's veins,
whose weaving peace into the harassed mind
mounts a sweet trickster, skilful to unbind
the galling knots and cords of here and now—
thou art no niggard, and no chooser, thou!
At the first wooing yielding all thy fire,
thee not the longest love can wholly tire.
None too uncomely are, nor commonplace,
for thee to greet; thou wrappest up disgrace
in the same mantle of oblivion
that feasted honour puts so warmly on.
Good fortune's fellow, by old ties invoked,
adversity beholds thee unreproached.
Mistrust salutes in thee the only fair
that will not play him false, nor is despair
quite without hope, commending himself to thee.
O courteous bottle, humbled to a fee!
and wearing amongst humankind such crass
constraints as those they bid thee awhile unloose.
    So, drinking flowers, Rebecca drank content.
But now no longer to the inn she went,
where all she saw, the ceiling smoked with soot,
the tramped-out oilcloth roses underfoot,
the beer-ringed table and the almanack
telling what moons lit nineteen-twelve, brought back
too shrewdly memories of former drought;
of evenings when the rain splashed down without,
and all, even the earth, might drink but she;
who creditless sat among the company,
and dully fawned, and heard the pendulum,
sneering and calm, go adding up the sum
of time twitched from her hope that one of these,
if not from kindness, from contempt might please
to lean from Abraham's bosom to her lip.
Those who can buy whole bottles soon outstrip
the common tavern cheer of such as wrench
their ease from sitting crowded on a bench,
while draughts incessant round their ankles chide,
214 and a coarse closing time waits just outside.

Closing time, pooh! What was it now to her?—
a sweet alarum and remembrancer
to fill again, a vagrant nightly story
that passed, and left her midway in her glory.
    'There sits Rebecca, grown too proud to souse
but with her cat,' said they. A new carouse
pride taught her, who from lonely drinking drew
deeper delighting, and a mystic grew.
Order, solemnity, and ritual
beseemed her drinking, and at each nightfall
she like a priestess trod the kitchen floor.
The blind must be drawn down, and locked the door,
the lamp well-trimmed set on its crochet mat,
plumped up the cushion, and shut out the cat,
and sometimes she'd wash hands, and comb her hair.
Meanwhile the bottle, so she was aware,
watched from the keyhole of its cupboard shrine.
While yet in darkness it began to shine
self-lit, and tingled with awakening fire,
and bulged its conscious flank to her desire.
And fetched, and poured, with its own ardour tame,
into the glass the meek and mastering flame
lapsed with what suppleness, with what silken pace
cringed up the bowl, and to itself a grace
before drinking murmured, until being come
to the brim it lay for every rapture dumb.
Harmless as any bride it lay, and wooed
her down with stillness; lip would be too rude
to crash against such crystal, sense too meagre
such an awaiting promise to beleaguer—
it should be possible not to drink but drown!
Slow the invincible circle wooed her down,
until the smell encountered, living and rank,
struck like a wave, and drowned her, and she drank.
    So meek untasted, what a termagant
thrust its wellmet against her tongue, with rant
and dance and riot through her veins deployed!
Oh, this was youth, and youth must be enjoyed
roughly, for youth is short! How shall the rose
have joy of its brief petals if there blows
no wind to scatter them? Ravish the glass!
For youth is short, and shorter yet, alas!
this revenant wildfire conjured from the ash,

this pixie-light dancing on rotting flesh.
Make haste, make haste! Not even liquor may
burn long thus bright in the candlestick of clay,
nor pipe old mutton back again to lamb,
nor cheat your wise threescore. And though you swam
in drinks to-night, and sweet, you would not taste
another glass like this. Make haste, make haste!
   Fill up once more, Rebecca. Though the first
glass will not come again, you have your thirst
still with you, and the night before you spread
deep and obsequious as a feather bed.
How well the steadfast lamplight fills the room!
How all the sights of everyday assume
what shapes of quaint reality! How wise
a countenance the clock's, how point-device
the row of cups along the dresser hung,
which seem to hang in air! And though the young
may think they own content, they only glance
at it, who round their painted maypole prance.
What pleasure theirs, on whom pleasures are dealt
violent as an August thunder-pelt,
that smites upon the field, but leaves it dry,
and presently is in a mist gone by?
How shall their liquor scrambled-down be matched
with the embalming fervour you have hatched
from your advised and contemplative booze?
Savour it well, sip cunningly, nor lose
one feather's weight of the enormous joy,
fixed on whose mounting tide you bob and buoy;
while round you chairs and pots and pans, entrapped
into such looks of stillness as the rapt
landscape of heaven wears, corroborate
by their continuance your blest estate.
   Youth you have pledged; that's gone; along your veins
nuzzles the toast to age; a third remains—
a deeper glass. How deep the night has grown!
At such an hour to such as drink alone
a guest arrives, with pomp and mystic riot
travelling from India. Out of the quiet
he mounts, he looms, he marches, and the blood,
in the ears' watch-tower, with its rub-a-dub
drums his approach, and at his meinie's shout
air whets its shrillest silence all about.

Fill to this guest, Rebecca, drink once more!
How soft his leopards pad your kitchen floor!—
and with their thick tails buffet you, and thresh
sharp waves of joy along your drowsy flesh.
Lovely they are, and affable, and tame,
and fawn and sidle round you, as the flame
fondles the log, owning you one on whom
their lord looks kindly. In your shabby room
how vast and calm a shade his ivy throws!—
dusky as wine outpoured, and to repose
weighing the thoughts of them who sit secure
in its inviolable clear-obscure.
Steeped in that shadow, sit, Rebecca, long!
Lost to the world, to you all worlds belong;
your bartered being for the glowing ghost
that in this hour apparels you, well lost,
and by this hour, that in an hour must hence,
even for its very fleeting recompensed.
Sit long, and deepen to the triumphing tide
that surged about an island and a bride;
drink onward, in this visiting glory arrayed
by him to whom your darkened vows were paid.
Drink the bright leopards, and the sacred shade!

   As moorland farmers drive their wedge of tilth
into the waste, outwitting with stern stealth
the casual might around their sally laid,
Rebecca set her husbandry to invade
the waste of winter. On till the first frost
the field was hers, but in a night was lost.
Against this iron, what could her annuals do—
her summer soldiers, who had wantoned through
an easy warfare since the first of May?
Mauled and dispersed the sixpenny squadrons lay,
their vigour bruised, their flaunt wilted and burned,
their fatness to a dismal jelly turned,
until the traitor sun, who was their friend,
smote with his midday scorn, and made an end.
Sad as a broken bottle was the sight;
and she through many a chilled and sober night
sat studying for a scheme to countervail.
Next year she planted honesty, whose frail
undaunted bucklers silver at the blows

of frost but yet hold out, and monthly rose,
whose scarlet not the longest night benumbs,
and tinfoil asters, and chrysanthemums.
   These last-fruits proved the best of all her gear;
for autumn is a dying time of year,
and those who mourn, and feel the world's eye fixed
on their lament, don't hesitate betwixt
this penny and that, but spend as lavishly
as though each week would bring a legacy.
Even the dying, from whose hearts had died
all other passions, felt a stir of pride
forecasting all the braveries whose date
hung upon theirs; as in the old estate
of kings, entombed with such a retinue
of tributary deaths, it seemed they drew
toward no victor's but an equal's court.
   Love Green knew this. And so when the report
that Mrs Merley and old Isaac Hay
were both near death enriched a winter's day,
the common voice enquired, 'What will they do?
Rebecca won't have flowers enough for two.'
Long was the contest, for, intensely prayed,
death like a simpering girl his choice delayed.
The rival houses with defiance met,
stoutly dissembling an unfeigned regret
to hear new tidings of less hope; all ranged
to sides, and bets and bulletins exchanged,
while in this losing game for vantage lost
fretting, the sufferers, in their balance tossed,
envied each hearsay pang the other bore.
Only Rebecca, numbering her store
of present blooms and bottles yet to come,
preserved a courteous equilibrium.
   What though the patriarch was stale in vice,
renowned for ancient rape and present lice,
and Bet had held her head up with the best
until her seventh bit her in the breast
and graffed a cancer there?—to neither cause
she leaned, death's partisan, not his or hers.
Why should she draggle to the strife impure?—
her gin was sure as death, and death was sure.
One should be taken—so the Holy Writ
218 avouched, and her impartial fancy knit

the wreaths, and to a grave in blank despatched.
Meanwhile some wayside profit might be snatched.
Of either faction the ambassadors
she welcomed, and conducted them indoors,
parried the devious hint, and took the bribe
before the indifferent witness of her tribe
of housed chrysanthemums, englobed and bland
as fireside cats musing on cream-jugs, and,
while they yet gloated, whisked them from the view
with a deft, 'Well, I'm sure I feel for you.
But the poor soul—who knows?—may yet be spared.'
A poor soul was. For while his backers declared
that Isaac would not see the morrow's sun,
Bet Merley, bandaged in oblivion
of morphia, moaned and vomited and died;
nor knew in her departure the wished pride
of dying first, but into Sheol passed
defrauded. 'He laughs loudest who laughs last,'
her rival said, hearing the death-bell send
the news, and from that hour begin to mend,
and called for meat, but called in vain, for all
his house were gone to see the burial.

    Dark was the day, and vexed with coming storm.
The mourners shrugged and shuffled to keep warm,
and gathered their cheap sables closer round.
A south-west wind strewed dusk upon the ground,
and delved the shadow of the open grave.
Borne on its wings the tramp of the sea wave
tolled through the sentences, and in the gale
the vicar's surplice rattled like a sail.
Leaf on last leaf whirled through the creaking air,
the cypress writhed its summit like despair.
Pale and aghast the headstones gathered near;
pale and aghast, as though a mortal fear
had quenched their living white, bedaubed with clay,
tumbled on the cold ground, the garlands lay,
and heard the doom of man as though their own
pronounced: *He cometh up, and is cut down
like*—and the wind went by and snatched the word
and scattered it upon the air unheard.

    Was this the end indeed?—would not death's clutch
spare even these fine flowers that cost so much?
So thought the widower: though he'd buried Bet

the wreaths might keep a little longer yet,
and do him honour, were they but housed fast
out of the weather till the storm were past.
At graveside lingering till all were gone
save Dennie Foot the sexton shovelling on,
he nudged his arm, and spoke, but nothing loud,
and pointed to the wreaths, and to the cloud,
and to the porch; and Dennie slapped his pocket
and cried, 'Don't fear. I shall be sure to lock it.'
      The grave was filled, the sods rammed down awry—
so soon the impatient darkness took the sky,
knocking day on the head as though day were
a crack-legged rabbit squirming in a snare.
People within-doors, by the fireside brave,
were glad they were not lying in a grave
on such a night; even Rebecca, not
much given to fancy, thought how poor a lot
was hers who in this nightfall must be gone
to a new house, and settle in alone.
—A moping thought . . . it would not let her be;
it watered down her gin as weak as tea,
and dimmed the flaring lamp, and hollowly spoke
within the chimney-breast, and puffed with smoke
into the room, and stared from the bereft
green indoor bower that had no blossoms left.
Let them be gone! She had their price instead!
She poured it in her lap, and dull as lead
it sank on her, and wearily as clay.
What ailed the gin tonight?—as well drink whey!
It had no power, no fire. Let the wind roar,
come such a storm as never came before,
she'd to the *Hand and Roses* and buy more.

      Strange was the night, and strange the road well-known;
everything strange, as though the wind had blown
thin the substantial world; and still it blew.
In the close tap she saw the things she knew,
heard casual greetings, and her own reply,
as though she were some traveller standing by,
whose glance, exact and unconcerned, sees plain
the seen-by-chance and never seen again.
      When she set out for home the moon was up.
It shone in heaven like a brimming cup;

unspilled in all the turmoil of the storm
smoothly it hastened through the jostling swarm
of clouds that snatched at it. With a pale fire
it brimmed before her, stinging her desire,
so that she laughed aloud, and hugged the freight
of her four bottles, where inviolate
under the dark slumbered a fire that soon
would brim her full and merry as the moon.
Now by the church she passed, and a whim took
her mind to visit the new grave, and look
once more upon her flowers. Ay, and she'd show
the bottles forth to them, that they might know
they were not plucked, and thrown to earth, and taught
the lesson of a winter night for naught.
　　The gate clanged to behind her, and she stepped
into a dream. The blanched earth was so swept
with a black lightning where the elm-trees tossed
their shadows that the look of graves was lost.
Scythed by that dark they crumbled and reshaped,
were, and were not, hollowed themselves and gaped
before her feet, and in an instant reared
back to reality. Onward she peered,
and, as she went, grave after grave was twitched
out of her sight as though she were bewitched.
It must lie hereabouts. Not this. The next.
The next, then. 'Twas the shadows that perplexed
her pathway, and the frantic moonlight poured
in the brief interval the clouds restored
that blotted out with its extremity
of light the whiteness where her wreaths must lie.
Not this; the next. Not this; not this . . . she found
her footsteps stumbling at the new-made mound
that covered Bet. Raw it heaved up, as mean,
lank, and undecked as she in life had been.
Gone! Not a petal left. The flowers were gone!
　　Still mocked the moon, and still the wind raved on.
Deep within her dumbfounderment there stirred
the echo of a prophecy, a word
of flowers, the with double meaning would menace
man too: *The wind goeth over, and the place
thereof knows it no more.* Down fell the dark.
The moon was gone, blown out, a dwindled spark
receding through interminable cloud.

She clenched her limbs to shriek her loss aloud,
but in the gale's dominion words came not.
And wherefore shriek, and shriek to whom? And what
loss should she howl for, and what thief accuse?
And what this loss that was so deadly to lose?
Cry for a mess of flowers, and blame the wind?
No, it was more, was more!—and her robbed mind
knew itself sickening over an abyss
where all must to unreason sink if this
moment of loss were not revoked. She knelt,
and pawed and searched the grave, but only felt
heaped earth, and sticky clods, and shrivelling grass.
Robbed and betrayed! Down there the felon was,
who with her dead hand could reach forth to blight
flowers out of being. Always one for spite
was Bet, and even a corpse she'd have her will.
Ah, cunning one, couched there so snug and still,
where are those wreaths that you have filched away?
Answer me, or I'll rout you from your clay,
unkennel you, while I have nails to scratch
and breath to cry Halloo; I'll be your match,
for all your death, and all your powers of death!
Close to the grave she spoke; and from beneath
travelling through the ground, answered a sigh.
    Waveringly it breathed, yet the outcry
of tempest could not tread it underfoot;
failing, it left a silence absolute
as though the last wave trembling to the shore
of time had come, and lapsed for evermore.
What, must it cower away with nothing told?—
a listless mockery beneath the mould?
Was there no engine to compel the dead?
Suddenly, all the churchyard was bespread
with moonlight, and the net of shadow blithe
as ever capered under boughs a-writhe.
Noosed in that net a glittering something grinned,
and beckoned her; unparcelled by the wind
the bottles lay, and to their mistress blinked.
On her illumined mind they shone distinct—
the sought-for engine, the awakening trump
that should uprouse the sleeper from her dump
and warm her lips to speech. Let her but taste,
222 and she'd tell all. On a tombstone in haste

she cracked a bottle neck, and pledged, and poured.
Over the sod with tricking pace explored
the gin, and sank, mouthed by the greedy clay.
But mute and glum the mannerless drinker lay;
and the first bottle, drinking turn about,
was drained, and cast, a dead-man, down, to flout
death's other wastage, and a second broached,
and wellnigh quaffed before sigh reproached
the air, as dragged out of a heart constrained,
and loth and wearily a voice complained.
  'What is this talk of flowers? No flowers are here.'
'Yet sorrowing neighbours laid them on your bier.'
'Neighbours I have who nothing feel for me.'
'In course of time they'll grow more neighbourly.'
'Time may the living ease; us it helps not.'
'You should lie easy now, your cares forgot.'
'My cares were me. While I endure, so they.'
'Ay, you'd a mort of troubles in your day.'
'And seven my womb drove out, like days to know.'
'The seventh was avenged on you, if so.'
'Life grinds the axe, however we may end.'
'Are all the dead doleful as you, my friend?'
'How are the living? Look in your own heart.
Farewell.'
                The voice was gone. But like a dart
it stuck fast in her mind, and would not out.
The wind's incessant clamour could not rout
it from her hearing, nor the inward thud
of her alarumed and embattled blood
tread out its permanence. Cowed as a slave
who hears the whip she sat upon the grave,
but knew not where she sat, nor why she clutched
a bottle; blind, she saw the moonlight smutched
with vapour, and the trees, that groaned for pain,
toss back to grapple with the wind again;
and uncomplying, felt herself alive.
  Why must she live, and why must all things strive
counter to endless onslaught, and the stress
of the long gravitational weariness
that bids all to the ground? Better at once—
since soon we must—lie down, and the strife renounce.
Yet did we so, little were mended by it.
Bet's seven would rage on, though Bet lay quiet:

Nor could she, mated to the earth, keep long
her long virginity, for worms would throng
the city of her corpse, and whatso their
capacity, its fill of living bear,
and the weak grass thrust from her mound to quail
before the anger of another gale.
What sucked this life forth? What insatiate drouth
held evermore creation to its mouth,
and drank the human hurt like a sharp wine?
And that full moon, which she beheld so shine
and brim unspilled through cloud—what hand unseen
toward that terrible thirst bore its serene
renewing draught? Drunk as a lord must be
the Lord of heaven and earth! He, it was he,
who in his bottomless mixed cup pell-mell
poured all things visible and invisible;
who feasting drank the wind, and to the worm
stooped down his lip; whose revel had no term,
whose thirst unquenched begot its own allay
unstemmed, who was inebriate with clay,
with flowers, with fire, with the slow diamond squeezed
from time, with tigers, and the never-eased
genital pain, and the fixed Indian snows;
into whose cup the stars like bubbles rose
and broke; who in immortal fury trod,
alone, the winepress, and drank on, a God.
   Drank! She could drink too, in her little time
be drunk as he, unquestioned and sublime,
ay, and surpass him. Fuddle as he might,
he could not drain his cellar in one night,
nor, bound in husbandry of omnipotence,
be drunk beyond his means and damn the expense.
She, in this winter midnight, in this place
of death, fit tavern for one of mortal race,
with her two bottles left her, and the drear
unblossomed months of soberness drawn near—
patient as wolves, and grim, and sure—their threat
confronting and transcending to a whet,
would teach this God a lesson how to drink.
Let him look down, and envy her, and slink
crestfallen back to his eternity!
And in this exploit of mortality

she, with her mite, to be magnanimous

as he with all his might, befitted. Thus,
as from his cup driblets of glory run
through man, to that slighted and sorry one
who lay beneath a wassail should abound:
had she more gin, she would stand drinks all round.
So would she revel out her night; so pull
down to her lips the brimming bountiful,
gin-coloured moon. Already it stooped low,
swam, swooned towards her, warmed her with its glow
even in this night of chill. Nearer it swooned—
Now it was two! Two bottles and two moons!
Quick, glass on stone! The dead in their neglect
would stir for doom, so shrill the bottle cracked . . .

   The coroner summed up as you'd expect:
Drink is a failing which the state deplores.
If drink you must, then please to drink indoors.
   Such was his gist. He then grew fatherly,
opined the jury would be glad of tea,
and with the air of one who's cleared a botch
went with the doctor for a double Scotch.
The empty bottles brought as evidence
to show the cause of death were carried hence
by Mr. Merley as a perquisite.
Comfort he needed in his widowed plight;
comfort they gave, for added to the tale
of those his wife had emptied in this vale
of tears they brought the total to the exact
sum of his years and hers—a striking fact,
and manifesting clearly to his mind
cosmic arithmetic at work behind.
   Diversely scheme we the creative plan.
Olivia Drumble, who was anglican,
perplexed her spouse with talk of sacrilege,
God's acre and what not. Meanwhile God's hedge
suffered a serious breach, where cognoscenti,
thinking it best to make a private entry,
crawled in to snuff about Bet's grave, and snare
the rich embalming odour lingering there.
For a full week the sods breathed out a smell
unmatched—mortality had spiced it well—
but with time's handling lost the lovely wraith,
and yielded, even to the nose of faith,

a smell like any other grave; like hers,
whose frolic death bequeathed the villagers
a tale that flashed awhile, and presently
waned, and was laid aside, extinct as she.
None broke a twig to view that resting-place.
Her legatees shrugged off the brief disgrace,
and with a briefer hope the name of Christ
bought on a label reasonably priced.
A larger label, saying: 'To be Sold
this Eligible Property Freehold,'
bleached for a twelvemonth over the green neglect
that had been flowers, till fate chanced to direct
a couple by. 'This is the place,' said they.
'It's picturesque, and stands on the highway.
That green stuff cleared, gravel put down, some quaint
checked curtains, and a lick of orange paint,
and within-doors some mugs and warming-pans—
this is the very cottage of our plans.'
   I passed the cottage some few weeks ago.
Where once the flowers had been there was a row
of tottering iron tables where no one sat.
Couched in the hedge I saw Rebecca's cat.
Out of the lifeless house there brayed a hoarse
aerial voice announcing cricket scores,
and a lean lady watched me loiter by
with a discouraged but attentive eye.
Beside the threshold where no traveller calls
a painted board said 'Teas and Minerals';
and at the inn I heard it told that these
newcomers did so poorly with their teas
that they had set out cots, one in the pantry,
to house the well-dowered by-blows of the gentry.
   I wish I had not gone that way, to smear
with aspect of the present the once clear
image of other summer when I first
saw the brave garden, and was told how thirst
had planted it. Then on Love Green I looked
as children on an open story-book,
and the best-painted picture it could show
was still Rebecca's stratagem a-blow.
Now from the page the picture blurs and dims,
wavers, discolours, perjures itself, dislimns.

The flowers are withered, even from my mind,

their petals loosed, their scent gone down the wind;
and she, to whom they such allegiance bore—
I knew her once, and know her now no more.

BOXWOOD
(1960)

I

Out of the silent rock the spring came welling
And air gave it a voice immediately.
I am free, it sang, I am free to hurry away.
But here is happiness, said the fern, in this cool dell—
Stay!
Here is security, said the swaying tree—
Dwell!
Never, never, never! sang the spring, I must go on my way
    though I know not whither.

Gravity, said the listening fox, the force of gravity,
Necessity, planetary influence, something of that sort,
    governs us all;
Trees to their earth rivetting, bantling brooks to ocean
    hurrying,
Me, I think, to a breakfast on this fine morning impelling.
Lightly he trotted away.

II

In ground that neighbours ground
They tilled in their lifetime
Our churchyard folk sleep pretty sound
Winter and summer.
They lie where they did look to lie,
With parents, mates, old friends, old foes, near-by.

Easter awakes them with sound
Of *Alleluia*,
And then *We plough the fields* comes round
At Harvest Festival,
Then Christmas with *The First Nowel*,
And in between they sleep knowing all's well.

III

Playing among the boughs that were
So high and out of mind last year,
The children seem in a sleep-walking dream
As though they played in upper air.

IV

The book I had saved up to buy
Was come, and I
Unwrapped it and went out to be
In privacy,
As though to read such poems were
A kind of prayer.
And any bank, and any shade,
Will do, I said,
To be the temple of this hour—
So why not here
Where these old creaking chestnuts frown?
There I sat down
And read the poems; but the tree
Spoke them to me.

V

All day, all day,
Nothing came that way.
No footfall on the mossy path,
No hand on the gate.

No hand, no footfall,
Nothing to see at all—
But a queen's presence when the night
Stepped out of the wood.

VI

All in a night, remote,
Dreamlike, scarcely to be known—
The contemptuous white beauty of a swan
Enforced upon the gaunt
Tussocky hillside which had grown
Sadder and shabbier as the year ran out;
A fall of snow . . . Thus, Milton wrote
Of that accustomed dead woman:
Methought I saw my late espousèd Saint.

VII

Hold up awhile, ye gates.
Swing on perished hinges, ye ghostly doors,
And the King of England shall come in.
Who is the King of England?
King Bracken with his meinie
Of stag and hind and coney;
Green and golden was his ancient reign.
He was the forefather
Of King Brutus and King Arthur,
And at the story's ending King Bracken will come again.

VIII

Lovely is the meadow now,
But it will be lovelier yet
When the child who plays therein
Remembers it.
Greener, greener will grow the bough,
    Whiter the white violets.

Spinning thread from thistle-stalks
Eve among her gipsy children,
Eve who once had dwelt therein,
Told them of Eden.
Ever more sheltered grew the walks,
More well-watered the garden.

Never was there a wilderness
So lovely-lonely as our desert,
Said her children in their turn,
Remembering it.
Never, never, were hours so spacious
Nor bramble-berries so sweet.

IX

People whom I never knew
In the house below the hill
That so many years ago
I looked down on through the bushes
Live, and prune their roses still,
Live, and brush the new year snow
Off their doorstep, live, and strew
Crumbs for robins, tits, and thrushes,

Live, and watch the blossom falling
On the grass-plat newly mown,
And the swallows reinstated;
Safe from living and from dying,
Never and forever known,
Not begotten but created,
Tea-time, Luke, forever calling—
Coming, Lucy, still replying.

X

The fire; the cushion, and the toy,
The curtained room
And my sweet milk to come—
All mine by right feline—
Is this not joy?

The wind, the dangerous dark, the sway
Of bough to ride,
The midnight world so wide—
All mine by right feline—
Is that not joy?

XI

The horse that stands in silhouette
Upon the summit of the hill
Is just the common height of horse;
He seems so nobly large because
The hill itself is rather small.

A horse at any time is grand;
But yet he seems sublimely tall,
Timelessly calm, as though he were
Related to that other horse
Cut in the turf of another hill.

XII
Dr. Johnson's Cat

When the house has cleaned itself at last
Of its diurnal human,
When the black man and the blind woman
Both have groped their way into the dark
And the dwindling watchman has gone by,
I have heard him waken, and sigh.

I have heard the bedstead twang and creak,
And the bed-curtains swaying,
And he sprawled down on his knees, praying:
O Jesu pie, salvum me fac!
Whether that same Jesu heard him or no,
My ears attended to his woe.

XIII

With a wide face
And an anxious nose
The owl sits in the ash tree
Thinking of all he knows—
Thinking of all he knows,
And his quiet feathers
Sit duteously around him
Like good scholars.

And below, on the willow bough
That spans the water-course,
Treads the poacher, wrapped in dead moles
And shod with a dead horse—
Shod with a dead horse
His footsteps reel and clatter.
What is this mild moony visage
Watching him from the water?

XIV

Some Joneses, Prices, Morgans, all in black
Troop to the chapel of Llangibby fach—
A parallelogram of yellow suet
That's finished off with a small vinegar cruet;

And other blackened Morgans, Joneses, Prices,
Who prefer litanies and such devices
Attend Saint Dogwell's church of the same parish—
In Rhineland Gothic, neat but somewhat garish;

And all the blackbirds into the mountain are flown
Where the wind preaches from a pulpit of stone:
A vexed doctrine, full of contention and cavil
But in such Welsh spoken as none can rival.

XV

Out of these trees a bird flies down to meet a bird,
And through the lake a leaf rises to kiss a leaf;
But though the autumnal woods burn in the water,
Cold it remains. Ice forms, and severs the playmates.

XVI

Not long I lived, but long enough to know my mind
And gain my wish—a grave buried among these trees,
Where if the wood-dove on my taciturn headstone
Perch for a brief mourning I shall think it enough.

XVII

If I had turned aside
Under that beckoning bough,
I should have found the glade,
The rushy mere, the old boat-house—
And I suppose
We should have fallen in love then, as we have now.

Then as now, you would
Have learned to fret and fear
And wish that you were dead
And recall books, dreams, freedom of mind,
As poor interim stuff—
But then your kind
Angel stood in the path and waved me on elsewhere.

XVIII

Enter if you will.
The door will not gainsay;
The dancing hooves are still,
The riders ridden away.
Mare, gelding, stallion,
The black, the roan, the bay, the flea-bitten grey,
All are gone.

The house beyond the wall,
The lighted long array
Of windows great and small
On rowdy Christmas Day,
Groom, gardener, scullion,
Gallants and ladies gay, children at play,
All are gone.

At morning and nightfall
The henwife comes this way,
But she has nothing to tell;
It was before her day.
Crest, motto and scutcheon,
The glory and decay, are only hearsay:
All is gone.

XIX

The wand was in the elder-bush,
The music was in the elder-wand,
I cut the wand and carved a whistle
As good as any man could wish;
But the only tune that it would play
Was *Over the Hills and Far Away*.

XX

Here, Death tumbled a girl,
Lowered a grey-beard there—
Long, long ago, but still
Their headstones declare it.

And the stones recoiling,
One this way, one that way,
Might be read as a gloss
On the doctrine of Predestination.

Yet it was not bliss or perdition,
Recoil of sex or age,
But the impartial roots of the tree
That so arranged them.

XXI

This year, last year . . . Leaf falls on leaf, life treads on
    life,
Innovation subsides upon innovation,
Time's lap hushes them all. Only the dragonflies
Flitting over the moat, or visiting children
Finding a story-tale, enter here as by right.

KING DUFFUS AND OTHER POEMS
(1968)

[KING DUFFUS]

When all the witches were haled to the stake and burned;
When their least ashes were swept up and drowned,
King Duffus opened his eyes and looked round.

For half a year they had trussed him in their spell:
Parching, scorching, roaring, he was blackened as a coal.
Now he wept like a freshet in April.

Tears ran like quicksilver through his rocky beard.
Why have you wakened me, he said, with a clattering sword?
Why have you snatched me back from the green yard?

There I sat feasting under the cool linden shade;
The beer in the silver cup was ever renewed,
I was at peace there, I was well-bestowed:

My crown lay lightly on my brow as a clot of foam,
My wide mantle was yellow as the flower of the broom,
Hale and holy I was in mind and in limb.

I sat among poets and among philosophers,
Carving fat bacon for the mother of Christ;
Sometimes we sang, sometimes we conversed.

Why did you summon me back from the midst of that meal
To a vexed kingdom and a smoky hall?
Could I not stay at least until dewfall?

'ON THIS PLAIN HOUSE ...'

On this plain house where I
Dwell and shall doubtless die
As did my plain forefathers in time past
I see the willow's light-limbed shadow cast.

I watch in solitude
Its flying attitude
Laid on that brick and mortar soberness
Like the sharp imprint of a fleeting kiss.

Just so, I think, your shade,
Alien and clear, was laid
Briefly on this plain heart which now plods on
In this plain house where progeny is none.

'LIKE AN OLD BEGGAR . . .'

Like an old beggar
White-beard Winter comes
Wrapped in a threadbare weed
Of ravels and thrums.

With a crazy hand
He knocks on every door,
But when the door is opened
No one is there;

Or motionless in a field
All day he will linger
Watching with mild blue eyes
The birds die of hunger.

'ENVY TO THE COUNTING-HOUSE . . .'

Envy to the counting-house
Ran, and pulled the Banker's sleeve.
Dreamy Banker, don't you grieve
These small deposits are not yours?

Do you think me poor?—the Banker said.

Am I one of those whose round
Brings them here on market day
Paying in with anxious joy
Penny as endeared as pound?

Oh, how I am robbed!—the Banker said.

'IN THE HIGH FIELD . . .'

In the high field, watching the sun go down,
Miranda said, I like to stand like this
And feel that I am sticking out into space.
On rolled the world and presently she walked on,
A moving turret among stationary towers,
Pylons, trees of secular growth and pyramids.

[TIME ON TIME]

Here in Yarnbury Camp, said the man, his shadow falling
Across us sunned and silent, they dug up a Roman soldier.
Complete with all his gear they found him, even to the
    rivets,
Brass—bronze, I should say—that fastened his leather
    sandals.
I'm interested in these things myself, whenever I come
    here
I make a special point of looking in all the rabbit-holes.

He paused a little, and went; and after him came the
    Roman,
Shadowless stepping the turf that hid him unsunned and
    silent,
Here in Yarnbury Camp, saying, we dug up a Briton,
Buried with all his goods, his worked flints and his amber.
Mortality is a strange thing, I muse and ponder about it
As I stand here on my watch, so still that at dusk the
    coneys
Nibble the grass at my feet, heeding me no more than a
    dead man.

I looked at your wrist, at the transient flesh and the bone
    beneath it,
And time bound dancing there with a viper's-tongue
    flicker.
To that coranto, I thought, north-east of us the shadows
Of Stonehenge veer onward into another evening.

'WHEN SHE WAS YOUNG ...'

When she was young she sang all day.
I told her she was like a wren,
So small the case, so ardent the voice.
Wait till my dying day, she'd say,
And then, then,
You'll hear me singing like a swan.

After midsummer birds fall silent
Or lose their tune, but she not so.
Still I could trace her by her voice
Through house and ground. But in the end
Like a swallow
Twittering softly she did go.

'ESTHER CAME TO THE COURT ...'

Esther came to the court
Of the Eternal.
Her good deeds followed her
Like menservants and maidservants;
The tears of her children
Sparkled on her like emeralds,
The sighs of her husband
Billowed out her garments.

When Esther beheld
In the sackcloth of a widow
With a sword across her knee
Judith of Bethuliah,
She cast off her ornaments,
She bowed herself low,
Down to the foot that had arched
Over the blood of the tyrant.

['SILENT WITH TIGERS THEY OBSERVE ...']

Beside a baby water-course,
Under a pine-tree roof that's hoarse

244 From argument with winds which blow

Spiked with repartees of snow
From Kinchinjunga and Kien-Shan,
An old man, and an older man,
And a third man who's older yet
Sit watching what the times beget.

Silent with tigers they observe
The mountain's mantled outline swerve,
The river's scaling voice blown loud
On the same wind that rocks the cloud.
These are the signs, who knows?—of day,
Or the day's earthquake on its way.

Below, below, far below,
The sun must rise, the river flow,
Beneath, beneath, far beneath,
The fire frets in a stone sheath.

Onward the Yellow River flows,
The yellow tiger cleans his toes.
One day much like another day
Begins, I heard the eldest say.

'AND PAST THE QUAY . . .'

And past the quay the river flowing;
And I not knowing
In what gay ripple, ambling and sidling,
The tears you wept for me go by me.

And in the ripples the bridge flaking;
Making and unmaking
Its grey parapet, and I not knowing
How in your mind I am coming and going.

And to my heart the wise river
Murmuring, Oh, never
Under the same bridge of any river
Does the wave flow twice over.

[ANNE DONNE]

I lay in in London;
And round my bed my live children were crying,
And round my bed my dead children were singing.
As my blood left me it set the clappers swinging:
Tolling, jarring, jowling, all the bells of London
Were ringing as I lay dying—
John Donne, Anne Donne, Undone!

Ill-done, well-done, all done.
All fearing done, all striving and all hoping,
All weanings, watchings, done; all reckonings whether
Of debts, of moons, summed; all hither and thither
Sucked in the one ebb. Then, on my bed in London,
I heard him call me, reproaching:
Undone, Anne Donne, Undone!

Not done, not yet done!
Wearily I rose up at his bidding.
The sweat still on my face, my hair dishevelled,
Over the bells and the tolling seas I travelled,
Carrying my dead child, so lost, so light a burden,
To Paris, where he sat reading
And showed him my ill news. That done,
Went back, lived on in London.

'AS RIVERS THROUGH THE PLAIN...'

As rivers through the plain
Widen and turn not back again
Descending man forgot
The ark on Ararat.

Grounded before the gale
Its swarthy timbers split and failed.
Its voyaging profile was
Blunted with vines and moss.

Emptied of all the prayers
Hymns and Te Deums of its passengers

246

No voice remained in it
But Noah's old she-cat

Praising her spotted young;
Save once at midnight came a long
Slow wing-beat through the dark,
And closed upon the ark.

Presently there spoke
The raven, dying: Out alack!
News of Elysium
I bring, but they are gone.

' "IF I CAN'T GET IT FROM HIS PURSE . . ." '

'If I can't get it from his purse
I'll get from his skin,'
Is an old saying among usurers.
After long meditation,
Research, and convocation,
Holy Church pronounced that usury is no sin.

When my rich joys were at an end
Love who their capital
Had loaned still held me to a dividend.
Paying in long starvation
Love's due of desolation
I acknowledge the righteousness of it all.

[LADY MACBETH'S DAUGHTER]

Your flesh sits featly on the bone
As sit the feathers on the swan,
Your brow is bravely broad and tall
As a new-masoned castle wall,
And well you are your father's daughter!
So sang my mother, the Thane's wife of Cawdor.

You shall have beads of gold and amber
And mock the wind in a warm chamber,
A rich relic you shall have

And a priest your soul to shrive,
So much you are your father's daughter!
So sang my mother, the Thane's wife of Cawdor.

You shall have the prayers of the poor,
And eat the red grouse from the moor,
And wipe your hands on a silk napkin
And wed a king's son for your liking
As shall befit your father's daughter—
So sang my mother, the Thane's wife of Cawdor.

The castle walls are slighted down,
The pretty martlets all are flown,
My beads were scattered in the fray,
The king's son stole my relic away.
Barefoot I trudge through mire and sleet
To gather nettles for my meat
And the poor's curses rattle after
Poor me, that am my father's and my mother's daughter.

'SHALL I BUY A DEAD BIRD? . . .'

Shall I buy a dead bird?
Shall I buy a dead fish?
Shall I buy a curly brown calf's head
John-Baptised in a dish?

The bird wears a feathered coat,
The fish wears a mackintosh,
The bull calf's innocent hood
Is gentle as plush.

But they must be plucked, skinned, singed,
They must be bared and neat,
They must be robbed of living looks
Before they are fit to eat.

Only man is buried
In boots and battle-dress.
Only man is buried
248 Without plea of nakedness.

In the merry black market,
Thick as maggots in a cloth,
The people stand gazing at so much
Death, at so much death, at so much death.

So shall I buy a dead Daddy?
Or shall I buy a dead son
Or shall I buy this curly brown calf's head
For me and my little one?

[FOUR POEMS]
i
Become as little children,
Said the Recruiting Sergeant;
With every hope as frantic,
With every fear as urgent.
Be seen and not heard
While the cannon volley
As sleep when you are bid
By Death, your tall Nannie.

ii
Five sons I have begot to part
In anxious feud the goods I leave.
My neighbour made a work of art
Which will not toil and cannot thieve.

iii
The infant's hand is raised in wrath,
The infant's face is red with lust,
The infant devastates the hearth—
And didst Thou make it of the dust?

iv
The Sleeping Beauty woke:
The spit began to turn,
The woodmen cleared the brake,
The gardener mowed the lawn.
Woe's me! And must one kiss
Revoke the silent house, the birdsong wilderness?

'THERE IS A MOUNTAIN'S-LOAD OF TREES . . .'

There is a mountain's-load of trees in the water.
From bank to bank the river is brimmed with trees.
Perhaps because of the smooth brushwork of the water
They do not seem to be this year's trees.

The river has no room for the shape of the mountain.
Beneath that glass runs no warrant of place or time.
It is plumed with the trees of no particular mountain
And green with a summer of no time.

This passing summer writes no word on the river
Except where a few small apples bob on the tide,
Cast off by some wilding further up the river
And carried onward by the tide.

'THE WINTERS HAVE MELTED . . .'

The winters have melted with their snows and gone.
Along the mossy walk
By the edge of the wood you beckoned me on
To hear the wooing cock pheasant talk
To his silent hen
On a young evening in May.
There I stood, leaning against you, listening—
I have never been away!

TWELVE POEMS
(1980)

AZRAEL

Who chooses the music, turns the page,
Waters the geraniums on the window-ledge?
Who proxies my hand,
Puts on the mourning-ring in lieu of the diamond?

Who winds the trudging clock, who tears
Flimsy the empty date off calendars?
Who widow-hoods my senses
Lest they should meet the morning's cheat defenceless?

Who valets me at nightfall, undresses me of another day,
Puts it tidily and finally away?
And lets in darkness
To befriend my eyelids like an illusory caress?

I called him Sorrow when first he came,
But Sorrow is too narrow a name;
And though he has attended me all this long while
Habit will not do. Habit is servile.
He, inaudible, governs my days, impalpable,
Impels my hither and thither. I am his to command,
My times are in his hand.
Once in a dream I called him Azrael.

THREE POEMS

i
Experimentally poking the enormous
Frame of the universe
This much we know:
It has a pulse like us.

But if it lags for woe,
Quickens for fever
Or calm euphoria measures it for ever
Other astronomers must show.

ii

Learning to walk, the child totters between embraces;
Admiring voices confirm its tentative syllables.
In the day of unlearning speech, mislaying balance,
We make our way to the grave delighting nobody.

iii

Fish come solid out of the sea,
Each with its due weight of destiny.
The purposed sprat knows what it would be at,
The skate, twirling in its death agony,
Is the embodied wave that flopped down
On the fisherman's coble and left him to drown.

DORSET ENDEARMENTS

'My Doll, my Trumpery!'
O sleepy child lulled on the jogging knee
With eyes brilliant as gems new-fetched from the gloom
Of the mine you stare about the cottage room.

On the ceiling badged with smoke the flies crawl.
The flowery paper sags from the damp wall,
The wind bellows in the dark chimney throat, the rain
Darkens the dish-clout stuffed in the broken pane.

Tick-tock. Tick-tock.
Time drips like water from the alarm-clock
That jars your Daddy from bed for the milking at five,
And will do the same for you if you live and thrive.

And before the narrow fire on the wide hearth
She sings to her child, her jewel new-fetched from the dark
Of the womb, and dandles him on a weary knee:
'My Doll, my Trumpery!'

BALLAD STORY

When I was young
And went to the school,
I saw Kate Dalrymple,
Who was so tall,
Who was so tall,
So laughing and lily-smooth
That I loved her before I knew
What it is to love.

What it is to love
I have studied since then,
But never so deeply
As that midnight when,
With day-break departing,
I betook me alone
To lie at her doorstep
And kiss the stone,

And kiss it and kiss it,
That dumb doorstone
Where her foot would be set
When I was far and gone.

Then I was gone
To learn to be a man,
To make a fortune
According to plan;
And according to plan
And forty years after
I came back by air
Who had gone by water.

Ebbed and flowed the water
While Kate Dalrymple
Crossed the same doorstone,
Heard the years ripple,
Heard the years trample,
Till at last she was led
Into the hospital
To lie on a high bed,

To lie on a high bed
And look at the wall.

GRAVEYARD IN NORFOLK

Still in the countryside among the lowly
Death is not out of fashion,
Still is the churchyard park and promenade
And a new-made grave a glory.
Still on Sunday afternoons, contentedly and slowly,
Come widows eased of their passion,
Whose children flitting from stone to headstone facade
Spell out accustomed names and the same story.

From mound to mound chirps grasshopper to grasshopper:
John, dear husband of Mary,
Ada, relict, Lydia the only child,
Seem taking part in the chatter.
With boom and stumble, with cadence and patient cropper,
The organist practises the voluntary,
Swallows rehearsing their flight sit Indian-filed,
And under a blue sky nothing is the matter.

With spruce asters and September roses
Replenished are jampots and vases,
From the breasts of the dead the dead blossoms are swept
And tossed over into the meadow.
Women wander from grave to grave inspecting the posies,
So tranquilly time passes
One might believe the scything greybeard slept
In the yew tree's shadow.

Here for those that mourn and are heavy-laden
Is pledge of Christ's entertainment;
Here is no Monday rising from warm bed,
No washing or baking or brewing,
No fret for stubborn son or flighty maiden,
No care for food or raiment;
No sweeping or dusting or polishing need the dead,
Nothing but flowers' renewing.

Here can the widow walk and the trembling mother
And hear with the organ blended
The swallows' auguring twitter of a brief flight
To a securer staying;
Can foretaste that heavenly park where toil and pother,
Labour and sorrow ended,
They shall stroll with husband and children in blameless
    white,
In sunlight, with music playing.

EARL CASSILIS'S LADY

Meeting her on the heath at the day's end,
After the one look and the one sigh, he said,
Did a spine prick you from the goosefeather bed?
Were the rings too heavy on your hand?
Were you unhappy, that you had to go?
No.

Was it the music called you down the stair,
Or the hot ginger that they gave you then?
Was it for pleasure that you followed them
Putting off your slippers at the door
To dance barefoot and blood-foot in the snow?
No.

What then? What glamoured you? No glamour at all;
Only that I remembered I was young
And had to put myself into a song.
How could time bear witness that I was tall,
Silken, and made for love, if I did not so?
I do not know.

DECEMBER 31st ST SILVESTER

Silvester, an old harmless pope,
Stands at the year's end and gazes outward;
And time his triple crown has shredded
And winters have frayed out his cope.

He is white as the weathered blade-bone;
Bleached in the rim of his name like winter honesty
He rattles on the stem of history
And is venerated at Pisa alone.

But green in his hand is a twig of olive;
For in his reigning days he devised a reign
Of peace with the Emperor Constantine;
And he watches the years to see it arrive.

IN APRIL

I am come to the threshold of a spring
Where there will be nothing
To stand between me and the smite
Of the martin's scooping flight,
Between me and the halloo
Of the first cuckoo.
'As you hear the first cuckoo,
So you will be all summer through.'
This year I shall hear it naked and alone;
And lengthening days and strengthening sun will show
Me my solitary shadow,
My cypressed shadow—but no,
My Love, I was not alone; in my mind I was talking with
    you
When I heard the first cuckoo,
And gentle as thistledown his call was blown.

GLORIANA DYING

None shall gainsay me. I will lie on the floor.
Hitherto from horseback, throne, balcony,
I have looked down upon your looking up.
Those sands are run. Now I reverse the glass
And bid henceforth your homage downward, falling
Obedient and unheeded as leaves in autumn
To quilt the wakeful study I must make
Examining my kingdom from below.
How tall my people are! Like a race of trees
They sway, sigh, nod heads, rustle above me,
And their attentive eyes are distant as starshine.
I have still cherished the handsome and well-made:
No queen has better masts within her forests
Growing, nor prouder and more restive minds
Scabbarded in the loyalty of subjects;
No virgin has had better worship than I.
No, no! Leave me alone, woman! I will not
Be put into a bed. Do you suppose
That I who've ridden through all weathers, danced
Under a treasury's weight of jewels, sat
Myself to stone through sermons and addresses,
Shall come to harm by sleeping on a floor?
Not that I sleep. A bed were good enough
If that were in my mind. But I am here
For a deep study and contemplation,
And as Persephone, and the red vixen,
Go underground to sharpen their wits,
I have left my dais to learn a new policy
Through watching of your feet, and as the Indian
Lays all his listening body along the earth
I lie in wait for the reverberation
Of things to come and dangers threatening.
Is that the Bishop praying? Let him pray on.
If his knees tire, his faith can cushion them.
How the poor man grieves Heaven with news of me!
Deposuit superbos. But no hand
Other than my own has put me down—
Not feebleness enforced on brain or limb,
Not fear, misgiving, fantasy, age, palsy,
Has felled me. I lie here by my own will,

And by the curiosity of a queen.
I dare say there is not in all England
One who lies closer to the ground than I.
Not the traitor in the condemned hold
Whose few straws edge away from under his weight
Of ironed fatality; not the shepherd
Huddled for cold under the hawthorn bush,
Nor the long, dreaming country lad who lies
Scorching his book before the dying brand.

A JOURNEY BY NIGHT

'In this last evening of our light, what do you carry,
Dark-coloured angels, to the cemetery?'
'It is the Cross we bury.

Now therefore while the last dews fall,
The birds lay by their song and the air grows chill
Follow us to the burial.

'It was at this hour that God walked discouraged
Seeing his olive-grove with a new knowledge
While man hid from his visage;

'It was at this hour the dove returned;
It was at this hour the holy women mourned
Over the body in clean linen wound.

'So God in man lay down, and man at long
Last in the sepulchre was reclining
And the dove laid her head under her wing;

'Only the poor Cross was left standing.

'Scarecrow of the reaped world, it remained uncarried and
    unwon;
With no companion
But its warping shadow it endured on,

'Till in this final dusk even that shadow,
Stealthy and slow, stealthy and slow
Faded and withdrew.

'So was the last desolation accomplished
And the Cross gave up the ghost.
Look on it now, look your last;

'See how harmless it lies, now it is down;
A shape of timber which in a tree began
And not much taller than the height of a man.'

It lay there, naked on the bier. It was black
With tears, blood, martyrdoms, with jewels decked,
And rubbed smooth with wearing on a child's neck.

Shouldering their burden, the angels went onward,
Like a wreath of mist moving unhindered,
And like a mourner I followed.

Time was no barrier to us, for time was no more;
The tideless sea lay muted along the shore,
The city clocks registered no hour,

The last echo had ebbed from the church bells;
Silent were the barracks, silent the brothels
And the water slept in the wells.

Rivers we forded and mountain-ranges crossed;
Silent were the reeds in the marshes we traversed;
Silent as they we came to a coast

And smelled the sea beneath us and walked dry-footed
On air—gentle it was as a bird's plumage—
And a shooting-

Star went by us on its errand elsewhere.
I knew neither astonishment nor fear
Till land glimmered below me, and an austere

Sea-board turf, shaggy as a wolf's pelt,
Bruised my being as I grounded with a jolt
On the prison-floor pavement

Of earth-bound man. The angels went smoothly on
Through a wilderness where each successive horizon
Was another sand-dune.

Time held out no promise, for time was no more.
Bones and bleached tree-roots lay scattered everywhere;
The dusk waited in vain for a star.

Suddenly the Cross scrambled off the bier.

Shouting like a bridegroom it bounded
On its one foot towards a pit dug in the sand—
A dark hole like a wound.

Poised on the edge of the pit, it began to sing.
'Lulla—lulla—lullaby' it sang. 'I am home again.'
And leaped in.

I saw the sand close over the pit and the suspended grey
Dusk convert to darkness in the twinkling of an eye.
'Now wake,' said the angel, 'and go your way.'

APPENDIX, NOTES AND INDEX OF FIRST LINES

APPENDIX

'WOMEN AS WRITERS'

[The following is the text of the Peter le Neve Foster Lecture which Sylvia Townsend Warner delivered to the Royal Society of Arts on 11 February 1959. It was later published in the *Journal of the Royal Society of Arts* (May 1959, pp. 378-86), and is reprinted here by kind permission of the editor of the *Journal of the Royal Society of Arts* and the estate of Sylvia Townsend Warner. C.H.]

When I received this invitation to lecture to the Royal Society of Arts on 'Women as Writers' (and here let me express my thanks to the responsible committee, and to the shade of Peter le Neve Foster, whose family founded the lectureship, and to my Chairman) —when I received this invitation, it was the invitation that surprised me. The choice of subject did not. I am a woman writer myself, and it never surprises me. Even when people tell me I am a lady novelist, it is the wording of the allegation I take exception to, not the allegation itself. One doubt, it is true, crossed my mind. It was inevitable that I should remember a book called *A Room of One's Own*, by Virginia Woolf. What had I to add to that? But *A Room of One's Own*, I thought, is not so much about how women write as about how astonishing it is that they should have managed to write at all. As they have managed to, there might still be something I could add. But then I reread my invitation, and became the prey of uneasiness. Women as Writers. *Women* as Writers. Supposing I had been a man, a gentleman novelist, would I have been asked to lecture on Men as Writers? I thought it improbable.

Here was an implication I might or might not resent. Here, at any rate, was an obligation I couldn't dodge.

It would appear that when a women writes a book, the action sets up an extraneous vibration. Something happens that must be accounted for. It is the action that does it, not the product. It is only in very rare, and rather non-literary instances, that the product —*Uncle Tom's Cabin*, say, or the *Memoirs of Harriet Wilson*—is the jarring note. It would also appear that this extraneous vibration may be differently received and differently resounded. Some surfaces mute it. Off others, it is violently resonated. It is also subject to the influence of climate, the climate of popular opinion. In a fine dry climate the dissonance caused by a woman writing a book has much less intensity than in a damp foggy one. Overriding these variations due to surface and climate is the fact that the volume increases with the mass—as summarised in Macheath's Law:

> One wife is too much for most husbands to hear
> But two at a time sure no mortal can bear.

Finally, it would appear that the vibration is not set up until a woman seizes a pen. She may invent, but she may not write down.

Macheath's Law explains why the early women writers caused so little alarm. They only went off one at a time. If a great lady such as Marie de France chose to give her leisure to letters instead of embroidery, this was merely a demonstration that society could afford such luxuries—an example of what Veblen defined as Conspicuous Waste. No one went unfed or unclothed for it. Nor could she be held guilty of setting a bad example to other women, since so few women were in a position to follow it. So things went on, with now and then a literate woman making a little squeak with her pen, while the other women added a few more lines to Mother Goose (about that authorship, I think there can be no dispute). It was not till the retreat from the Renaissance that the extraneous vibration was heard as so very jarring. By then, many women had learned to read and write, so a literate woman was no longer an ornament to society. Kept in bounds, she had her uses. She could keep the account books and transcribe recipes for horse pills. But she must be kept within bounds; she must subserve. When Teresa of Avila wrote her autobiography, she said in a preface that it had been written with leave, and 'in accordance with my confessor's command'. True, she immediately added, 'The Lord himself, I know, has long wished it to be written'—a sentiment felt by most creative writers, I believe; but the woman and the Lord had to wait for permission.

The French have always allowed a place to Conspicuous Waste, it is one of the things they excel at; and Mme de La Fayette rewarded this tolerance by giving France the first psychological novel, *La Princesse de Clèves*. But Molière was probably a surer mouthpiece of public opinion when he made a game of literary ladies. It is more damning to be shown as absurd than to be denounced as scandalous. It is more damning still to be thought old-fashioned. Margaret, Countess of Newcastle, was derided not only as a figure of fun but as a figure out of the lumber-room. (Much the same condemnation fell on Lady Murasaki, a most eminent woman writer, whose nickname in the Japanese court of the early eleventh century was Dame Annals.) In eighteenth-century England, a woman of fashion wrote at her peril (I doubt if Pope would have laid so much stress on Lady Mary Wortley-Montagu being dirty if she had not been inky). A woman who wrote for publication—by then, a fair number did—sank in the social scale. If she wrote fiction, she was a demirep. If she wrote as a scholar, she was a dowdy. However, as men of letters had also gone down in the world, writing women gained more than they lost. They gained companionship, they approached a possibility of being judged on their merits by writers of the opposite sex.

Too much has been made of Dr Johnson's opinion of women preachers, not enough of the fact that Mrs Chapone and Elizabeth Carter contributed to *The Rambler*, nor of his goodwill towards Mrs Lennox, and the hot apple pie he stuck with bay leaves in her honour. In the case of Fanny Burney, Johnson showed more than goodwill. He showed courage. Fanny Burney was his friend's daughter, and a virgin. And Fanny Burney had written a novel. Not even a romance. A novel.

The speed with which women possess themselves of an advantage is something astonishing. Such quantities of virtuous women turned to novel-writing that Jane Austen was able to pick and choose among them, to laugh at Ann Radcliffe and Mary Brunton, to admire Miss Edgeworth. It was an Indian summer, the last glow of the Age of Reason. Jane Austen could inscribe her title-page with that majestic, *By a Lady*. The Brontë Sisters, not so. They were born too late. The barometer had fallen, the skies had darkened. They grew up in an age which had decided that women had an innate moral superiority. As almost everything was a menace to this innate moral superiority, it was necessary that women should be protected, protected from men, protected from life, protected from being talked about, protected from Euclid—Mary Somerville the mathematician has recorded how hard put to it she was to expose herself to Euclid—protected above all from those dangerous articles, themselves. You couldn't have women dashing their pens into inkpots and writing as if they knew about life and had something to say about it. Determined to write and to be judged on the merit of their writing, women put on men's names: Aurore Dudevant became George Sand, and Mary Ann Evans, George Eliot, and Emily Brontë consented to the ambiguity of Ellis Bell.

I think I can now venture a positive assertion about women as writers. It is a distinguishing assertion; if I were talking about Men as Writers I could not make it. Women as writers are obstinate and sly.

I deliberately make this assertion in the present tense. Though a woman writing today is not hampered by an attribution of innate moral superiority, she has to reckon with an attribution of innate physical superiority; and this, too, can be cumbersome. There is, for instance, bi-location. It is well known that a woman can be in two places at once; at her desk and at her washing-machine. She can practise a mental bi-location also, pinning down some slippery adverb while saying aloud, 'No, not Hobbs, Nokes. And the address is 17 Dalmeny Crescent'. Her mind is so extensive that it can simultaneously follow a train of thought, remember what it was she had to tell the electrician, answer the telephone, keep an eye on the time, and not forget about the potatoes. Obstinacy and slyness still have their uses, although they are not literary qualities.

But I have sometimes wondered if women are literary at all. It is not a thing which is strenuously required of them, and perhaps, finding something not required of them, they thank God and do no more about it. They write. They dive into writing like ducks into water. One would almost think it came naturally to them—at any rate as naturally as plain sewing.

Here is a non-literary woman writing in the nineteenth century. She wrote under her own name, for her sex was already notorious:

> There were three separate registers kept at Scutari. First, the Adjutant's daily Head-Roll of soldiers' burials, on which it may be presumed that no one was entered who was not buried, although it is possible that some may have been buried who were not entered.
>
> Second, the Medical Officer's Return, in regard to which it is quite certain that hundreds of men were buried who never appeared upon it.
>
> Third, the return made in the Orderly Room, which is only remarkable as giving a totally different account of the deaths from either of the others.

I should like to think that Florence Nightingale's work is not yet done. If it could be set as a model before those who write official reports, the publications of Her Majesty's Stationery Office might grow much leaner, much time and money might be saved. But this is by the way.

Here is another, writing in the seventeenth century:

> Take a pint of cream, three spoonfuls of rice flour, the whites of three eggs well beaten, and four spoonfuls of fine sugar. Stir these well into your cream cold; then take a few blanched almonds and beat them in a mortar with two spoonfuls of water, then strain them into your cream and boil it till it comes from the skillet. Then take it up and put in two spoonfuls of sack, and wet your cups with sack and put in your custard, and let it stand till it is cold.

From a cookery book, as you will have realised—but a piece of tight, clear, consecutive writing.

Here is a woman writing from Norwich in July 1453:

> And as for tidings, Philip Berney is passed to God on Monday last past with the greatest pain that ever I saw a man; and on Tuesday Sir John Heveningham went to his church and heard three masses and came home never merrier; and said to his wife that he would go say a little devotion in his garden and then dine; and forthwith he felt a fainting in his leg and slid down. This was at nine of the clock and he was dead ere noon.

Here is another Norfolk woman, writing, or possibly dictating, towards the close of the previous century:

> And after this I saw God in a Point—that is to say, in my understanding; by which I saw he is in all things. I beheld and considered, seeing and knowing in sight, with a soft dread, and thought: What is sin?

I really have not cheated over these examples. The two notable women, the two women of no note, I chose them almost at random, and went to their writings to see what I would find. I found them alike in making themselves clear.

As far as I know, there is only one certain method of making things clear, and that is, to have plainly in mind what one wishes to say. When the unequivocal statement matches itself to the predetermined thought and the creative impulse sets fire to them, the quality we call immediacy results. Immediacy has borne other names, it has even been called inspiration—though I think that is too large a term for it. But immediacy has this in common with inspiration, that where it is present the author becomes absent. The writing is no longer propelled by the author's anxious hand, the reader is no longer conscious of the author's chaperoning presence. Here is an example; it is a poem by Frances Cornford:

> The Cypriot woman, as she closed her dress,
> Smiled at the baby on her broad-lapped knee,
> Beautiful in a calm voluptuousness
> Like a slow sea.

One does not feel that the woman has been written about. She is there.

Women as writers seem to be remarkably adept at vanishing out of their writing so that the quality of immediacy replaces them. Immediacy is the word in *La Princesse de Clèves*, that masterpiece of emotion laced up in the tight embroidered bodice of court dress. Madame de Cleves's heart is laid open before us, and we hang over it; not even pity is allowed to intervene between us and the demonstration. Immediacy is the word when Jane Austen keeps a bookful of rather undistinguished characters not only all alive at once but all aware of each other's existence. In *Wuthering Heights* immediacy

269

makes a bookful of almost incredible characters fastened into a maddeningly entangled plot seem natural and inevitable, as if it were something familiar to us because of a dream. When the goblins fasten on Lizzie and press the fruit against her clenched teeth; when Orlando finds the man in Mrs Stewkley's room, the man who turned his pen in his fingers, this way and that; and gazed and mused; and then, very quickly, wrote half a dozen lines—and no more need be said, with our own eyes we have looked on William Shakespeare; when Murasaki's Genji takes Yugao to the deserted house where the ghost steals her away from him; when, at the close of Colette's *La Chatte*, the girl looks back from the turn of the avenue and sees the cat keeping a mistrustful eye on her departure and the young man playing, deftly as a cat, with the first-fallen chestnuts, it is not the writer one is conscious of. One is conscious of a happening, of something taking place under one's very nose. As for Sappho, I cannot speak. She rises in my mind like a beautiful distant island, but I cannot set foot on her because I haven't learned Greek. But I am assured that immediacy is the word for Sappho.

While all these splendid examples were rushing into my mind, I realised that a great many examples which could not be called splendid were accompanying them: that when the gust of wind flutters the hangings and extinguishes the solitary taper and Mrs Radcliffe's heroine is left in darkness, it is a darkness that can be felt; that in George Sand's writing, for all its exploitation and rhetoric, George Sand may suddenly be replaced by the first frost prowling under cover of night through an autumn garden; that the short stories of Mary Wilkins, a New England writer of the last century whose characters appear to be made out of lettuce, can remain in one's mind and call one back to a re-reading because one remembers a queer brilliant verisimilitude, the lighting of immediacy.

There is, of course, George Eliot. She makes herself admirably clear and her mind, such a fine capacious mind, too, is stored with things she wishes to say; but in her case, immediacy does not result. We remember scenes and characters, but do they ever haunt us? She dissects a heart, but something intervenes between us and the demonstration—the lecturer's little wand. There is a class of women writers, praiseworthily combining fiction with edification, and among them is Mrs Sherwood of *The Fairchild Family*, Mrs Gatty of *Parables from Nature*, Mrs Trimmer . . . it seems to me that George Eliot insisted upon being a superlative Mrs Trimmer.

Still, George Eliot apart—a considerable apart—I think one might claim that this quality of immediacy, though common to either sex, is proportionately of more frequent occurrence in the work of women writers. And though it is impossible in judging the finished product to pronounce on which pages were achieved with effort, which came easily, the fact that even quite mediocre women writers will sometimes wear this precious jewel in their heads/seems to indicate that it is easier for a woman to make herself air and vanish off her pages than it is for a man, with his heavier equipment of learning and self-consciousness. Perhaps this is really so, and for a reason. Suppose, for instance, that there was a palace, which you could only know from outside. Sometimes you heard music playing within, and the corks popping, and sometimes splendid figures came to an open window and spoke a few words in a solemn chanting voice; and from time to time you met someone who had actually been inside, and was carrying away under his arm—it was always a man—a lute or a casket or the leg of a turkey. And then one day you discovered that you could climb into this palace by the pantry window. In the excitement of the moment you wouldn't wait; you wouldn't go home to smooth your hair or borrow your grandmother's garnets or consult the Book of Etiquette. Even at the risk of being turned out by the butler, rebuked by the chaplain, laughed at by the rightful guests, you'd climb in.

In something of the same way, women have entered literature—breathless, unequipped, and with nothing but their wits to trust to. A few minutes ago, or a few centuries ago, they were writing a letter about an apoplexy, or a recipe for custard. Now they are inside the palace, writing with great clearness what they have in mind to say—for that is all they know about it, no one has groomed them for a literary career—writing on the kitchen table, like Emily Brontë, or on the washstand, like Christina Rossetti, writing in the attic, like George Sand, or in the family parlour, protected by a squeaking door from being discovered at it, like Jane Austen, writing away for all they are worth, and seldom blotting a line.

Do you see what we are coming to?—I have put in several quotations to prepare you for it. We are coming to those other writers who have got into literature by the pantry window, and who have left the most illustrious footprints on the windowsill. It is a dizzying conclusion, but it must be faced. Women, entering literature, entered it on the same footing as William Shakespeare.

So if women writers have what might appear an unfairly large share of the quality of immediacy which is sometimes called inspiration—and in the case of Shakespeare we all agree to call it so—it is not, after all, original in them—like sin. It derives from their circumstances, not from their sex. It is interesting to see what other qualities, also deriving from circumstance, the circumstance of entering literature by the pantry window, they share with Shakespeare. I can think of several. One is their conviction that women have legs of their own, and can move about of their own volition, and give as good as they get. Lady Macbeth, and Beatrice, and Helena in *All's Well*, could almost be taken for women writers' heroines, they are so free and uninhibited, and ready to jump over stiles and appear in the drawing-room with muddy stockings, like Lizzie Bennet.

Another pantry window trait is the kind of workaday democracy, an ease and appreciativeness in low company. It is extremely rare to find the conventional comic servant or comic countryman in books by women. A convention is *pis-aller*, a stop-gap where experience is lacking. A woman has to be most exceptionally secluded if she never goes to her own back door, or is not on visiting terms with people poorer than herself. I have said before—but as the remark has only appeared in Russian I can decently repeat myself—Emily Brontë was fortunate in being the daughter of a clergyman, because the daughter of a clergyman, with her duty of parish visiting, has wonderful opportunities to become acquainted with human passions and what they can lead to. Another trait in common is a willing ear for the native tongue, for turns of phrase used by carpenters, gardeners, sailors, milliners, tinkers, old nurses, and that oldest nurse of all, ballad and folklore. Just as Mme de Sévigné was always improving her French by picking up words and idioms from her tenants at Les Rochers, Colette listened to every trade, every walk in life, and kept dictionaries of professional terms beside her desk—while Edith Sitwell's poetry reaches back through centuries of English poetical idiom to *Nuts in May* and Mother Goose.

These traits, as you will have noticed, are technical assets. They affect presentation, not content. Their absence may be deadening, but their presence does not make their possessor any more eligible to be compared with Shakespeare. The resemblance is in the circumstances. Women writers have shared his advantage of starting with no literary advantages. No butlers were waiting just inside the front door to receive their invitation cards and show them in. Perhaps the advantage is not wholly advantageous; but circumstances do alter cases. It was not very surprising that young Mr Shelley should turn to writing; it was surprising that young Mr Keats did, and his poetry reflects his surprise, his elation. It is the poetry of a young man surprised by joy. So is the poetry of John Clare. But though the male entrants by the pantry window possess the quality of immediacy just as women writers do, are at ease in low company and in the byways of their native language, they do not employ these advantages with the same fluency—I hesitate to use the word *exploit*; I will say, they are not so much obliged to them. I see a possible explanation for this, which I will come to presently.

But first I must come to the present day, when women, one might think, have so well established themselves as writers that the extraneous vibration must be hushed, and the pantry window supplanted as an entrance to literature by the Tradesman's Door. No woman writer should despise the Tradesman's Door. It is a very respectable entrance, the path to it was first trod by Mrs Aphra Behn, and many women have trodden it since, creditably and contentedly too. I should be failing my title if I did not remind you that we now have women newspaper reporters working in such vexed places as Cyprus—a signal advance. Yet, when we use the term *hack-writer*, we still feel that it must apply to a man; that a woman is once and for always an amateur. In the same spirit, if she happens to make a great deal of money by a book, well and good, it is one of those lucky accidents that happen from time to time, no one is the worse for it, and she is unexpectedly the better. But if she earns her living by her pen, we are not so ready to accept the idea. If we are polite enough to dissemble our feelings/we say that it is a pity that with so much talent she should be reduced to this sort of thing. If we are candid and pure-souled, we say that it's outrageous and that she ought to become a hospital nurse. If she marries—again it's a pity—a polite pity that she will have to give up her writing. So much pity is ominous.

And in fact, the vibration may start up at any moment. Macheath's Law still holds; not for numbers, perhaps, but for area. It is admitted that women may write very nearly what they please, just as, within limits, they may do what they please: though I suppose it will be a long time before they can enter the priesthood or report football matches on the BBC. But this liberty is zoned. It applies to women belonging to the middle classes. You know those shiny papers one reads in waiting-rooms, and how, every week, they show a photograph of a woman of the upper classes, with a little notice underneath. One has just come out. One has recently married. One wins prizes with her Shetland ponies, another has a charming pair of twins, another is an MFH. But despite Edith Sitwell and Dorothy Wellesley, one does not expect to read below the photograph that the lady is a poet. Take it a step higher. Suppose that a royal princess would not tear herself from the third act of her tragedy in order to open a play-centre. People would be gravely put out, especially the men who had been building the play-centre, men who have taught their wives to know their place, and who expect princesses to be equally dutiful.

273

A working-class woman may be as gifted as all the women writers I have spoken of today, all rolled into one; but it is no part of her duty to write a masterpiece. Her brain may be teeming, but it is not the fertility of her brain she must attend to, perishable citizens is what her country expects of her, not imperishable Falstaffs and Don Quixotes. The Lord himself may long have wished for her books to be written; but leave has yet to be granted. Apart from one or two grandees like Mme de La Fayette, women writers have come from the middle class, and their writing carries a heritage of middle-class virtues; good taste, prudence, acceptance of limitations, compliance with standards, and that typically middle-class merit of making the most of what one's got—in other words, that too-conscious employment of advantages which I mentioned a few minutes ago, and which one does not observe in Clare, or Burns, or Bunyan. So when we consider women as writers, we must bear in mind that we have not very much to go on, and that it is too early to assess what they may be capable of. It may well be that the half has not yet been told us: that unbridled masterpieces, daring innovations, epics, tragedies, works of genial impropriety—all the things that so far women have signally failed to produce—have been socially, not sexually, debarred; that at this moment a Joan Milton or a Françoise Rabelais may have left the washing unironed and the stew uncared for because she can't wait to begin.

UNPUBLISHED AND UNCOLLECTED POEMS

All dates and place names which appear in the notes are as found on typescripts in Sylvia Townsend Warner's own hand. Where she made any changes to a poem in typescript, the original wording is noted here.

p.3 'Queen Eleanor' [London, 1926] Eleanor of Castile was the wife of Edward I, who erected the Eleanor Crosses to mark her body's resting-places from Lincoln, where she died, to Charing Cross.

p.4 'East London Cemetery' [London, 1927]

p.5 'I thought that love . . .' [London, 1927]

p.5 'Ornaments of Gold' [1928]

p.5 'Early one morning . . .' [1928]

p.7 'Eclogue': first published in an anthology of Christmas prose and verse by the Cresset Press, 1928.

p.8 'A Burning' [Dorset, 1929]

p.8 'Pleasure is so small a place' [London, 1929]

p.9 'O staring traveller . . .' [1930]

p.10 'Trees' : first published in *The Countryman*, vol.8 (January 1934) pp. 376-77.

p.11 'Building in Stone': first published in *The Saturday Review of Literature*, 15 February 1930. Included in *Modern British Poetry*, ed. Louis Untermeyer (1936).

p.13 'Fair, do you not see . . .': first published as 'Fairy Tale' in *New Republic*, 24 June 1931.

p.14 'At the first meal . . .' [Winterton, Norfolk 1931]

p.17 'Of the young year's disclosing days . . .' [Winterton, 1931]

p.18 'Here, in the corner of the field . . .' [Chaldon, Dorset 1931]

p.19 'Woman's Song': first published in *The Countryman*, vol.4, no. 3, p. 414 (October 1931).

p.20 'Squat and sullen . . .' [1933]

p.21 'Cottage Mantleshelf': first published in the *London Mercury*, vol. 31, no. 186 (April 1935), pp. 526-27.

p.22 'Mangolds': first published in the *London Mercury*, vol. 31, no. 186, p. 527.

p.23 'Making the Bed': first published in *The Spectator*, vol. 151, p. 846 (8 December 1933). Later published in *The Literary Digest*, vol. 117, p.13 (17 March 1934).

p.24 'The vinery has been broken . . .' [Frankfort Manor, 193?]

p.25 'Fie on the heart ill-swept . . .' [Norfolk, 1934]

p.26 'A Man in a Landscape' [Chaldon, 1935]

p.40 'Summer is going . . .' [1940]

p.40 'An Acrostical Almanack, 1940' : the acrostic reads, VALEN-
TINE TIB ('Tib' was a nickname for Sylvia—see 'Vale', p.27).
'Envy to the counting-house . . .' and 'Esther came to the court'
were both included in *King Duffus*, but are repeated here to
keep the acrostic intact.
'Broceliande': 'Broceliande was the foremost Elfin Court in all
Western Europe, the proudest and most elegant.' (*Kingdoms of
Elfin* (1977), p.56-7).

p.53 'The Story of a Garden': first published in *The Countryman*,
vol.22, no.1 (October 1940), p.35.

p.54 'Recognition': first published in *The Nation*, vol.153, p.644,
(20 December 1941).

p.55 'The Visit': first published in *New Republic*, vol.104, p.626,
(5 May 1941); also published in *The New Yorker*, vol.17,
p.24 (2 August 1941).

p.56 'Twelve Poems in the manner of Bewick' [1943] : also included 'As rivers through the plain . . .' and 'Like an old beggar . .'
which appeared later in *King Duffus*, and 'With a wide face . .'
later included in *Boxwood*.

p.57 'Death of Miss Green's Cottage' [Dorset, 1944]

p.58 'In East Anglia' and the next poem, 'Song from a Masque' were
first published as no.3 in the fourth series of 'The Grasshopper
Broadsheets' (Kenneth Hopkins, Derby) March 1945.

p.59 'Song from a Masque': see above.

p.59 'I Said to the Trees': first published in the *London Mercury*,
vol.31, no.181 (November 1934), p.6.

p.61 'We Accuse' [1945]

p.62 'Trial of Marshal Pétain': l.37 (ts):
       For every fault a good repentance,

p.65 'Five British Water Colours' [1946-47] : the other two poems,
'King Alfred's Country' and 'St. David's Country', were included as poems number XI and XIV in *Boxwood*.
'Mr Gradgrind's Country': first published in *The Countryman*,
vol.33, no.2 (summer 1946), p.222. l.16 (ts):
       There were silver rose-bowls, asparagus tongs, and inlets of
          real lace,
'John Craske's Country': John Craske was a Norfolk fisherman
and artist whose work was patronised by Valentine Ackland
and Sylvia Townsend Warner.

p.68 'Seven Conjectural Readings' [1948] : another three in this
group were 'Lady Macbeth's Daughter', 'Anne Donne' and
'King Duffus', all included later in *King Duffus*. No seventh
'conjectural reading' is marked among the tss.
'The Wife of King Keleos': in her wanderings to recover her
daughter, Persephone, Demeter, disguised as an old woman,
was taken in by King Celeus of Eleusis and his wife, Metaneira. 277

She was interrupted whilst holding their child, Demophon, in the fire to endow it with immortality, and thus her own divinity was uncovered. The Eleusian Mysteries were instituted in her honour.

'Monsieur de Grignan': Mme de Sévigné's correspondence with Mme de Grignan, her beloved daughter, forms the bulk of Sévigné's *Lettres*.

p.70 'Through all the meadows . . .' [12 June 1950]

p.74 'The birds are muted . . .' [1950] l.5 (ts):
O breast, too deep in peace for song or saying,

p.74 'Bubbles rise . . .': originally a fourth in the group which appeared as 'Three Poems' in *Twelve Poems*.

THE ESPALIER

[All dates given for poems in *The Espalier* are as marked in Sylvia Townsend Warner's hand in her own copy. C.H.]

The Espalier was dedicated 'to P.C.Buck' who taught music at Harrow School and was, with Sylvia, one of the editors of *Tudor Church Music*.

p.77 'Quiet Neighbours' [London, 1923]

p.78 'London Churchyard' [London, 1923]

p.79 'Country Churchyard' [1922]

p.80 'In the Parlour' (i) [Essex, 1922]

p.81 'In the Parlour' (ii) [London, 1923]

p.83 'An Afternoon Call' [London, 1924]

p.83 'Wish in Spring' [London, 1924]

p.84 'The Virgin and the Scales' [Idbury, 1924]

p.89 'I Bring Her a Flower' [1924]

p.90 'Caves of Harmony': The Cave of Harmony was a London nightclub best-known for its music.

p.90 'Old Man' [London, 1922]

p.91 'Song from the Bride of Smithfield' [1923] : anthologised in Louis Untermeyer's *Modern British Poetry* (1936).

p.91 'Let Me Go!' [1923]

p.92 'Country Thought from a Town' (i) and (ii) [London, 1922]

p.93 'The Green Valley' [1923]

p.94 'Ghosts at Chaldon Herring' [1923] : Chaldon Herring, or East Chaldon, was the Dorset village where T.F.Powys lived.

p.95 'The Traveller Encountered' [Essex, 1922]

p.97 'The Repose' [Essex, 1922]

p.97 'The Traveller Benighted' [Essex 1922]

p.98 'The Happy Day' [1920]

p.99 'Nelly Trim' [London, 1923-24] : anthologised in *Modern British Poetry*, ed. Untermeyer (1936). On her first visit to East Chaldon, Sylvia Townsend Warner heard the following story:

'We followed the track along to the top of the Five Maries ridge, and pointing to the opposite hillside Tommy [Stephen Tomlin] told me of Nelly Trim, a dairy maid who, it was said, would yield herself to any wanderer who chanced to come to her lonely dwelling. Towering wreaths of mist were following each other along the valley, and I thought how glad the cold traveller would be of a warm woman . . .' 'Theodore Powys and Some Friends at East Chaldon', *The Powys Review*, no. 5, p.15.

TIME IMPORTUNED

Time Importuned was dedicated 'to Victor Butler'.

p.141　'The Load of Fern': used by Alan Bush in his song cycle, 'The Freight of Harvest' (Bush, Opus 69).

p.147　'The House Grown Silent': included in *Modern British Poetry* ed. Untermeyer (1936) under the title 'After He Had Gone'.

p.153　'Elizabeth': included in *Modern British Poetry*.

p.153　'The Red Dress': first published in *The Saturday Review of Literature*, vol.3, p.875 (4 June 1927).

p.157　'Triumphs of Sensibility' (iii): included in *Modern British Poetry*.

p.158　'Sad Green': included in *Modern British Poetry*.

p.162　'The Rival': ditto

p.164　'Song': ditto

p.167　'Allegra': Lord Byron was a pupil of Harrow School, where Sylvia Townsend Warner lived as a child.

RAINBOW

Rainbow was no.2 of 'The Borzoi Chap Books', published by Alfred Knopf in New York. The poem was illustrated by Ervine Metzl.

OPUS 7

Opus 7 was one of 'The Dolphin Books', published by Chatto & Windus, a series which also included *The Only Penitent* by T. F. Powys and Samuel Beckett's *Proust*. *Opus 7* was dedicated 'to Arthur Machen': Machen was Sylvia Townsend Warner's uncle by marriage.

p.195　l.4: 'Love Green' —the setting of the poem, and the subject of an article of the same title which appeared in *The Nineteenth Century and After*, vol.112, pp.220-26 (August 1932). Besides the Powysian names, there is much to connect Love Green, and its rector Mr Pagan, in Warner's article with Powys's village, East Chaldon, and the Rev. Joseph Staines Cope, who features prominently in all Sylvia Townsend Warner's reminiscences of the village and about whom she wrote a long poem in *Whether a Dove or Seagull*.

BOXWOOD

Boxwood was a collection of engravings by Reynolds Stone 'with illustrations in verse by Sylvia Townsend Warner' and appeared in two editions. The first contained sixteen engravings and sixteen poems
and was designed by Ruari McLean of The Monotype Corporation,

which published it in 1957, as a specimen for a new typeface, Giov-
anni Mardersteig's Dante Roman and Italic. This edition also contained a foreword by Beatrice Warde. The 1960 edition, used here,
was published by Chatto & Windus and included five extra engravings and poems.

Boxwood is dedicated 'to Janet' [Janet Stone].

p.235 XI: entitled 'King Alfred's Country' in ts (see note on 'Five
       British Water Colours') where there are the following var-
       iations; after l.5, stanza omitted:

> The people walking down the lane
> Observe him neither less nor more
> Than any other thing of course.
> I noticed him myself because
> I have not been this way before.

l.8 (ts): Timelessly calm, as though he was

p.235 XIII: originally one of 'Twelve Poems in the Manner of Bew-
       ick' (see note). l.3 (ts):

> The owl sits in the willow-tree

l.9 (ts): Below him on the willow-bough

p.236 XIV: entitled 'St. David's Country' in ts (see note on 'Five
       British Water Colours'). l.1 (ts):

> Some Joneses, Prices, Morgans, wearing black,

l.8 (ts): Whose gothic is both reach-me-down and garish.
l.9-12 do not appear in ts. After l.8: 3 stanzas omitted:

> The Celt who like a saint adores, an angel sings,
> Has no more architecture than a pig has wings.
>
> But on the bar of the Cross Keys
> A cat licks up the cider lees
> Whose bulk is vaulted, vast, and grave
> As any echoing Norman nave,
> Whose soaring tail, whose rounded apse,
> Whose rose-windowed flamboyant chaps,
> The Great Original proclaims
> Of Chartres and Westminster and Rheims.
>
> And him the week-day Prices, Morgans, Joneses,
> Stroke with admiring hands and praise with moanses.

KING DUFFUS AND OTHER POEMS

King Duffus and Other Poems was printed privately for the author in
1968 by Clare, Son & Co Ltd (Wells). None of the poems in the
pamphlet were titled. I have provided titles in square brackets in the
text for poems given titles in ts or previous publication.

p.241 'King Duffus': King Duffus of Scotland (961-5) was the earl-
       iest recorded victim in Great Britain of witchcraft practised
       through the making of a wax figure. He fell ill of a myster-

ious sickness, and when a girl hinted at the cause, the Guards were sent to her mother's house where they found 'some Hags, such as herself, roasting before a small moderate Fire, the King's picture made of Wax. The design of this horrid Act was that as the Wax by little and little did melt away, so the King's Body by a continual sweating might at last totally decay. The Waxen-Image being found and broken, and these old Hags being punished by death, the King did in that moment recover.' [Buchanan, *History of Scotland* (1722), I, p.245, quoted by Margaret Murray in *The God of the Witches*, ch. V, p.132 (Oxford University Press, 1970).]

p.242   'Like an old beggar . . .': one of 'Twelve Poems in the Manner of Bewick'. l.10 (ts):
             Light-long he will linger

p.242   'Envy to the counting-house . . .' part of 'An Acrostical Almanack, 1940' (see note for p.40). The last line of the two versions varies.

p.243   'Time on Time': given this title at its first publication in *The Countryman*, vol.15, p.61 (April 1937).

p.244   'Esther came to the court . . .': part of 'An Acrostical Almanack, 1940' (see note for p.40).

p.244   'Silent With Tigers They Observe . . .': given this title in ts.

p.246   'Anne Donne': in ts, one of the 'Seven Conjectural Readings'. The author seems to have drawn on two separate stories about Donne, both recorded by Walton. Donne had unwillingly left his wife, Anne More, who was expecting another of their children, to go to Paris with Sir Robert Drury. One evening Donne is reported to have told Drury: 'I have seen a dreadful Vision since I saw you: I have seen my dear wife pass twice by me through this room, with her hair hanging about her shoulders, and a dead child in her arms' (Izaak Walton, *The Lives of John Donne, . . . Robert Sanderson*, World's Classics, 1956, p.40). Walton also says that Donne concluded the letter which told his wife of his dismissal by Sir Thomas Egerton, later Lord High Chancellor, in 1602 with the words 'John Donne, Anne Donne, Vn-done' (ibid., p.60). Sir James Prior, in his *Life of Edward Malone* (1860, p.396), relates another version of this story. He tells how the newly-, and surreptitiously-, married Donnes fled to Pyrford, where 'the first thing he did was to write on a pane of glass—John Donne An Donne Undone. These words were visible at that house in 1749.'

p.246   'As rivers through the plain . . .': in ts, one of 'Twelve Poems in the Manner of Bewick'.

p.247   'Lady Macbeth's Daughter': in ts, one of the 'Seven Conjectural Readings', where it is given this title. l.3 (ts):
             Your brow is buirdly broad and tall

TWELVE POEMS

Twelve Poems was published by Chatto and Windus in 1980, with a foreword by Sir Peter Pears. The poems had been printed privately for the author in 1978 as a pamphlet entitled *Azrael*.

p.253 'Azrael': first published in *PN Review* 7, vol.5, no.3 (1978), p.57; also published in the *Telegraph Sunday Magazine*, 25 February 1980.

'Azrael' in Jewish and Muslim mythology is the angel who severs the soul from the body at death.

p.253 'Three Poems': first published in *PN Review* 7, vol.5, no.3, p.57.

p.254 'Dorset Endearments': first published in *The Countryman*, vol.37, no.1 (Spring 1948) p.60, as 'Words to a Wessex Child'.

p.256 'Graveyard in Norfolk': first published in *The Countryman*, vol.9, (July 1934), pp.413-14, as 'Delectable Mountains'.

p.257 'Earl Cassilis's Lady': first published in *PN Review* 7, vol.5, no.3, p.58.

p.257 'December 31st St. Silvester': first published in *PN Review*, vol. 5, no.3, p.58.

p.258 'In April': first published in the *Telegraph Sunday Magazine*, 25 February 1980.

p.259 'Gloriana Dying': first published in *PN Review* 7, vol. 5, no.3 p.58.

p.260 'A Journey By Night': l.12 (ts):
In the Aramithian ground.

INDEX OF FIRST LINES